KT-567-797

SHOAL WATER

BY THE SAME AUTHOR

Published by
Ward, Lock & Co., Ltd.

BERRY AND CO.
JONAH AND CO.
AND BERRY CAME TOO
THE BROTHER OF DAPHNE
THIS PUBLICAN
THE COURTS OF IDLENESS
THE STOLEN MARCH
ANTHONY LYVEDEN
VALERIE FRENCH
AND FIVE WERE FOOLISH
AS OTHER MEN ARE
MAIDEN STAKES
SHE PAINTED HER FACE
GALE WARNING
PERIOD STUFF

Published by Hodder & Stoughton

ADELE AND CO.
BLIND CORNER
PERISHABLE GOODS
BLOOD ROYAL
FIRE BELOW
SAFE CUSTODY
STORM MUSIC
SHE FELL AMONG THIEVES

SHOAL WATER

BY

DORNFORD YATES

WARD, LOCK & CO., LIMITED

LONDON AND MELBOURNE

First published in 1940
Reprinted 1942

MADE IN ENGLAND
Printed in Great Britain by Butler & Tanner Ltd., Frome and London

To

Jill

who does all things well

The characters of this book are entirely imaginary and have no relation to any living person.

SHOAL WATER

CHAPTER I

WHEN I came down from Oxford in 1936, to enter the family business in Crutched Friars, my uncles let me see that, though they were bound to make me their junior partner, they did so against their will.

I do not blame them at all. They were grave, elderly men, to whom business was a religion and the service of Solon and Solon the article of their faith. Since I was twenty-two and had nothing to show for my costly education—unless you count six oars and one very good friend—they naturally looked askance at a colleague so young and so unpromising, for though I let the firm down, I could not be dismissed, but must remain in authority, to set a shameful example to those who could.

It was this overt suspicion as much as anything else which made me determined to show them that I could be worth my salt, and no man ever worked harder than I did for nearly two years. The business was so well established that, fortunately for me, routine duties were all that had to be done: but these were numerous. I laboured early and late, and, except for an odd week-end, I had no holidays: when one of my uncles fell sick, I did his duty, too, for nearly three months : and, most important of all, I honoured a list of rules which must, I think, have been printed before my father was born.

And then, one evening in June, I opened the following note.

My dear Jeremy,

If I may say so, my brother and I have been very favourably impressed by the devotion to duty which you have shown for nearly two years. At the same time we cannot lose sight of the fact that 'Youth's a stuff will not endure,' and we feel that this year you should take a considerable holiday. Since the summer is, as you know, the season in which we are least busy, we suggest—and indeed desire—that you should absent yourself for the next three months. The rest and change will do you a deal of good. I enclose a cheque for six hundred pounds, which we hope will enable you to take some friend away with you and to spend a really enjoyable time. Let us say from the first of July to the thirtieth of September.

Your affectionate uncle,

John Solon.

To this very handsome treatment I owe the fact that I have a tale to tell, for I made up my mind that night to wander abroad and six days later I purchased a second-hand car. This was a 'guaranteed' Lowland—a swift, all-weather coupé, with an enormous boot : she proved as good a bargain as ever a driver made. Since coupés are built to seat two, I did my best to persuade my friend, George Laking, to bear me company. But he was at work in Paris and could not join me for more than a long week-end. Still, he said he would meet me at Rouen, if I could go by that way; and since I very much wanted to see him again, I made arrangements to ship the car to Dieppe.

So it came that I drove out of London at five o'clock on a Thursday, the seventh day of July, taking the road to Newhaven and meaning to cross that night. Newhaven . . . Dieppe . . . Rouen—where George was due to meet me the following day.

The afternoon was hot, and I took things easily, trying the Lowland's paces and taking stock, as I went, of a beautiful countryside: indeed, I well remember the pleasure I found in picturing Crutched Friars and contrasting my labours there with the leisure my good old uncles had bundled into my arms. Still, I had time to waste, for the ship did not sail till ten and I had until eight to bring the car alongside.

Just before half-past seven I stole through Lewes and on to the Newhaven road; and it must have been ten minutes later that I saw a black coupé ahead by the side of the way and a girl who was wearing grey trousers, full in my path.

As I set a foot on the brake, she lifted a hand, and when she was sure I was stopping, she stepped to one side and stood waiting for me to come up.

As I brought the Lowland to rest, she opened her mouth.

"I'm dreadfully sorry," she said, "but will you help a damned fool?"

"Where is he?" I said, and made to get out of the car.

She smiled.

Then—

"Don't get out. I want a gallon of petrol. You see, I'm crossing to-night: and if you've got any petrol, they take it out on the quay. So an old hand tries to run it as fine as ever he can—and fetch up with a teaspoonful. But this time I've been too clever, and now I'm stuck."

I looked at my petrol-gauge. This showed that more than nine gallons were still in my tank. And Newhaven was three miles off. Of course, I was not an 'old hand.'

In silence I showed her the gauge, and she covered her mouth.

I sighed.

"D'you mean to say they just take it—and give you nothing at all?"

"It's an old Channel custom," she said. "And then they expect you to tip them for pumping it out."

As soon as I could speak—

"But *we* have no pump," said I. "So, though we've nine gallons between us, we've got to buy more."

She nodded cheerfully.

"Without delay, too," she said, "if I'm to be there by eight."

As I let in my clutch—

"I promise," I said, "to be as quick as I can."

I was as good as my word—for my sake, as much as

for hers. I wished to see more of my lady. Never before had I met so unusual a girl.

She was tall and slim, and she moved and stood very well. Over her well-cut slacks she was wearing a white silk shirt ; and, to keep her hair in place, she had bound a gay, green handkerchief over her chestnut curls. Wimple and gorget in one, this suited her perfectly : but while any face so framed must have looked its best, her beauty was so outstanding that I was all agog to see the handkerchief gone. Her nose was aquiline, and her eyes were the clearest gray ; her clean-cut chin was firm and her mouth had an exquisite curve : but her gaze was so level and fearless and her manner so quiet and so sure that I knew I had had to do with a very exceptional type—a girl with the charm of a maid and the drive of a man.

I was back in a quarter of an hour : and when I had poured the spirit into her tank and had taken the price I had paid, because I dared not refuse, she waited for me to turn round and then drove off before me, " because I know the ropes and I'll lead you on to the quay."

Half an hour later the cars were tied to their trays and my nine gallons of petrol had been withdrawn. (Never expecting such bounty, they had to send for more cans, to take it away.) And since we could not go aboard for an hour and a half, I asked my lady to dine with me at the hotel.

She shook her head.

" I'll eat on the boat," she said. " You go and have some dinner—unless you'd care for a walk."

"Yes, please," I said. "But I think you should put on a coat."

For a moment she made no answer.

Then—

"Perhaps you're right," she said slowly, and turned to go back to her car. "And what about you?"

I helped her to put on a woolley that matched her scarf: then I put on a jacket myself, and we left the quay.

As we crossed the railway lines—

"My name's Solon," I said; "and I'm trying to be a merchant in Crutched Friars."

My companion looked at me.

"That sounds all wrong," she said.

"I'm not sure it isn't," said I. "But so many better men would be thankful to have my job."

"Of course. But you're young and fit. And you don't look as if you had more than one mouth to feed."

"I haven't," said I. "But—damn it the job was there. A junior partnership. There's nothing the matter with that."

"There never is—with a mess of pottage," she said. "But you have to pay for it—Esau. Rank heresy, of course. And damned impertinence. But that's your fault. 'Trying to be a merchant' got me under the ribs."

"May I ask why?"

She regarded the heaven, aglow with the setting sun.

"Well, I think one tries *not* to be a merchant. If there's nothing for it—yes. But I'd rather lie out as a shepherd than fatten in Crutched Friars."

"Am I fat?" said I.

"Not yet."

I laughed.

"If you saw me in Crutched Friars, you wouldn't say that." I threw a look round about me and took a deep breath. "This is the life that is going to make me grow fat."

"How long have you got?"

"Three months."

"Three months. That's not too bad."

"It's the first leave I've ever had."

"Is it, indeed?" she said. "Oh, well, there's hope for you yet."

But when I asked what she meant, she would not say.

She was leading me into the country which lay to the north and east, and everything looked so peaceful and seemed to offer so much that I was quite sorry that I was going abroad.

When I told her as much, she nodded.

"I know," she said. "I always feel just the same. 'Are not Abana and Pharpar, rivers of Damascus, better than all the waters of Israel?' But the change of scene is good. And my father lives in France. He's—not very strong: and I go to see him a lot. And now tell me where you're going and what you're going to do."

I told her as much as I knew.

"I should go south," she said. "I shouldn't waste time at Rouen, but pick up your man and get on. It's glorious down there now—wherever you like to go, south of Angoulême."

" But he can't stay on," said I.

" Then send him back from Bordeaux and go on alone. Wander down to the frontier and then turn east. And when you can smell Marseilles, turn west by north."

It was clear that she knew France well, and I led her on to speak of routes and places and all the things that a wayfarer ought to know. But though she seemed glad to be with me and talked so naturally, she never gave me her name or told me where she was going or where her father lived. Instead, she made me talk—at least, I found myself telling her many things and how for the last four years I had had to shift for myself, because my father and mother had lost their lives in the air.

After a while, as though to do me pleasure, she took her green handkerchief off and gave her curls to the breeze, to look like some nymph by Boucher and make me more proud than ever to bear her company : but, though she must have known how lovely she was, she gave herself no airs and seemed to expect no kind of deference.

Dusk had come in before we got back to the quay : and when we had shown our passports, we went aboard. And there we sat down to an excellent, simple meal of cold meat, cheese and beer, which, frankly, suited me better than any elaborate repast.

When she learned that I had no cabin, she looked at me soberly over the rim of her glass.

" You need looking after, Esau. How and where were you meaning to spend the night ? "

" I had meant to sit up," I said.

" What a dreadful thought. I'm going to go to bed and be called at seven o'clock. Breakfast at eight, and at nine I shall be on the road."

" That's much more like it," said I.

With that, I sent for a steward and asked him to find me a cabin and take a certain suitcase out of my car.

As he left to do my bidding—

" I frankly admit," I said, " I've a lot to learn."

" More than you think," said the girl. " That's the direct result of trying to be a merchant in Crutched Friars."

" You mean——"

" That I very much doubt if your uncles know their world. And they are three times your age. Maybe, they're happier so. But I don't believe you would be. I may be wrong."

" Do you know your world ? " said I.

" More or less. Probably less. But I move about a lot, and that is the way to learn."

I gave her a cigarette and took one myself.

" I've three months," I said, " in which to improve my mind. May I send you a letter to say how I'm getting on ? "

She put up a hand to push back her shining hair.

" I have no address to give you. I'll be by Bordeaux to-morrow—I'm joining a party there. But after that —who knows ? I've no idea of their plans."

I sat very still.

It was clear that she meant our acquaintance to end

at Dieppe. I had served her a turn for an evening—because there was nobody else. But I must not know where to find her or who she was, in case I should reappear and put her to shame.

I had not believed that she would treat me like that. It had not entered my head. I would have sworn that she was above such things. . . . But so would any fool—who was trying to be a merchant in Crutched Friars.

I laughed shortly.

"Perhaps you're right," I said, and called for the bill.

When we left the table, she led the way to the deck: but though we strolled, I did not feel like speaking, and she, I suppose, thought it best to leave me alone. It was dark now and we had the place to ourselves, for ours were the only cars and the boat-train was not yet due. Time and place, in a word, would have favoured the making of love: but no man wants to make love when he has been kicked in the face.

And then, to my great surprise, the girl slid an arm under mine.

"Try not to hate me, Esau."

"I could never hate you," I said, and wondered why that was true.

"I'm glad of that," she said quietly. "I—I couldn't bear you to hate me. I'm not as tough as you think."

"That's all right," I said somehow. "After all, it's up to you. But you've done enough damage to-day to make me upset to think that I'm not going to see you again."

I heard her draw in her breath.

Then her arm slipped away and she put out a little hand.

" Good-night, Esau," she said. " I'm going to bed. Sleep well, my dear, and—thank you so very much."

I took her hand in both mine.

" Won't you give me a name," I said, " to remember you by ? "

She looked away over the water, swaying black under the stars.

Then—

" I will—to-morrow," she said.

My heart leaped up at that, for it showed that she was relenting and might go further still the following day. Indeed, I forgot my resentment, which now seemed unfair to her, and after a moment I put her hand to my lips.

As I kissed her fingers, I felt them close upon mine.

" Breakfast at eight ? " I said, smiling.

" And don't be late," she said gravely. " By half-past eight you'll have to be off the ship."

With that, she was gone.

As she reached the companion, she turned, and the light of some naked lamp fell on to her face. She smiled and lifted a hand. Then she turned again and passed out of my sight.

... ...

I suppose I must have been tired, for I slept that night like a log. Though the boat-train arrived, whilst

I was unpacking my things, I was asleep before we put out to sea: and I never heard us arrive at the port of Dieppe, when there must have been noise enough to have woken the dead.

When the steward called me at seven, he brought me some tea—and there, on the tray, was a note, to which the man drew my attention, because I was half asleep.

"I was to give you this note, sir, directly you waked. Those were the lady's last words, before she went off."

I sat up and stared at the man.

"'Went off'?" I said slowly. "D'you mean to say that she's gone?"

"That's right, sir. You can get off, if you like, at half-past five. She got off then, an' her car was cleared before six."

"I see," I said, and put a hand to my head.

"You'll be taking breakfast, sir?"

I nodded.

"Yes, I suppose so," I said. "I'll come in about eight."

"Very good, sir."

The man withdrew, and after a little while I opened the note.

Esau dear,

You've made it so very hard for me to do the right thing. Good-bye. And the best of luck always, wherever you are.

Katharine.

... ...

I remember that the first thing I did was to look at my watch. Five minutes past seven. I had to rise and dress and to clear the car. I might, I reckoned, be on the road by eight. But Katharine had been on the road by six. That meant she had two hours' start —on roads that she knew. All the same . . .

And there I remembered George Laking. George was to meet me at Rouen at half-past two.

I lay still and thought things out.

Katharine was now beyond Rouen, heading for Chartres. Even if I started at eight, it was one chance in ten thousand that I should overtake her before she came to Bordeaux. I had the faster car, but she knew the roads. If, on the other hand, I waited at Rouen for George, any chance of catching her up would, of course, no longer exist. All the time, I knew in my heart that I could not break my engagement and let George Laking down.

After a little I decided that George and I together should take the road for Bordeaux. He probably knew the way—which would be a great help. And if we left Rouen at three, we could be at Bordeaux that night. We would follow, but not pursue. And George's counsel would be invaluable.

I put my letter away and began to get up . . .

It will be observed that I had but one idea—to find my lady as soon as ever I could. I cared for her and I knew that she cared for me. Of course she would never have said so, had she not known that she was to see me no more: but, safe in that knowledge, she had 'returned' the interest she knew that I took in her.

She had shown her hand—and that was enough for me. I meant to find her somehow. And when I had found her, then I would have things out—and smash this spectre at which her conscience had shied. I could have moved mountains, if mountains had stood in her path. 'You have made it so very hard for me to do the right thing.' Very well. I would make it easy—easy to do the right thing, and see herself in my eyes.

It occurred to me that she had bade me go south—to send George back from Bordeaux and go on alone. *Bordeaux.* That was where she was going. 'Wander down to the frontier and then turn east.' A thousand to one that was what she was going to do. Oh, of course. The thing was clear. And if I slipped down to the country south of Bordeaux and kept an eye on the road which led to the south, one day I should see a black coupé rounding a bend . . . and a flash of green and chestnut, as it went by.

By eight o'clock my appetite had returned.

There was now no need for haste, so I took things easily. It was nearly ten before I ran out of Dieppe, and past eleven before I had come to Rouen and found the hotel at which George and I were to meet.

Now if we were to drive to Bordeaux and to waste no time by the way, to take some food in the car seemed the wisest plan: so, when I had had a drink, I set about buying provisions from which we could make a good meal by the side of the road. I bought far more than we needed, because in the shop which I entered everything looked so nice, and the people were kindness itself and sent out for bread and butter and even for fruit. When they heard that I should not be leaving till three o'clock, they offered at once to keep all the stuff until then, because, as they pointed out, the Lowland was not a larder and the day was extremely hot. To this I gladly agreed: and I made a like arrangement with a very pleasant fellow who sold me six bottles of beer: these he put into his ice-box before my eyes, so that when I came for them later, they should be thoroughly cold.

Then I berthed the car and visited the cathedral and strolled the ancient streets until it was time to lunch—and perceived how wise I had been to wait for George. For one thing only, the fact that I could not speak French would have been enough to weight me out of the race. Had I had to ask my way, I could, perhaps, have made myself understood: but, unless they had been very simple, I could not have understood such directions as I received. That sort of thing does not matter when you have time to spare, because, if both parties are patient, liaison can be achieved: but, as I had found that morning, such fences cannot be rushed. But George could speak excellent French.

I finished my lunch by two and took my seat in the lounge, to glance at an English paper and keep an eye on the door. But I need not have been so zealous, for more than an hour went by, but George never appeared.

I was out on the pavement by now, because I could not sit still: but I should have done better to go to the porter's desk.

I saw the telegram there at a quarter past four. It

had been there *since ten o'clock*. But it had not been given to me, although I had given my name.

Terribly sorry detained till this evening coming by train reaching Rouen eleven o'clock.

I could have screamed the house down—and have shoved the hall-porter's face through the back of his head.

Had I been given the wire when first I arrived, I should, of course, have set out alone for Bordeaux. I could not have faced the prospect of wasting another twelve hours. But now, through no fault of my own, I had wasted five. Was I to waste seven more and start my adventure equipped with a valuable squire, or was I to start it at once and set out alone ?

I put my head in my hands and argued the pros and cons. . . .

Here perhaps I should say that I was so wild with George for letting me down—I frankly admit, a most unfair point of view—that I felt no compunction whatever about leaving him behind : all that I sought to decide was whether by waiting for him my interests would best be served.

At last I decided that they would. George could speak French. If he did not know the road, at least he could read the map, whilst I was driving the car. He could sleep as we went : and then, if I grew sleepy, could take the wheel. And when we got to Bordeaux—well, George was a proper man and would pull his weight.

Having made my decision, I had to try and kill time.

Of this I made a bad business, because I was so much upset, wandering to and fro, till I was too tired to stand up, yet quite unable to rest, because a black coupé I knew was doing a steady forty a great way off. In fact I never passed a more miserable afternoon, wondering all the time if I had done right to wait and cursing poor George and the porter, until I ran out of oaths.

At seven o'clock I picked up my food and my beer and stowed them away in the Lowland for what they were worth : but I could not get away from the fact that, let alone George, if I was to drive all night, I should be fit for nothing the following day, and that common sense was suggesting that we should stop, say, at Chartres and get four or five hours' sleep in a decent bed before going on. The idea of such further delay sent me almost out of my mind, and yet I knew it was better than its alternative.

In this winter of discontent I ordered and later sat down to a something pretentious dinner at eight o'clock, but at half-past eight I was once again walking the streets, because to sit still inactive was more than I could endure.

The night was breathless—more oppressive, in fact, than the day had been, and it must have been ten o'clock when I made up my mind that I must have a long, cold drink before I went down to the station to meet George's train. I, therefore, turned my steps towards the hotel, near which the Lowland was waiting —had waited most of that day.

I knew the direction to take, though I did not know

the way: but I had not far to go and had plenty of time. This was as well, for I took a narrow, paved street, where the houses were very high and seemed very old, but when, after two or three minutes, I came to its end, I found that it was a blind alley, or, rather, did no more than run into a very small square.

I was looking round this, to be sure there was no way out, when I saw a discreet-looking café in one of its sides. There were no tables outside, and its blinds were drawn, but a slant of very good music was stealing out of its doors and, as I stood listening, I heard the pop of a cork.

At once I saw no reason to wait for my drink and, since I was sick of the sight of the lounge of the hotel, I determined to enter the café and then go straight to the car. With that I crossed the square and walked into the place.

For a moment I thought I had entered a private club, for all looked up as I entered and watched me choose a table and take my seat. But when a waiter came up, he took my order and never asked my name, so I lighted a cigarette and began to look round.

There was a dancing-floor, but the band was playing *Tosca*, and playing it very well: it was playing it very quietly, so that to listen or not was a matter for you. And everyone seemed to speak quietly: no voice was raised. There must have been thirty customers, sitting alone or together—nearly all men: but, most surprising of all, with one or two exceptions, they did not seem to be French.

As they were looking at me, I looked at them.

English faces I saw and clear American—to be quite honest, some of them not too good. Some were well turned out, and some were shabbily dressed: the girls . . .

And there I saw Katharine . . . whom I had supposed to be three hundred and fifty miles off . . . sitting, staring before her, with a frozen look on her face.

CHAPTER II

SHE was sitting sideways to me, with her back to the wall, at a table laid for three, at which dinner was being served. She was wearing a very smart frock of, I think, black silk and a small black hat, which suited her lovely hair. On either side of her was seated a man, and, when I saw her, both men had their eyes on her face. One had his back to me: but the other I saw very well. His face was large and pale, his graying hair was sandy, the rims of his eyes were red: he had the grimmest mouth that ever I saw, but worse than this was the sinister light in his eyes. These seemed to be on fire—I can put it no other way. And to see so dreadful a gaze bent upon Katharine released my primitive instincts as nothing else could have done.

How she came to be here, I neither knew nor cared. She was in trouble—in peril: and I was at hand. The pricks I had kicked against had all the time been goading me up to her side.

I put out my cigarette and rose to my feet. Then I walked across to the table at which she sat.

"I'm awfully glad," I said, "to see you again."

The man whose back was towards me was looking up into my face: but the eyes of the other man were fast upon Katharine.

Very slowly she turned her head. . . .

Then she looked me up and down.

" By God," she said slowly, " I thought I'd got rid of you."

Her words and her manner of speaking hit me over the heart. Indeed, I was so much dumbfounded that I think that I should have turned and walked out of the place, if the man looking up at me had not seen fit to laugh.

The snigger made me see red.

" I don't think you mean that," I said. " I think——"

The contents of her champagne-glass caught me full in the face. . . .

The man on her right was speaking—the man with the dreadful eyes. His tone was curiously silky.

" Why interrupt him, Formosa ? We've heard what he doesn't think : let's hear what he thinks."

As I wiped the wine from my face—

" Pray go on, my young friend," he drawled. " I'm sure in her heart Formosa——"

" Speak for yourself," snapped Katharine. " God knows——"

" I know He does," flashed the other. " And I want to know, as well. I want to know what he thinks —your nice, young man."

The position was intolerable : but nothing on earth would have made me leave Katharine now. She was playing some part, of course : and something was terribly wrong. She was, I was sure, afraid of the man on her right.

I addressed myself to her, as though she were sitting alone.

"I'll go back to my table," I said. "Perhaps, later on . . ."

With that, I bowed and turned.

As I passed to the seat I had left, I noticed that the band had stopped playing, that everyone in the café was sitting as still as death. The atmosphere was hateful. I never felt more self-conscious in all my life.

My beer was waiting for me, but I was too shaken to drink. Instead, I took out cigarettes. . . .

I saw Katharine leave her seat, her underlip caught in her teeth. For a moment I thought that she was making for me; and so, I think, did her companions, for the man on her left started up, as though in pursuit. As I rose in my turn, he stopped, for, instead of coming to me, she sped to an archway which gave to the ladies' room, and, parting the curtains which hung there, passed out of our view.

I sat down again at once, and he returned to his seat; but this time he slewed himself round, for so he could see the curtains through which my lady must come.

Here, to my great relief, the band began playing again, and I noticed that general movement which always means that tension has been relaxed.

As I lighted my cigarette, I saw a man making his way to the table which Katharine had left. Though I had seen no sign given, he had been clearly summoned by the man who had sat on her right, for he stood by his side, as a servant who has been sent for and now awaits the order which he expects to receive. The other spoke over his shoulder : and since, as soon as he spoke, his myrmidon looked at me, there could be no doubt at all that I was the object of his instructions.

That this made me feel uneasy, I must most frankly confess, for the fellow was heavily built and looked a criminal. However, there was nothing to be done : and I watched him leave his master and pass to a seat by the side of the entrance-doors. As he went by, I saw a girl glance at her neighbour and purse her lips.

I think every eye in that café was watching the curtains which shrouded the ladies' room. Sooner or later, Katharine was bound to come out : and with her coming, something was going to happen—and something big. In a word, the scene was set for a first-class row.

I began to wish very much that I was not alone. I know how to use my hands and I am a powerful man : but I had the definite feeling that everyone there was against me, because they dared not offend the man with the dreadful eyes. And I would have been glad of someone, to set his back against mine.

And something else I wished. That was that the little square to which the café belonged was not at the very end of a long, ill-lighted and lonely *cul-de-sac*.

And then, without any warning, the whole of the lights went out.

I shall never forget that moment.

The valse which the band was murmuring died a discordant death : a girl cried out 'My God' ; and a general rustle suggested that all were up on their feet.

I know I was up on mine, for I at once assumed that this had been done on purpose to give my friends a chance of coming to grips with me before I could see they were there. And I was just going to move, to try and get my back to the wall, when I felt a hand close on my wrist and Katharine breathed in my ear.

"Come."

I could not think how she could see, for I was blind, but she haled me rather than led me across the dancing-floor and behind the bar.

As we went, confusion broke out.

I heard an ice-pail go crashing, and somebody tripped and fell. This might have been the signal for uproar, for chairs began to go over and oaths to rise and a pile of metal dishes slid on to the floor. As their hideous racket subsided, a girl cried out again and a dozen men were cursing and calling for lights. And a voice that I knew was blaring "Close the doors."

As we rounded some screen, the pallid beam of a torch leaped out of the dark behind.

We were in a passage now, and a waiter collided with Katharine and drove her back on to me. At once he began to abuse her; but she thrust on. The fellow sought to detain her—without success, for I hit him under the jaw and I heard him fall. Through the kitchens we went, where a scullion was lighting a candle and a *chef*, his back towards us, was raving like any madman over the fate of some dish. So down another passage and into a broad courtyard, at the end of which a shaft of light from some lamp which I could not see was shining on to the cobbles and silhouetting some man.

We came to gigantic doors which were keeping a *porte-cochère*: in these a wicket was open and a nigger in uniform was speaking with someone without. As we came up, he turned: but before he could close the wicket I hurled him aside, and Katharine stumbled out, with me on her heels.

Somebody shouted behind us, and the nigger gave tongue in reply: but we were out in a street—*a street that I knew.*

There was next to no one about, and I saw no policeman: but the Lowland was standing silent, some sixty yards off.

I put my arm under Katharine's and ran her up to its door.

"Inside," I panted. And, as I flung in behind her, "Where shall I go?"

"Anywhere. Quick. Straight on. You've no time to turn."

This was the truth.

As I fitted the key to the switch, I saw a man running towards us and two or three standing by the wicket through which we had come.

To go straight ahead was to meet him and pass by them; but because the devil was driving, we had no choice. If only the car had been facing the opposite way . . .

My faithful engine started like any highwayman's mare, but the man was but five paces off when I let in my clutch. I recognized him as the tough, with the criminal face.

As he sprang for the running-board, I put down my foot. . . .

He had, of course, aimed for the door : but, because the Lowland leaped forward, he met the side of the boot and the off hind wheel—a very disagreeable encounter, to judge from the bump on the car and the screech which he let.

I changed into second . . . third. . . .

As we tore past the wicket, the light was falling full on a big, pale face. This might have been a mask, the eyes of which were lighted by some supernatural means.

"Which way now?" I breathed.

"Straight on, for the moment. I'll tell you. Put on your lights." I did as she said. "Turn to the left at the bottom, and then go straight."

We streaked down the empty street and swung to the left. I remember I heard some clock chiming and saw the masts of ships standing up on my right.

"Let her right out," breathed Katharine. "They've got a racing Merk. And Judas has gone to get it. I saw him go."

Although her voice was steady, the flood of light from an arc-lamp showed me the fear in her face. This was turned towards me. Her eyes were fast on the window in the back of the hood.

"Judas be damned," said I. "He hasn't a hope."

But I did not like the sound of 'a racing Merk.'

We flashed the length of the quay. Then, by her direction we bore to the right, fell down a cobbled cutting and whipped up a broad highway. Bend was succeeding bend, but the Lowland knew how to sit down and I never lifted my foot.

"Left, in a minute," said Katharine; "and up the hell of a hill. We must get over the river, before we play any tricks."

"Are you sure we hadn't better turn off—and let them go by?"

"No, no. I—I've heard them talking. I know I'm right."

The hill was serpentine, and I lost time badly there, because it was dark and I did not know the road. And then we were out on some uplands, and I was able again to give the Lowland her head.

With the needle pointing to eighty, we dived at a long decline. . . .

As at last I slowed for a bend—

"Quick," said Katharine. "I see the glow of their lights."

I bit my lip.

"Where is this damned river?" said I. "I thought——"

"Not very far now. But we must be over the bridge, before they come on."

The mile or so that followed, I cannot remember at all. Poplars, I think, and some houses: but I cannot be sure. My brain was not recording. I drove instinctively. All my wits were focussed on whether or not the next bend was masking the bridge.

"Are they coming up?" I breathed.

"I—can't be sure."

From that I knew that they were, and I set my teeth.

And then I saw the bridge coming—and saw its length.

"God Almighty," I groaned—and put down my foot.

"All you know," said Katharine. "They're—not very far."

As we left the road for the bridge, she spoke again.

"You're coming slap into a town. Cobbles. Bear right and stand by to brake and to put out your lights. I'll tell you when to do it. We're going to turn off."

Off the bridge and into a cobbled street.

As I lifted the Lowland up for a sharp ascent—

"Brake at the top of this and turn sharp to the right."

"My lights?"

"Put them out when you've seen the turning."

With her words, it came into view—a turn and a half: and I put out my lights and took it—on two of my wheels.

"And now switch off."

As I switched the engine off, I heard the wasp-like note of the racing car.

I heard her leave the bridge and the hum turn into a snarl as she leapt at the cobbled street. The snarl swelled into a roar. . . . And then she bore to the left . . . and the snarl slid into a mutter . . . and she was gone.

I turned to Katharine: but she was still listening intently, straining her ears.

I began to listen, too, to hear what I could.

Suddenly, out of the silence, I heard the mutter flare up—for one instant of time.

I saw Katharine nod her head.

"That's right," she said. "They've changed down. They're taking the Evreux road."

There was a little silence.

Then—

"And we, my dear?" said I. "Which road do we take?"

"God knows," said Katharine.

She clapped her hands to her face and burst into tears.

... ...

I naturally did what I could.

I did not talk, but I put my arm about her and held her close: but it wrung my heart to see her in such distress.

After a little, however, she drew away from me and lifted her head: and before five minutes had passed, she opened her mouth.

"There's something," she said, "there's something the matter with me. Never mind. We've got to get on. Get her going again. I'll tell you the way to go."

As I switched the engine on, I glanced at the clock in the dash, to see that this had stopped at twenty minutes to eleven o'clock. But when I looked at my wrist-watch, this said the same. And then I realized that the clock in the dash had not stopped—that it was but thirty-five minutes since I had walked into the café that stood in the little square.

Digesting this startling truth, I let in my clutch. . . .

Except that she took me south, I do not know where we went: but I drove as hard as I could for over two hundred miles. Two or three times we stopped; but never for more than five minutes, to stretch our legs: and we had no need of petrol, because my tank had been full.

In all this distance we hardly spoke at all, because, I think, what had to be said was too big to be said whilst we were driving at such a speed. Besides, we were fugitives—not from justice, of course, but from something that knew no law. At least, that was how I saw it: for Katharine was no fool and was taking charge as much for my sake as for hers.

I have said that the night was warm; and after some twenty miles, we lowered the hood: and I well remember how very pleasant it was to be free of the cool, sweet air as the Lowland sailed and darted, after the way of a bird.

The roads were very good and often as straight as a ruler for miles on end: but I could not, of course, see the country through which we went. There seemed to be no hedgerows: but wayside trees had been planted carefully, and every road was a decent avenue. Had we run short of petrol, we should, I am sure, have had to knock somebody up, for every town and village was fast asleep. If other cars were abroad, I never saw them: once in a very long while we would pass some lorry, pounding along the road, and then for twenty odd miles we would have the world to ourselves.

What astonished me very much was Katharine's quiet assurance as to the way we should go. She never asked for a map, and she led me through town after town with hardly a check. The roads were certainly 'posted' extremely well: but there could be no doubt at all that she knew the line she was taking and knew it perfectly.

And then, as the dawn came up, she told me to slacken speed.

"There's a place near here," she said, "where I've stopped before. I think I shall know the turning—it's just before or just after a tumble-down house."

"On the left or right?" said I.

"On the left. . . . There it is. And there's the old house beyond."

I braked and swung to the left, and after another two miles we came to a long stone bridge.

"Over this," said Katharine. "And two hundred yards farther on, you'll find a track on your right. You'll have to go carefully there, and I think I should put her in first."

The track was pretty steep, and its surface was bad; but it just accepted the Lowland, and that was as much as I asked. Almost at once it began to curl round to the right, until I saw that we were running down to the bank of the river which we had crossed a moment before.

A moment later the sides of the track fell away, and there we were on a decent patch of greensward, with room to turn and trees growing thick about us and, ten or twelve paces away, the bank of the river itself. My headlights showed me the water, flowing deep and steady, but making no sound at all.

I brought the Lowland to rest. Then I switched off her engine and put out her lights: and though it was dark where we were, I could see the heaven above now pale with light, and the woods across the water were taking shape.

Katharine left the car and I followed her out.

" We shan't be disturbed here," she said. " If only we'd got some food——"

" There's enough for six," said I, " in the Lowland's boot."

She let out a sigh of relief.

" There's luck and to spare," she said. " You haven't by any chance got anything hot ? "

" I'm afraid I haven't," I said. " But I think a glass of brandy would do you good."

" If you'll give me a little," she said, " I think it would."

I found my flask and poured a tot of brandy into its cup.

" Drink that down," I said, " and I'll give you a coat."

" It's just the dawn," she said. " I'll be all right as soon as the sun gets up."

But I made her put on a big coat that I had in the car; then I gave her a cigarette and began to get out the food.

It was a curious breakfast.

The sward was wet with dew, so she sat in the car; and a suitcase made her a table, set up in the driver's seat. Smoked salmon and bread and butter, and *pâté* and galantine—I served them as best I could, using the step as a side-board and thankful to see her eat. For drink, we had only the beer: but she drank a glass of that, and I think she enjoyed the cherries, which had kept remarkably well.

At length she slid out of the car and on to the sward.

"I've done, but you haven't," she said. "Could you possibly lend me a sponge? And soap and a brush and comb? If you could, I'll go down to the water and do my best."

I was glad to do as she asked, for only three days before I had bought myself a new outfit of 'toilet requisites.' But as she went off with these things and a cashmere scarf, which I had, to serve as a towel, I could not help thinking how miserable she must be—dressed up in a 'party' frock in which she had spent the night, yet quite unable to change so much as her stockings, because, of course, she had nothing else to put on.

And there it occurred to me that I had some new, gray trousers and plenty of sleeveless shirts. . . .

By the time she was back, I had a full change of raiment laid out on a rug—with a bath-dressing-gown and a toothbrush out of my store of spares.

I heard her cry of delight, as they met her eyes.

"Oh, Esau. How marvellous. Are these things really for me?"

"I thought," said I, "you might be glad of a change."

She stared at the clumsy apparel, finger to lip.

"I'll tell you what," she said. "Not now, but a little later, I'll have a bathe. And then, what joy—to be able to put on clean things."

"A bathe," said I, "would suit me down to the socks."

"But not for an hour. You've just been eating stone fruit. Wash your face and hands—and shave, if you feel that way. But don't be long."

I was back in a quarter of an hour, and, as I parted the bushes, I saw her before she saw me.

The cushions were out of the car, on the farther edge of the sward. Because of the rising woods, the sunshine was not yet falling upon the grass, but, because she was higher up, her head and shoulders were bathed in the blessed light. She was sitting, staring before her, with her knees drawn up and her fingers laced about them—and as desperate a look on her face as ever I saw. This was not drawn. She looked neither tired nor afraid. Indeed, with the sun about her, against the natural background of gay, green leaves, she made a most lovely picture, and one that I cannot forget. But her beauty was tragic—that of the nymph Oenone, who must have sat on Mount Ida with much the same look in her eyes.

Not knowing what else to do, I stole a few paces back. Then I advanced noisily. . . . As again I parted the bushes, I saw, to my relief, that the look was out of her face; and as I advanced, she met my gaze very gravely and then set a hand on the cushion that lay by her side.

"Let me get a pipe," said I. "And you'd like a cigarette."

"Very well."

A moment later, I took my seat beside her, glad of the sun. Then I lighted her cigarette and unfolded my pouch.

"You don't look tired," I said. "And yet you should be all in."

"So should you," said Katharine, "driving all night."

"For some reason I'm not. I imagine that later on we'll both be glad of a rest."

"I expect so. And we can have it. I don't want to leave here till dusk." She regarded the palms of her hands. "And now, if you please, let's tell one another the truth. The air has got to be cleared, so we'd better do it at once. I'm not going to keep anything back—it's too late now. And I'm not going to throw any stones, for the fault was mine. *I should never have sent you that note.* You'll say 'Oh, yes, you should': but I'm the best judge of that. It was the damndest folly: and all the good it's done is to let the two of us in. But I thought it was safe—because I had laid the drag. I could have sworn that you would make tracks for Bordeaux. . . . I pictured you flicking through Chartres and having some dinner at Poitiers or Angoulême. And then I looked up and saw you walk into that cursed room. . . . As I say, I don't blame you at all. But how in God's name did you manage to run me to earth? I mean, I had gone to ground before you were called."

I told her all that had happened the day before: how the one idea I had had been to get to Bordeaux and to find her there; how George and the porter, between them, had let me down; how I had arranged to leave Rouen as soon as ever George came; and how the merest chance had taken me into the café in which she was.

"I was killing time," I concluded. "I meant to drive all night to get down to Bordeaux. But George's train wasn't due till eleven o'clock. And so I was walking the streets, because I couldn't sit still. Then I landed up in that square from which I couldn't get out, and, seeing a café there, I decided to have a drink before retracing my steps. I never saw you at first: but when I did, I could hardly believe my eyes."

Katharine sighed.

"I wish you hadn't," she said. "And I'll tell you another thing. That you should have entered that café means that your guardian angel—well, wasn't earning his keep."

"To be honest," I said. "I thought that some of the customers looked a bit queer. But it seemed all right from outside. In fact, it looked better than most."

"Now and again," said Katharine, "a 'non-member' does blow in. It doesn't often happen. *The Wet Flag*'s not in the books and it's right off the beaten track. But it has been known to happen. And unless he is answered for, unless some 'member' can say that he is all right—well, I don't know what happens to him: but he never comes back."

"'Member'?" said I, staring. "Then my first impression was right. It is a club of sorts—this place that you call *The Wet Flag.*"

Katharine raised her eyebrows.

"Yes," she said, "it is. It is 'a club of sorts.' In fact, it's a thieves' kitchen—to use the traditional term. And I am a member . . . because, you see, I'm a crook."

CHAPTER III

I HAVE taken some knocks in my time: but this revelation of Katharine's, so bluntly and casually made, actually set my ears singing—and that is the downright truth. I sat there, staring upon her, 'as a sheep before her shearers is dumb,' while she and her background seemed to retreat before me and grow very small and, though I was out in the open, I seemed to need air to breathe.

I knew that the sun was shining, the sky was blue; but these things no longer counted: her statement had taken heaven and left the earth. And my brain could not accept this—this hideous fact. It was shying, jibbing, backing away from the truth. And with it my senses were reeling. . . .

Then the sweat broke out on my forehead, my vision cleared, and something that seemed like a wave sank back into place in my head.

As I wiped my face, I began to review the facts. Grisly or no, they simply had to be faced.

This glorious, well-bred creature belonged to the criminal class: my most attractive companion, of whom I had been so proud, was nothing more or less than a common or garden thief: Katharine was Formosa: the girl whose hand I had kissed, who had left behind her that tender, pitiful note. . . .

'You've made it so very hard for me to do the right thing.'

It was the thought of that sentence that brought me up all standing, dispersed the facts I was facing and showed me, instead, two definite, flaming truths.

The first was this—though she gave herself that name, she was not by nature a crook. And the second —that I was in love with one of the criminal class.

"Takes getting hold of, doesn't it?"

I looked up to meet her gray eyes.

"It would," said I, "if it happened to be the truth."

"It's true enough—and you know it," said Katharine.

"Let me put it like this," said I, with my eyes upon hers. "For some reason or other, you may have done as crooks do. But that doesn't make you a crook. Nothing on earth, my dear, could ever do that."

She was looking down and away, with a hand to her head.

"That's—very handsome," she said. "But you can't get round it like that."

"I'm not getting round it," said I. "I don't care who you've run with or what you've done. Everyone there was a crook—I can see it now. But you are not of that kidney, and never were. That means that you had good reason for mucking in with that crowd. What that reason was, I neither know nor care. You had good reason—and that is enough for me."

"In fact . . . you believe in . . . Formosa?"

Her head was still turned away, and she spoke very low.

"With all my heart," I said gently. "I may not know my world, but I've seen the light in your eyes."

There was a little silence.

Then—

"I've never stolen," said Katharine. "I only carry the stuff. That's just as bad, of course: it's no good stealing a thing if you can't get it safely away: but, in fact, I have never stolen: and, nine times out of ten, I never set eyes on a jewel. I'm not excusing myself. By rights, I should be in jail. But . . . since you believe in Formosa, I'd like you to hear her side—for what it is worth. No one has ever heard it, and no one but you ever will. And no one but you would believe it—it's just a shade too fantastic for people who know their world."

"I'd love to hear it," I said. "But please don't think that I've got to. I know your hands are clean, and I don't have to have any proof."

Katharine looked at me.

"You're very sweet, Esau," she said. "Sometimes you make things easy, and sometimes you make them hard: but at least you've shown me I'm not so tough as I thought." She put out her cigarette and took up her old position, clasping her knees. "And now you shall have my story: I'll make it as short as I can.

"My father's an artist—a painter: at least, he was. If he had cared to paint portraits, I think he'd have made a big name: but he had a private income, and so he wouldn't bother, but painted whatever he pleased. He had a rare eye for beauty and all things fair. He never could bear ostentation of any kind, but simple, natural things were the breath of his life. Anything sordid or vulgar caused him genuine distress: and I want you to understand that this wasn't a pose. He was—and is—unusually sensitive.

"Well, he served right through the War, and, as you may well imagine, it left its mark on his soul. What left a still deeper mark was my mother's death. She died in 1918, when I was born. Bruised and broken-hearted, for my sake he held up his head: but the ways of the post-war world were more than he could endure, and so he began to wander, in search of some corner in Europe which had been spared. He found it in 1930, when I was twelve: and he came straight back to England, to fetch me and take me out, so that I could share with him his great discovery.

"Cardinal is a little hamlet, right in the heart of France. It's really very lovely, set on the banks of a river and sunk in magnificent woods. Its people are very simple and quite unspoiled, and they live and work as they used to in bygone days. But Cardinal's pride is its castle, a little pocket château, hung high above the village by someone who knew how to build in the fifteenth century. It was for sale, and my father bought it at once. And then he set to work to restore it. . . .

"He and the village masons did all the work. It took five years to do, and I saw it done. And when it was finished, it was the most perfect thing. It's like a fairy castle, built on very small scale. It hangs in the woods, directly above the village, with great trees all about it and two magnificent chestnuts growing in its courtyard. Its terrace and turrets and stairways, its coats-of-arms and battlements—I simply cannot tell you how perfectly lovely they are. And it faces south and it sleeps in the sun all day: and below it the water-wheels are running and the smoke from a score of chimneys lies like a veil in the treetops, because the air is so still.

"Well, as I've told you, it took five years to do. And when Cardinal was once again perfect in every way, my father went blind. One day he could see, and the next he had lost his sight. And that, irreparably.

"He took it wonderfully. 'I'm sorry,' he'd say, 'but it might be so very much worse. I'm here at Cardinal, and I know its beauty by heart. I know the view from the ramparts: I know the hamlet below and the meadows beyond. I can feel the sun hot upon the terrace and hear the song of the water-wheels running below. And I shall be happy here, with the speech of the birds about me and the lisp of the wind in the trees.' The servants were very faithful—we've only four: and, as I was careful to see that everything went the same, he really survived very well this great catastrophe. He knew the castle so well that soon he could move about as he did before: his clothes were laid out, as always: the meals were served as usual, with Conrad —that's the butler—standing behind his chair: and after six weeks, Esau, if you had dined there with us, I honestly do not believe that you would have known he was blind.

"But one thing he could not do, and that was business. His correspondence was small; but he couldn't sign cheques or write letters, and things like that. Not that it mattered, because I took all that on. I was seventeen then, and though I knew nothing before, I very soon picked things up.

"There wasn't much to pick up. What savings he had had gone on Cardinal: but he couldn't touch his income, for that was settled on me. It was fifteen hundred a year—and more than enough, for Cardinal only costs a thousand a year to run. So, as I say, I soon got the hang of things. . . . And then, on my eighteenth birthday, I opened a note from his Bank. It was very politely worded, but very firm. 'No more cheques could be honoured, until my father's account was in credit again.' This shook me up, for I knew that we weren't overdrawn. And there I was wrong. We were: for no income had been paid in for nearly six months.

"To cut a long story short, the money was gone. A trust company had crashed, and we had nothing at all—except an overdraft of two hundred and fifty pounds.

"I never told my father—he doesn't know to this day: but I had a pretty bad time for the next few days. The thought of his leaving Cardinal was something I could not face: and yet I had to face something far worse than that—a blind man, lodged in some alley where rooms were cheap, while his daughter tried to earn money to buy them bread. Deprived of all he set store by—had always had . . . peace, and beauty and comfort . . . servants and home: unable, because of his affliction, to meet the blow: and bound, because of his nature, to feel it far more than most; my father must surely die—or go out of his mind.

" Well, I managed to cover up somehow for twenty-four hours: and then I left for London, to sell my jewels. They had been my mother's, of course, and I worked out that they'd make twelve hundred pounds. That would pay off the overdraft and carry Cardinal on for the better part of a year. And before that time was up, I guessed I could marry money and get the man to settle the income I had to have. That was the general idea. The special idea was to get as much for my jewels as ever I could. I didn't know where to take them: and I was mortally afraid of being done down.

" And then a strange thing happened.

" We had a fearful crossing—the Channel was at its worst. And one poor woman on board was terribly ill. To make matters worse, she had a little girl with her, and though the scrap wasn't ill, she was frightened to death. I happen to be a good sailor and so I took charge of the child. It wasn't much to do: but when we were safe ashore and her mother was able to speak, you might have been forgiven for thinking I'd saved her life. She couldn't thank me enough, and all she wanted to do was to prove her gratitude. And then, on the way to London, she used these words.

" ' I know my place, and it's no good asking you out. But I'll tell you what, my dear—if ever you want a fine brooch, or a bracelet or diamond ring, never you go to Bond Street. You write to me. My husband's in Hatton Garden: and when he knows what you've done, he'll get you whatever you want and let you have it at cost.'

" Well, that was good enough. There and then I told

her that I had come to London on purpose to sell my jewels and that, if she meant what she said, here was her chance to help me to do a good deal. To say she jumped at it means nothing at all. Her husband was at Victoria, and before I left the platform, I'd arranged to be at his office at noon the following day.

"I went—to get the shock of my life. He examined the jewels with the greatest possible care: then he said he would try to get me six hundred and twenty-two pounds.

"He proved his case all right. He showed me other gems and then turned them up in his books and showed me the prices he'd paid. But that didn't temper the wind: it only satisfied me that I was up against it far more than I'd dreamed. And what with all I'd been through, this unexpected punch put me down and out. I fainted properly. And when I came to, I was lying flat out on a sofa and he and another man were bathing my temples and wrists.

"Who the other man was I had no idea: but I took him to be some magnate, for he was issuing orders and taking charge, and my friend—Mr. Cohen—was fairly twittering. Then he sent Cohen off for brandy, and when he was gone, he asked what my trouble might be.

"I told him some of the truth—because I wasn't myself: but I had had no one to talk to, and he was a business man. I didn't like his looks: but any port in a storm. He might be able to help me—you never knew.

"Well, he listened carefully. Then he asked me where I was staying and how long I should be there:

and then Cohen came back with the brandy, and soon after that I cleared out. Two days went by, and then I received a note. It was from the magnate all right, and he said if I'd come and see him, he had a suggestion to make. Hatton Garden again, but a different house. I went, and he made his suggestion. Two thousand a year and expenses, if I would do as he wished. 'Smuggling,' he called it: for nearly three months I really believed it was. And then, one day, I found that it wasn't 'smuggling.' . . .

"My impulse was to go to the police, and I wish to God that I had: but, you see, my hands were not clean, and I dreaded the awful exposure which must result if I did. So I went to—my employer, instead. I told him what he was fit for and pitched the stuff down at his feet. And then I walked out. . . .

"I didn't get very far. That night I was in a cabin, on board a ship in the stream. The door was locked and I couldn't open the port-hole, and I didn't like the look of the nigger who came when I rang the bell. 'He' came to see me an hour before the ship sailed. He said I could take my choice—carry on as before, or sail for Buenos Ayres . . . to take on a different job.

"And so I went back.

"I tried again, later on. By that time I was afraid to go to the police. I was involved too deeply—he'd seen to that. And so I just disappeared. And after lying low for ten days, I ventured to Cardinal.

"A letter was waiting for me. . . .

"Till then, I had never dreamed that he knew my true name and address; for I'd taken my mother's name and I'd always been so careful to cover my tracks. But he knows—everything.

"The letter was very short. It simply said that, if I did not return, he was coming to Cardinal. 'I must make your father's acquaintance. In a sense he is my protégé. I have kept Cardinal going for more than a year. And when he knows this . . .'

"Well, I couldn't face torture like that. And so, once more, I went back."

She put her hands to her temples and pushed back her shining hair.

"And that was how I learned what I might have perceived before—*that, having begun, I had simply got to go on.* When I reported for duty, he rammed that home. 'Don't do it again,' he said, 'lest a worse thing befall. You're worth the trouble you've given—*but not any more.*' I realized then that I'd never be permitted to clear, because I knew too much. You see, I know a great deal—that shouldn't be known. I know the thieves and receivers: I know the big men and small: I know their habits and customs and where they are to be found: I know how the police are outwitted and see the mistakes they make: when a crime's done, I can tell you who planned it as well as who carried it out—because I am in on these things. . . . And once you are in on those things, you've got to stay put. You can't retire—they won't let you: they've simply got to have you under their eye. I'm not at all sure that I blame them: but any way there you are. You've got to go on or go under—there's no other way."

"What d'you mean—'go under'?" I said.

Katharine shrugged her shoulders and picked up a cigarette.

Then—

"Lose your life," she said slowly. "I can't put it plainer than that. Twice my life has been spared, because—well, because it was worth it. You see, I'm valuable. Because of my birth and my breeding, I am 'above suspicion,' and I can go anywhere. For that reason, too, he's always played straight with me. But now he's through. I know it. He's got a good many faults: but he never speaks twice."

There was another silence—a much longer one than before. Her cigarette was half smoked before I opened my mouth.

"I'm afraid I've torn it," I said.

"Fate has torn it," said Katharine. "It wasn't your fault."

"The point is—it's torn," said I.

Katharine gave a short nod.

"Yes," she said. "It's torn. When you walked up to my table, the veil of the temple was rent." She threw down her cigarette and covered her eyes. "When I saw you come in, I was gravelled—I couldn't think what to do. I knew you were bound to see me: and once you'd seen me, I knew you were bound to come up. And that was, of course, what happened. . . .

"I hardly know what I said, but I tried to force you—to blast you out of that room. If you'd turned on your heel and gone, I think they'd have let you go. But when you stood your ground—well, that was about as good as walking on to the drop. You would have been, er, rendered unconscious and then dropped into the Seine.

"Well, something had to be done. The door was hopeless, of course: but I knew the back way out. Most of us know it—in case: but it's not allowed to be used. I mean, that's understood. . . . The question was how to make it, and take you, too. And then I thought of the switchboard. I knew that was fixed in a cupboard, inside the ladies' room. Well, that was all right; but I had to be able to see, whilst everyone else was blind. So I shut my eyes for two minutes: then I put up my hand and pulled the main switch down: then I shut and locked the cupboard and took the key: and then I got hold of you, and you know the rest."

"You saved my life," I said.

"Perhaps. But what else could I do? If you had been placed as I was, you couldn't have let me go down."

"And, as a result, you're 'wanted.'"

Katharine gave her short nod.

"We're both of us 'wanted'," she said. "The Shepherd wants us—that's the man with the eyes. And—it's no good not facing facts—he usually gets what he wants."

"Does he, indeed?" said I—and felt as ripe for murder as ever I did in my life. "Was he the swine who 'engaged' you three years ago? When you were right up against it and ready to sell your soul?"

"Yes, it was he."

I sucked in my breath.

"It's as well for us both," said I, "that I didn't

know that last night. Never mind. Some other time. If he tries as hard as you say, we shall probably meet."

Katharine caught my arm.

"My dear, you're out of your mind. You've about as much chance with The Shepherd as a baby would have with a tiger who'd lost his kill."

"I know," I said. "I'm not going after him. I don't believe in throwing one's life away. But if somebody's after you—well, the time may come when it suits you to let him come up."

"I'm afraid I can't see that time coming. I know my—my colleagues too well."

I rose to my feet and stretched.

"And I actually thought," I said smiling, "that I had torn everything up."

Katharine stared up at me.

"What has happened to change your mind?"

"Reflection," I said. "Nothing else. Upon reflection, I see that I've done you a very good turn."

Katharine sighed.

"If you can see that," she said, "you must have damned good sight."

"No," said I, "it sticks out. You may have saved my life; but I've lost you your job."

"I see. The Salvation Army. I'm much obliged."

"No," said I. "Just Esau—speaking as he has been taught. I think your mess of pottage has cost you enough."

She lowered her eyes.

"That's just," she said. "I've sold my birthright, I know. But don't rub it in."

I put out my hands for hers, and after a moment or two she gave me them both.

"You only pledged it," I said. "And Fate and I, between us, have got it out."

"That's a shade too Quixotic, Esau—even for you. I told you about my father, because I wished you to know how I came to do what I've done. But if ever we get out of this—and I can't quite see how we shall—well, a merchant in Crutched Friars can't be friends with a well-known crook."

"That's tripe," said I, "and you know it."

"It isn't tripe. In certain—circles, Formosa is very well-known. And if anyone liked to squeak, a warrant would issue to-morrow for my arrest."

"In which case," said I, "the merchant would bail you out."

"How nice for Solon and Solon! And didn't you say that you were a member of White's?"

I drew her up to her feet, and looked into her eyes.

"I'm sorry, my lady," I said, "but you shouldn't have sent me that note."

"Don't be a fool. I was trying to temper the wind."

"That's all I'm doing," said I. "Let's leave it at that."

... ...

Twelve lazy hours had gone by.

We had bathed and slept, and Katharine was wearing my clothes, which, because they were far too big, made her look like a beautiful child. For the time, she went barefoot, because she was sick of her shoes and there, of course, my wardrobe had broken down.

The change and the rest had refreshed her: and, as she sat by my side on the sunlit sward, propping herself on one arm and considering one of my maps, I found it hard to believe that this was indeed Formosa, who had flouted the police of Europe for three long years.

After a while she looked up.

"Listen, Esau," she said. "We've had a nice, quiet day, and, if things were what they look like, we'd pack up our traps and go to some good hotel. But things aren't what they look like, and, though you mayn't believe it, we're in a hell of a jam. For the moment we're off the map. But we've got to *stay* off the map for some considerable time. For at least a month they'll ransack France for us both: and it's no good our clearing out, for they'll watch the ports. The Shepherd has wires he can pull all over the place. And *The Wet Flag*'s like an Exchange. Last night the news went out that Formosa had cut and run and, what is much more to the point, that The Shepherd would like her back. And, as The Shepherd's worth pleasing, that means that petty crooks all over the place will keep an eye cocked for Formosa and, if they should see her go by, will try and follow her up."

I think that I must have shown the surprise which I felt, for I heard her expire and a hand went up to her head.

"Esau dear, get this. However absurd it seems, you must accept as gospel whatever I say. 'There are more things in heaven and earth, Horatio, Than are dreamt of in your philosophy.' That's what Shakespeare said—and here's my corollary. 'But if you could see the things which are under the earth, you would not believe your eyes.' For one thing only—and I could talk for hours—law-abiding people have no conception at all of the way in which news goes round in the underworld. Rumour, perhaps: but the rumour is always right. Nothing is ever written, so far as I know; but no system of information is half as quick or as good. The things they know about people would startle you out of your life. After all, it's a secret service: and the better the service is, the more money it makes.

"And now let's get back to the point—which is that our lives depend on our not being found. Well, we obviously can't stay here. We've got to have food and shelter, and I've got to have some clothes. In a word, we've got to start fair: and that is why to-night we must make for Cardinal."

I opened my eyes.

"But won't that be asking for trouble? I mean ——"

"I think he'll try elsewhere first. Only last night he told me a way to pass into Spain. And I think he's now going all out to stop that gap. I may be wrong, but I think he will make up his mind that Cardinal is the one place which I shall avoid. If I'm right, that will give us a breather. No more than that, of course; for when he's drawn blank elsewhere, he's certain to go to my home. But before then we shall be gone. I can warn the servants against him, and Cardinal's half a fort: but I don't think he'll trouble my father—he's past blackmail.

"It may have been a mistake to lie up to-day: but ask too much of the flesh, and the spirit will let you down. And I'd very much rather travel by night than day. Besides, to tell you the truth, when we got here this morning, I didn't know where to turn. It's only during the day that I've managed to work things out.

"Well, from here to Cardinal is three hundred and fifty miles. On the roads we are going to take, you'll have to drive very well to average thirty-five: and that works out at ten hours—which means, if we leave at dusk, that we ought to be in by six. I shan't like the last two hours, but it can't be helped. And, as I said just now, I think he'll rule Cardinal out for two or three days."

"I'm in your hands," said I. "But we'll have to take in petrol—twice, I'm afraid."

She bit her lip.

"I'm sorry for that. To-night doesn't matter a damn. But to-morrow morning does. It means knocking somebody up: and when you don't want to be noticed that's not the way to behave. Still, that's a drop in the bucket—of this appalling stew." She put her hands to her eyes. "I'm afraid to look at the future, because, if I did, I believe I should throw in my hand. Havoc's ahead all right, and I can't see any way through. But the obvious thing to do is to try and hang on to our lives—if only because, when we're dead, we can't do anything more."

With that, she turned again to the map and left me staring before me, regarding the efforts of a beetle to find a way off the blade of grass he had climbed, without turning back.

Sitting there, in that peaceful place, it was very hard to believe that we were in peril, let alone danger of death: and when I remembered the office in Crutched Friars, my pleasant, window-boxed chambers in Savile Row, the cheerful London traffic and all that went to make up the safe, untroubled existence which I had so lately led, I was almost prepared to wake up and find myself sitting at Rouen, still waiting for George's train.

I think I may be forgiven.

I had read of crime in the papers: I had never been into a police-court, had never seen an arrest: I had always supposed that, pickpockets apart, unless you had great possessions, no rogue on earth could be bothered to look at you twice: and I had firmly believed that no crook ever did murder, unless he had his back to the wall. I had heard of 'the underworld'; and it meant no more to me than the urban district council of Zanzibar. . . . And now I was 'wanted' by one of its leading men—the dent on the Lowland's boot left no doubt about that: because his writ ran in Europe, I must not drive by daylight over the roads of France: because I had encountered Formosa, I was to be put to death.

A gust of anger swept me. Who was this filthy sewer-rat to raise his hand against me? Who was this beast to pursue me, because I had dared to raise my eyes to his prey. His prey! A lady of high degree . . . of whom he had taken advantage, when she was down and out. *He called it 'smuggling.'* And when she had tried to withdraw, he had shipped her beautiful body for Buenos Ayres. . . . I felt the sweat break upon my forehead, as I pictured the stuffy cabin and The Shepherd dictating his terms. And then—blackmail. . . . A threat to break her father, to smash the life for which she had sold her soul. 'And so I went back.' Because he said so, she must 'go on or go under.' No *joie de vivre* for her: no love, no marriage, no hope: nothing but running the gauntlet, risking her name and her freedom, to carry his stolen goods. . . . The thing was intolerable. If Scotland Yard—— And then I saw that I could not call on the police . . . for Katharine was Formosa . . . and anyone in touch with Formosa would be just a shade too welcome at Scotland Yard.

"Have you got things straighter?" said Katharine.

I looked up to see her watching me, finger to lip.

"Yes," I said boldly, "I have: but I'm still a bit out of my depth, so I look to you. It's very kind of you to ask me to Cardinal: I'll love to meet your father and stay with you at your home. How we get there is, of course, a matter for you: but it seems to me a scandalous thing that in this year of grace, you and I should go in fear of our lives, because your late employer disapproves of our acquaintance. That sort of thing makes me feel that The Shepherd's death and burial are overdue: I mean, the man seems to me to have outlived his usefulness."

"There are many quarters," said Katharine, "in which that sentiment would be greeted with prolonged applause—provided, of course, that The Shepherd was out of earshot. But when, encouraged by this, you called for recruits, you'd find that all your supporters had something much better to do."

"That I can well believe. Of such is the kingdom of Hell. And as a result, we have got to bow to the storm. We must, of course—for the moment. And when we're at Cardinal, we'll talk about him again."

"Do you realize now why he wants to find you so much ?"

I shrugged my shoulders.

"Because, I suppose," I said, "I wandered behind the scenes."

"Let me give you his point of view, Esau. You followed me to *The Wet Flag* : you saw with half an eye that I was keeping—well, doubtful company : you determined to stand your ground and to get to the bottom of this : he, therefore, tried *and failed* to—shall we say, shut your mouth : result—you are at large and so at liberty, if ever you see him again, to point him out to the police and demand his arrest : add to all this that Formosa has thrown in her lot with you, and you must be able to see that, from his point of view, his mental and physical health depend upon your being found *and* silenced as soon as possible."

"Well, it's nice to think he's worried," said I.

"You may," said Katharine, "be perfectly sure of that. You see, he's a pretty big man. He's a beautiful flat in Town, and I don't think you'd believe me if I told you the name of his Club."

... ...

I had driven for nearly eight hours, and we had covered two hundred and thirty odd miles. The roads had been tricky, and some of them none too good: but it was the level-crossings that spoiled our time. How many we met I forget, but seven of these had been shut. Had it been day, this would have been bad enough; but in nearly every case the keeper was fast asleep and had to be roused. Of course if one goes across country at dead of night, one must, I suppose, expect to be badly served: but the waste of time was enough to break anyone's heart. I would have been thankful myself to open and close the gates, but, though I tried more than once, they were always locked.

And now the dawn was coming—the east was pale: and we had still to cover one hundred and seventeen miles.

The strain had told on us both, for we could not lose sight of the fact that we might be driving straight into the enemy's arms; and in any event we were heading for dangerous country, where neither could tell what a bend in the road might conceal. Then again the delays at the crossings had sickened our hearts, had made us feel that the stars were fighting against us, holding us up to serve the enemy's turn.

It was just a quarter to five when I put out my lights.

But I did not put out the hooded light on the dash. It was no good not facing facts. The petrol-gauge was a telltale I had to watch. And when I remembered the petrol which had been pumped out of my tank on a certain summer evening, a lifetime ago, I could not help feeling that Fortune must have her tongue in her cheek.

So for another ten miles, while the country about us unveiled and distance took shape and a crag on the left stood up like a mourning hatchment against the glow of the dawn.

At last I could bear it no longer, and cleared my throat.

"My dear," I said, "I'm sorry: but very soon we've got to take petrol in."

I heard her catch her breath and saw her eyes leap to the dash.

Then—

"How much does that say?"

"Just over a gallon," said I. "Say twenty miles."

She bit her lip.

"That means the next pump," she said. "And a hundred to one the fellow will be in bed. He'll never forget the people who had him up and out at a quarter past five."

"He needn't see both," said I. "You can walk on out of sight before I knock at the door."

"That's too easy," said Katharine. "I think perhaps we'd better make for a town." She picked up a map. "I think we're close to Volet. There may be an all-night garage: and any way there'll be any number of pumps. It's the lonely petrol-station that lets the fugitive down."

Volet was twelve miles off, and eighteen minutes later we entered its cobbled streets.

For two or three minutes we picked our way through the town, moving very slowly and peering to right and to left down ways which we passed: then our street curled into a *place* in which stood a decent hotel. By the side of this house stood its garage: and the doors of the garage were open, though those of the house were shut. What was still more to the point, in the jaws of the garage entrance some car was being fuelled—from a pump which was inside the garage and out of our sight.

"The luck that changed," said Katharine. "Who but a guest would use a hotel garage to fill his tank?"

The back of the car was towards us, and as I brought the Lowland to rest on the opposite side of the way, a man in clogs appeared, to play with the pipe for a moment and then lift it clear of the tank and screw the cap back into place. Then he re-entered the garage, to hang up the pipe. A moment or two elapsed, during which, no doubt, some payment was being made: then he appeared again, to watch the car into the road. As its driver moved slowly backwards, he waved him on with his hand.

I let the other get clear. Then I swung over the road, over the pavement and into the garage itself.

As I stopped where the other had stood, the man in clogs came shambling up to the door: but when I asked for 'petrol,' he only stared, for *petrole* is not petrol, but paraffin. Of such is the curse of Babel. . . . And Katharine had to lean forward and put me right.

For obvious reasons, I did not get out of the car: but I watched the petrol-gauge and I took my note-case out.

After a frantic calculation—

"How much shall I give him?" I whispered.

Katharine made no answer, and when I looked at her, I saw there was something wrong.

She was white as a sheet, she did not seem to be breathing, her eyes were shut.

"Good God," I said, "what's wrong?"

She did not speak, but I saw her open her eyes and look to the left.

I followed her gaze.

A glare of lamps was lighting the concrete sink, upon which a car could be washed. And a car was standing there, dripping—waiting on our convenience, before it was dried. And the car was 'a racing Merk,' which was painted an elephant gray.

CHAPTER IV

THAT I was 'rattled,' I make no shame to confess. Indeed, the shock was so great that I cannot clearly remember what happened next.

I know that the cap was screwed on and that when the man came to the door, I could not understand what he said and that Katharine had to tell me how much I must pay. Then I started the car and backed out, while the washer stood looking on and waving me back: and once I was in the roadway, I put the Lowland in first and drove straight on, careless of where I went, so long as I left that cursed garage behind.

At length—

"Perhaps he won't talk," I said. "Unless they—they ask him, there's no reason why he should."

"What does it matter, Esau, whether they ask him or not? They're here—at Cardinal's gates. If they breakfast at eight they can be there by half-past ten." She cupped her face in her hands. "You see, I'm a broken reed. I said they'd try elsewhere first: but I got them wrong. I'd hoped for a day or two's respite—a chance to rest and refit. And now, my God . . ."

"Tell me this," said I. "Are we on the right road?"

"For Cardinal? Yes."

"Good enough," said I, and put down my foot. "That brush was damned unpleasant—I'll give you that. But we do know where they are: and that to me, at least, is a great relief. And now let's look at it this way. As like as not, their visit has already been paid. The Cardinal covert's been drawn: and since it yielded no fox, they're on their way off. Of course they'll come back—very soon. But at least we shall have our respite—our chance to rest and refit."

"You may be right," said Katharine. "What if you're wrong?"

"We shall still have our respite," said I. "From what you said a while back, they can't force their way in. Let the swine wait our convenience. If, after thinking things over, we still consider it better to—to go our way, we'll choose our time and do so. I'm damned if I'll be rushed by a couple of burglars who happen to want my life."

Katharine made no answer, but I felt her eyes on my face.

I continued steadily.

"I'm not so sure you're right, when you say we must stay off the map. I see two things against it. First, if you're off his map, the enemy must be off yours: and that is very trying: at least, I think it would be—moving with your chin on your shoulder from morning to night. Secondly, some day or other you've got to come on it again. I mean, that stands to reason. I've only got three months' leave."

"Are you suggesting, Esau, that you should stand and fight?"

"I'm suggesting nothing," said I. "I'm thinking aloud."

"I don't like your thoughts very much. For one thing only, those two can play with a pistol: but you are not armed. And if they ran into us now, they'd bump you off, like brushing a fly off their nose. I mean that, Esau. France is not like England. They'd never hear any more of their—escapade."

"I'll take your word for that. But the honest truth is that neither you nor I will be fit to work out our salvation until we have had some rest. And when I say 'rest,' I mean a bath and breakfast. I don't feel a bit like sleep."

With the tail of my eye, I saw her give her short nod.

"There's common sense," she said. "We'll have things out when we've had a wash and brush up. But do get hold of this—that we are up against people who know no law. They'll go all lengths to get us—because they will not be able to take *their* rest until they know that we are no longer alive."

Since a girl should have the last word, I left it there: but I felt that that statement of hers had proved my case. Unless I stood and fought, I must prepare to be hunted for years to come. Which was absurd. The thing was to choose one's ground and to come to grips.

... ...

For the next two hours we ran through lovely country —hill and dale and woodland, with here and there a village, but never a town. The day being Sunday, the traffic was very slight; but the work-a-day world was awake by seven o'clock, and bells were ringing and peasants were going to Mass. The morning was very handsome: I never saw sunlight so brilliant in all my life: and the meadows were cloth of silver, because of a heavy dew.

Just twenty minutes later, the Lowland swam over some crest, to enter woods so thick that the view upon either hand was wholly obscured, and though the road twisted and turned and rose and fell, for the next two miles we never saw any country, but only the curtains of foliage hanging and swaying and glancing to right and to left.

Katharine was speaking.

"Lift your foot for a moment: we're coming to a break in the trees. It's round the next bend. Half a minute won't matter, and I'd like you to see—my home."

I did as she said.

As I rounded the bend at twenty, I saw the gap she spoke of some fifty paces ahead. Abreast of this I stopped. Then I looked to my right.

I was looking across a valley, the opposite side of which was as thickly wooded as ours. Below were lying green meadows, bordered with piled stone walls, and a stream was tumbling through them—I could see the flourish of foam, where a rock rose out of its bed. What caught the eye at once was the way in which woods and meadows were taking each other's ground, for the trees ran down in irregular lines and patches into the fields, to pay for this pretty trespass by casting their shade upon the grass, and now and again the meadows climbed up by linchets into the arms of the woods. And other things caught the eye. Astride the stream was lying a tiny village, whose walls were white and whose roofs were an old rose red: a pocket church was thrusting a little belfry, a toy of a bridge was spanning the busy stream, and a water-wheel was dripping with silver, and smoke was rising into the breathless air. As though to assert their seigniory, big trees were growing in the hamlet and turning it into a bower; and the patchwork of sunshine and shadow, of green and red and white—above all, the air of contentment and simple *amour propre* cried out for the pen of a Goldsmith, to catch a charm which I cannot hope to describe. And above the village was hanging a miniature castle, exactly as its mistress had said. Sunk in the living green, its old, gray stone looked finer than any jewel, and it made me think of a cameo, brooched to a handsome cloak. All the lovely detail was there—battlement, turret and mullion, the slender spire of a chapel, the terrace, the old stone steps: nothing had been omitted by the builders who set it up. Yet all was Lilliputian. It was a baby stronghold, ruling a baby town.

I turned to Katharine, to see the softest look in her fine, gray eyes.

"I don't wonder you love it," I said. "And its secret is safe with me; for if I told someone about it, he'd write me off as a liar and leave it there."

Katharine smiled—for the first time for fully four hours.

Then—

"Let's have a close-up," she said. "But don't expect too much. Cardinal has a guest-chamber : but you're the first guest we've had."

"*Force majeure*," said I, and let in my clutch.

"Yes, in a way, I suppose : and yet, that night at Newhaven, I wished so much that I could have shown you my home."

"No man could ask for a sweeter invitation than that."

Katharine looked straight ahead.

"You were nice to me," she said : "and you asked no—no payment at all. And what upset me was your eyes : they were down on the ground when they should have been lifted up. And Cardinal stood out so clearly as the ideal corrective for Crutched Friars."

... ...

Two hours and more had gone by.

I had bathed and changed, and Conrad, the English butler, had brought me a blessed breakfast of eggs and coffee and honey and new-baked bread. All this in two very small chambers, panelled with oak. Never before had I used apartments so fine : and the sunlight seemed the richer for falling upon such carving of wood and stone. And now I was down on the terrace, to which I had found my way, surveying the pageant before me and gladly admitting the force of my lady's words.

Cardinal *was* a corrective—and something more. You could not get away from the fact that the peasants that worked in the mills and the meadows below were better off than a merchant in Crutched Friars.

Then I put such thoughts aside and began to consider my surroundings from a fugitive's point of view.

Looking across the village, I saw the gap in the woods from which I had viewed the castle two hours before. From there, though I could not see it because of the trees, I knew that the road fell down unusually sharp, doubling upon itself, to gain the valley below. This descent being over, I saw it curl into the meadows some fifty yards south of the bridge, and from there I could follow with ease the line which it took—over the jolly water and into the village *place*, and then up a very steep hill which presently brought it up to the castle's gate.

Two other roads ran into the little *place*, but Katharine had told me that that by which we had come was the only road which led to the world outside.

We had, therefore, but one to watch : but I could not lose sight of the fact that what is sauce for the gander is also sauce for the goose. If we wished to drive out from the castle, we had but one road to take—a narrow way, that could not be taken at speed. Such roads are dangerous.

And there I turned to see Katharine, framed in a little doorway which gave to a flight of steep steps. She was wearing a blue and white dress which even I could see had a style of its own, for it looked so fresh and smart and yet was as plain and simple as any frock ever was. Her head and her legs were bare, and she wore no jewellery : but though, no doubt, the ladies who must have stood there in bygone days had boasted silk and satin and famous gems, I cannot believe that one of them looked so lovely or filled so well the rôle of chatelaine.

And then, to my dismay, I saw how very strained and weary she looked—far more so, in fact, than I had seen her before. She had been up all night, and our sharp experience at Volet had hit her hard: but I had expected, as she had, that, though she was short of sleep, the physical comforts which Cardinal had to give would have refreshed her spirit as well as her flesh.

As I stepped to her side—

"You were right," she said. "The enemy's been and gone. Someone inquired at the village yesterday afternoon. Whoever it was was on foot: so there must have been a car in the offing, which didn't appear."

"Good," said I. "Have you given the servants orders—to let no strangers in?"

"Yes. I've told Conrad—something." She put a hand to her head. "What's going to be so hard is my father. I've told him nothing so far. I don't know where to begin."

"My dear," I said, "don't jump till you come to the fence. Till things begin to happen, it would be the rankest folly to open your mouth."

"Blind leading the blind," said Katharine. "'Shall they not both fall into the ditch'?"

I bit my lip. Then—

"I think I ought to know what you've said about me."

"I've lied—as usual," she said. "I've had to do it for years; but it only seems to get harder as time goes by." She looked away, twisting her hands. "He thinks I'm a secretary—to a very big business man. Offices in London and Paris: that accounts for my flitting between the two. I call him 'Mr. Shepherd'—you see, it's all founded on fact. And now I've told him this—that you met me yesterday evening. You found me beside the road, with my car burned out. Everything I had with me had gone with the car, so, as you were only touring, you offered to bring me home."

I nodded my head.

"Is that all?" I said. "I don't want to let you down."

"I said that you were making for Carcassonne."

"Why Carcassonne?" I said, staring.

She put a hand to her head.

"Well, you had to be making for somewhere. I had to think of some name."

"That's all right," I said gently. "I only wanted to know." I glanced at a cushioned bench. "Before I meet him, d'you think we could have a talk?"

"That's why I'm here," she said. "He's down in the village now. A colt has hurt itself, and he is so strong and so gentle, they've sent for him. They always do, but I don't like his going much. He had an attack of angina two years ago; and any effort is bad when you suffer from that." She moved to the bench and took her seat on its arm. "We seem to have got our breather. How long do you think it'll last?"

"As long as we please," said I. "I'd no idea at all that Cardinal was so strong."

Katharine raised her eyebrows.

"I think you've no idea of a great many things."

I shrugged my shoulders:

"Perhaps you're right," said I. "But castles will be castles—you can't get away from that."

Katharine stared at the sky.

"I'm not going to stay here, Esau. I'm not such a fool."

I fingered my chin.

"In that case," said I, "there's nothing more to be said. What time d'you propose we should leave?"

"We must leave by night on foot—it's the only way."

"On foot?"

"On foot. It will never occur to them that we've dropped the car. No one—not even my father—will know that the car is still here: and Conrad will see that the village knows that we've gone. So when they come back, as they will, they'll leave again to try and pick up the car. And if you're as careful as I am——"

"One moment," said I. "Are you proposing that we should separate?"

"Of course I am. I want you to leave to-night."

"Why shouldn't you leave with me?"

Katharine leaned forward.

"Because I'm too young to die. I haven't much to live for—I'll give you that: but, as I said yesterday evening, I may as well try and hang on. Alone, we may escape notice. Together, wherever we went, we should take a risk."

"A man and a girl?" I said. "That combination is surely common enough."

"To you, it would be. But we are not dealing with merchants of Crutched Friars. I don't want to be too brutal—I know you mean well. But, frankly, I'm safer without you. I am extremely expert at lying low: but if you're to be round my neck. . . ."

I sat very still.

I had not believed that she would have spoken like that. After all, we had run together before the wind: we had exchanged confidences: together, we had considered terrible things. And now a hard-bitten Formosa was putting a sucking merchant where he belonged.

After a little silence—

"How long d'you suggest," I said, "that I should continue to play The Wandering Jew?"

"For the rest of your leave. I think—I believe that then you could go back to Crutched Friars."

I looked at her very hard.

"Talk about a *volte-face*," I said. "Four hours ago ——"

"I know. But I've—thought things over. If you disappear for three months—well, after all, they've got their living to earn. You are not very dangerous really, because you cannot betray them without betraying me. And when they cool down, they'll see that. And when they see that, I think they'll throw in their hand and let you go."

"I see," I said slowly. "And you?"

Katharine shrugged her shoulders.

"I shall come through. Cardinal's safe for two years—I've saved enough money for that. And two years is quite a long time. Formosa will be forgotten: The Shepherd may even be dead."

I regarded the palms of my hands.

"I'm not persuaded," I said. "I still believe that we should do better to stay and to have things out. In fact, I had worked out a plan: but it's no good telling it you, if you are determined to go. But I make one stipulation—that we shall go together. I will not leave you alone."

Katharine stared.

"But I've told you——"

"I know you have," I said quietly, and looked her full in the eyes. "But I don't think you've told me the truth."

"What on earth d'you mean?"

I rose to my feet.

"That if I go to-night, you're not going to leave this house. You're going to wait here till they come, and then *you're going to meet them and try to make some arrangement by which they will spare my life.*"

Katharine had gone very pale. I saw her moisten her lips.

"You flatter yourself," she said coldly. "In fact, to be perfectly honest, I think that I've done my bit. Two nights ago I literally saved your life. I did it—on the spur of the moment. All I saw was a man who'd been civil to me, and, *as a result,* was going to be bumped off. Well, I may be a crook ; but the instincts I used to have aren't entirely dead. And so—I did what I did . . . without waiting to count the cost. Having started, I had to go on. I had to take you and lead you, show you the way across country and where to hide."

"I've tried to say I'm grateful," I said.

"Wait a minute. Yesterday, because I was shaken—because I was out of my mind, I made a damned fool of myself and told you the truth. I told you—all about me and what I was. For once in her life, Formosa exposed her sores. God knows why I did it, but let that pass. I confided in a casual acquaintance—a man that I'd never set eyes on some thirty-six hours before."

I stood very still. I knew where I was now. And I felt as though a cold hand had taken hold of my heart.

"Do you write the same note," I said, "to every casual acquaintance you happen to make."

Katharine drew in her breath.

"My God, that note," she said. "Are you suggesting that I was in love with you ?"

"I may be a fool," said I ; "but I'm not such a fool as that."

"Then why bring that up against me ? If I liked to pick you up, can't I lay you down ?"

I set my teeth.

"You shall," I said, "as soon as you're out of the wood."

"I see," she said. "Till then I'm to hold your hand." She threw back her head and laughed. "I don't want to be too rough, but I'm not a shorthand typist who's missed her 'bus. I am—Formosa. Your uncles are over sixty, and I'm not twenty-two : but I begin, my friend, where, if they live to be ninety, they may leave off. But that's by the way. . . . You blundered into that café : and I went out of my ground to get you out. Well, isn't that good enough ? "

" I've said I'm grateful," I said.

" And you show your gratitude by running between my legs. Good God Almighty, haven't you done enough harm ? "

There was a little silence, broken only by the rustle of water and the gentle note of a wood-pigeon calling a friend.

" What d'you want me to do ? " I said.

" Drop this Quixotic drivel and face the facts. Digest the truth that I may be over my knees, but you are out of your depth. Which means that I can help you, but you cannot help me ; and that any efforts *you* make can only end in killing what chance I've got."

" I see," said I. " Anything else ? "

" One thing more. You let me down in Rouen. Well, please don't let me down here. I've told you that my father is blind. Well, blindness had made his other senses acute. And if you were to say or do something which made him so much as suspect that there was something doing of which he was unaware. . . ."

" You needn't go on," said I. " I may be out of my depth ; but, although I'm only a tradesman, I do know how to behave."

" I suppose you mean that I don't."

I put a hand to my head.

"No," I said dully. "Take it that way, if you must. I can only say such a thing never entered my head. If you like to hurt 'a casual acquaintance,' that's your affair: there's no reason why you shouldn't. But it doesn't necessarily follow that the casual acquaintance will endeavour to hit you back. But that doesn't mean he's no pride."

"Pride or presumption?" said Katharine.

"Pride," said I. "He'll—never presume any more."

Katharine said nothing to that, and, after waiting a moment, I stepped to the stone balustrade and stood looking over the valley which I had found so perfect ten minutes before.

I should not, I think, have been human, if I had not been stung to the quick by the 'whips and scorns' she had used: but I was as sure as before that once I was out of the way she did not mean to follow, but meant to face the music and do her utmost to save me at her expense. And this was unthinkable. If, on the other hand, she truly intended to leave before the enemy came, she would be better without my company: and if she made herself scarce for the next two years, there could be next to no doubt that she would escape. And Cardinal would be inviolate—The Shepherd was out for murder, not for blackmail. I alone should go down; for the number-plate of the car had given him my name and address; and when October came and I had to come out of hiding and go back to Crutched Friars. . . . But if I could see that, Formosa could see it, too: and, rail as she pleased, I knew she would never allow it, whilst she was alive. Whether she cared for me, I could not pretend to say: but she felt responsible for me, and that was enough.

I turned, to see her watching me, finger to lip.

For a moment I met her gaze. Then—

"Where are you, Kate?"

The pleasant voice came down the winding stair.

Katharine flashed to the doorway.

"Here. On the terrace," she said.

With her words, the speaker appeared—a man like a Viking, clad in an old, tweed suit, with his daughter's magnificent eyes and a pointed beard that was glowing with gray and gold.

Katharine was speaking.

"Jeremy, this is my father, Sir Valentine Scrope. Father, here's Mr. Solon, who's come miles out of his way to give your daughter a lift."

I took the outstretched hand and I met the great, gray eyes: I found it most hard to believe that they could not see.

"Any man who brings me my daughter is welcome here. There was a fellow of Merton who bore your name."

"That was my grandfather, sir."

"I'm glad of that. He was my classical tutor a good many years ago. And I used to sit at his feet, for he made the dead languages live. 'Get what class you like,' he'd say. 'It's nothing to me. I shall have done my job if, whenever you see the sea, you think of the Odyssey.'"

"I was at Merton, sir."

A hand came to rest on my shoulder.

"What fun," said the giant. "Did you row?"

For five minutes we strolled and talked, while Katharine moved beside us, but said no word. Then Sir Valentine cocked his ear, and I heard the church clock striking ten.

"You must excuse me," he said, "for a quarter of an hour. I want to prepare a stall for a mare that is coming to stay. And when I get back, we'll go on. I must make the most of your time, as you're leaving to-night. I'd have liked to have kept you here: but you mustn't let down the fellow you're joining at Carcassonne."

With a nod and a smile he stepped to a second stairway that gave to the court below—to leave me staring after, with an open mouth and one of my hands to my head. And when I turned to Katharine, my lady was gone.

CHAPTER V

FEW guests can have passed a more distracting day.

No one could have been nicer than was Sir Valentine Scrope. On his return, he took me all over the castle and showed me every detail of all its loveliness. And then we talked of Oxford, until it was time for lunch. And I had to play up somehow—take and display an interest in all he said.

There were times, indeed, when I felt that I could not go on. I was mentally and physically tired ; and my weary brain was obsessed with matters of life and death. Yet I had to discuss architecture and talk of the river and coaches and Oxford's eternal charm.

Katharine appeared at lunch : but the moment the meal was over, she said she was going to rest. I tried—and failed to do likewise, until it was time for tea : but though I then left my room, more dead than alive, she did not reappear, and I had to talk to her father till half-past six.

At last he rose to his feet.

"I wish you weren't going," he said. "I'd like to have kept you here. However, it can't be helped. You'll dine with us first, won't you ?"

I stammered my thanks.

"That's right. I've said dinner at eight. No changing, of course. I expect you're very wise to travel by night. Kate says it's the only way, and she ought to know. And now I must have my stroll." He threw up his head. "I love the meadows at sundown. To every kind of country, its special hour. Dawn on the uplands : noon in the heart of a forest : night on a river's breast."

I made some feeble reply, and he smiled and was gone.

For a quarter of an hour I sought Katharine, and sought in vain. Then I withdrew to my chamber and wrote her a note.

My dear,

Unless you go with me, I will not leave here to-night. How to break this to your father, I do not know. I never was very quick, and after the day I've spent, my brain is about as much use as a cough in a hurricane. But unless you come to my help, I shall have to do it alone. I'm going to sit on the ramparts till eight o'clock.

Esau.

When I had sealed this up, I called the butler and asked him to see that she had it at once. And then I went up to the ramparts, as I had said.

It was a beautiful evening, and the country before and below me might have belonged to a landscape which some great painter had dreamed of and then recorded on canvas a hundred years ago ; for the peaceful scene was stately beyond belief—an artless fable, rendered in deathless verse.

I never heard Katharine coming: but something made me look round, and there she was. And my heart leaped up when I saw the look on her face, for in that instant I knew that all her unkindness that morning had been put on, in one last, frantic effort to force my hand.

"I've come to beg you, Esau, to do as I ask."

"That's out of the question," I said.

"But my father is sure to suspect——"

"I don't see why he should. More than once he has said that he wished I could stay. What I propose to do is to ask if George can come here—and to do my best to get him as quick as ever I can. But if he does suspect something, it won't be my fault. Who, as the poet says, who tipped me into the muck?"

"Esau, listen. This morning I tried my utmost to force your hand. Perhaps I should have known better: but let that pass. To-night I am going to implore you not to discard the only chance that we have. I've told you that The Shepherd means business, and so he does. To stand and fight is hopeless: against such a man you haven't the ghost of a chance. To run is equally hopeless: he'll simply bide his time and get us both in the end."

I folded my arms.

"And so you propose to see him?"

She nodded.

"We've only one card, Esau. And that is Formosa's value, as one of The Shepherd's Crooks. He can't replace her—he knows that as well as I. And if, when he comes, you are really out of his ken, I think I can make your health a condition of my return."

"My dear——"

"One moment, Esau. I know what you're going to say. But what would become of my father, if anything happened to me? And unless I go back—unless I am taken back, whether I live or die, I shall be as good as dead. A fugitive can't earn money: and I shall never dare to return to Cardinal. Your life, my life and his welfare—all three depend on your leaving alone to-night. If you will do that, I believe I can bring it off."

"And I," said I, "should never see you again."

With the now familiar gesture, she pushed back her lovely hair. Then—

"Don't make it so hard, Esau. I'm—out of court, my dear: and you know it as well as I. What is the good of pretending—of picking the Dead Sea apples, when both of us know they'll be dust and ashes to eat?"

I took her two hands in mine.

"Do you really think," said I, "that I'm going to leave you now?"

The fine, gray eyes looked away.

"I hoped that you would—for my sake. You see, I've nothing to gain from your staying, but so much to lose."

"'Nothing to gain,' Katharine?"

She shook her head.

"Nothing, my dear. I mean it. You see, you can

do no good. You are up against something which doesn't belong to your world: and if you try to face it, you'll lose your life. And I . . . don't want you to die. That is the most I can hope for—that you should live. Formosa will carry on, and Cardinal, too. In fact, we'll be back as we were—if only you'll do as I say."

I set her slim hands on my shoulders.

"I've looked in your eyes," I said: "and I am not content for us to be back as we were."

"It's the most we can hope for, Esau. If it comes off, you and I will always remember the hours which we spent together, first in that fatal calm and then riding the storm. They'll always mean—a great deal to me. *Please* be content with that. Don't stake the pittance I've won—because you're bound to lose it, and I shall have nothing at all. In a sense, I'm a victim of Fate. But victims of Fate are doomed. They cannot be saved."

"It's too late now," I said gently. "I don't care what whirlwind I reap. I'm not going to give you up."

"But, Esau, be reasonable. Supposing, somehow or other, we found ourselves out of the wood. Say The Shepherd fell dead or something—I can't think of anything else. Well, that couldn't wash out the past. I should still be Formosa. And I couldn't accept your friendship, because——"

"I don't offer you my friendship," I said.

She lifted her eyes to mine.

"Esau, dear, listen to me. Some of us have a box, which is labelled 'What might have been.' You'll never have one, I hope. But I have . . . a very big one. It holds such a lot, and I think it's nearly full. Please, Esau, don't open that box. It does no good, and if ever I look inside, it hurts me terribly. You see, it's full of dead things, that should be alive. My heart's among them somewhere."

"D'you want to add mine to the collection?"

Her head went back, and her eyes went up to the sky.

"Esau, don't talk like that. It's only twisting my tail. We've had . . . a great time together. Let's always remember that. Sixty precious hours, which no one—not even The Shepherd—can take away. I think—I have a feeling, that if you will only fade out, I can pull things round. For God's sake, realize this—that that is the best we can hope for. To go for anything else is to court the most awful crash. You and I and my father—we'd all go down."

"You must always have known," said I, "that sooner or later some end was bound to come. I expect you fobbed off the spectre. But I think you knew that at last the end *had* come, when I walked into that café two nights ago. By so doing, I tore things up—you said as much yesterday. And now you talk of mending 'the veil of the Temple.' . . . Myself, I decline to believe that the thing can be done: and, in any event, I won't help. If I did, I'd be mentally sick for the rest of my life. Don't think I'm trying to save you—I never had that idea. But I do know what I want. And I'm not going to be ridden off by one of the filthiest blackguards that ever made use of a lady to save his creeping skin."

Her hands laid hold of my shoulders: her eyes met mine.

"Esau, I've told you——"

"Enough," said I, "to show me we're two of a kind."

"We're not. We're not." She tried to shake me: I felt her breath on my face. "We never can be, Esau. If The Shepherd fell dead to-morrow, we couldn't be that."

I put my arms about her and held her close.

"No," said I; "that's true. You'll always be a great lady, and I am a sucking merchant of Crutched Friars. But Fate has thrown us together, and that is enough for me. I loved you the moment I saw you: and after that note you sent me, I never should have rested until I had found you again. You see, it meant that you cared. Well, now I know more than that—that, no matter what it costs you, your one idea is to save me from possible harm. That can only mean that you love me—for that's how I feel about you."

She took my face in her hands.

"Yes," she breathed, "I love you. How could I do anything else? You are so natural, Esau. So simple and understanding, and so unspoiled. And it is because I love you, that, even if a miracle happened to bring us out of this jam, nothing on earth would make me become your wife. You see, Formosa's spoiled goods."

"Not in my eyes, my darling."

"I know. That's because you love me. The police would be less—broad-minded. And that is why I never could take your name. So, you see, we've no future, my darling. Our little love-affair is bound to—never grow up. And that being so, why won't you do as I say? You've been so sweet to me, and if I can straighten things out, I should be so very thankful to think that—no harm had been done. I say again, *that is the most we can hope for*, for no one can do any good. And if you stand and fight, you'll only be killed, my darling, and that'll be the end of Formosa and so of Cardinal."

I looked at myself in her eyes.

"I've told you, sweetheart," I said, "that if you insist on my going, I'll leave with you."

"Go alone, darling, for my sake: and spare us both. You've turned a muck-heap over and pulled an idyll out. Don't take it away from me, Esau—I've never had one before. Kiss me and go, beloved, before my father comes back. I'll tell him something—make some sort of excuse. And I'll let you out by the window which gives to the path in the woods. But go, if you love me, Esau; for even if we come through—and I know we can't—the day will come when you'll have to go alone."

"*Tant pis*," I sighed. "That's French. I learned it at school."

I bent my head and kissed her beautiful mouth. Then I let her go and stood back and away.

"Do we go or stay?" I said. "It's up to—my future wife."

"Esau, you're mad. We've life and death before us. Which do we choose."

"Life—and love," said I. "Things being as they are, the second must wait upon the first. But when The Shepherd *is* dead and Formosa is out of the wood, then we'll remember this evening—and bless the madness that made me choose as I did."

She lifted her hands, to let them fall to her sides.

"I've done my best," she said, "and you've turned it down. You are determined, Esau, to rush upon both our fates."

I shook my head.

"I just won't leave you," I said. "I'll run with you if you like: but I'd rather we stood our ground."

Katharine regarded me dumbly, as one who has shot her bolt. Then a tear rolled down her cheek and she put up an arm to her eyes, as a weeping child.

She was in my arms in an instant and her face was pressed close against mine.

"Don't cry," I whispered. "Don't cry. It tears my heart, my darling, to see you cry."

After a little, her arms went about my neck.

With an effort, she mastered her voice.

"I . . . don't want you to be . . . hurt. I couldn't bear . . . that. My life . . . doesn't matter. I've messed it up so much . . . it's only fit to be smashed. But I'd like to think . . . you were all right."

"I shall be, my blessed," I breathed. "Both of us will be—all right."

I felt her take a deep breath.

Then—

"The stuffing's gone out of me, Esau. Things are too much for me, and I'm not going to fight any more.

I'll do all you say, of course. But you have taken charge, and you'll have to play the hand. I daresay it's better so. I've not been myself since Rouen—Formosa went into that café, but Katharine Scrope came out." She sighed again. "And now you must let me go. I don't know much about tears, but I think I should bathe my face."

I watched her cross the ramparts and take the winding stair that led to the terrace below. And then I made haste to follow, because I had more to say.

As I began to go down, I heard her descending below me, just out of sight.

"Listen, Katharine," I said, and quickened my pace. "We haven't arranged——"

And there I missed my footing. . . .

After all, it was easy enough.

The ramparts had been full of light, but the stair was dim: and the steps were steep and worn, and I, who did not know them, was moving fast.

Be that as it may, I stumbled and put a foot wrong, and, because there was no handhold, I fell down the rest of the flight.

It was not far to fall, and, happily, she was clear: but I came to rest on the terrace, right on her heels.

Although I sat up, I did not attempt to rise, but leaned forward to nurse my left foot, which was hurting me very much.

Katharine was kneeling beside me: her face was cupped in her hands.

"Esau, you're hurt. What is it?"

"Give me a hand," I said, smiling.

She did as I said and I got to my other foot.

"But, Esau——"

"Cold, running water," I said. "That's all I need. And a bandage, later. But first the way to a tap."

"Lean on my shoulder, dear."

So we came to a tiny bathroom, which I afterwards found was hers. . . .

As the water streamed over my ankle—

"Does it still hurt terribly, Esau?"

I picked up her hand and kissed it.

"It's nothing at all," I said, "except a perfect excuse for not leaving for Carcassonne."

... ...

Sir Valentine made things easy. Before the words were out of his daughter's mouth, he had issued the invitation I wished to hear.

"Since you cannot go to Laking, ask Laking to come to you. Kate will drive you to Cruise—we have no telephone here: and from there you can speak to him and tell him how you are placed. We shall be delighted to have him—to have you both: and as you lived together at Oxford, I daresay, for once in a way, you won't mind sharing a room."

I thanked him suitably: and, after a word or two, he left me to bathe and change. But I sat still where I was, with a hand to my mouth. It had never entered my head that the nearest telephone was actually twelve miles off.

I confess that for two or three minutes I did not

know what to do. It was madness to leave the castle and take again to the road: yet, if I could possibly get him, I had to have George. That he was back in Paris, I had no doubt: neither had I any doubt that, if I could only convince him that I was in danger of death, he would throw everything up and come to set his back against mine.

And then, all at once, I saw that if we were to stand and fight, we simply must be able to come and go; and that if we were to be able to come and go, the very first thing to do was to get the car out of the castle and lodge her in some safe place to which we could walk when we pleased without being seen.

There and then I went off to find my lady and ask for a large-scale map: but I might have known that she knew the country by heart, and before we had talked for two minutes, I had the trick in my hand.

The castle hung in the woods on the spur of a mountainside, and all of its walls could be seen, except that which rose to the north. This wall looked on to the mountain and could not be seen from below or from either side, because of the foliage in which the castle was sunk.

Though there was no gate in this wall, there was a window one of whose bars could be dropped: since this was but six feet up, a man who meant to do it could easily pass either way: but the bar could not be moved, except by somebody standing within the walls. (This was, of course, the window, by which Katharine had wished me to leave.)

Once afoot in the forest, you had a choice of two

ways ; for thirty yards off lay a path which could not be seen. If, when you came to this, you turned to the right, six minutes' walk would bring you down into the valley, beyond and below the castle and east of the village itself. But if you turned to the left, a walk of an hour would carry you up and over the mountainside and so to the village of Ousse, which was, if anything, smaller than that of Cardinal.

Such was her information.

It was, therefore, perfectly clear that Ousse was the place at which to conceal the Lowland and that, since we had to drive out, the time at which to conceal her was after our visit to Cruise.

It follows that when, after dinner, we took our seats in the car, Conrad had been instructed that we should return on foot and that he must be ready to admit us by the window that gave to the woods.

Though we were making a virtue of necessity, I did not like the look of the venture on which we were setting out. In fact, I was most uneasy. I could not lose sight of the fact that the Cardinal road was as perilous as the castle itself was safe. Solitary, narrow and dark, it offered an enemy all that he could desire, and the very strength of the shelter which we were abandoning insisted on the nature of the gauntlet which we were proposing to run.

Could I have done so, I would have left Katharine behind : but, for one thing, she would not have stayed, and for another, I could not have done without her the things I was going to do. (I could, in fact, have driven, instead of her : but since I had before me a walk of two miles, it seemed better to rest my ankle until that came: then again, if trouble was coming, it was very much better that I should have my hands free.)

So I sat still by her side, with my foot strapped up and a hammer close to my hand, while she drove out of the courtyard and down to the sleeping hamlet and over the miniature bridge. We severed the sweet-smelling meadows and bore to the right. Then we entered the hanging forest, which might have been the cloak of darkness itself.

If I had been shaken before, it was the forest that brought my fears to a head. The place was the lair of Ambush: and we were proclaiming our presence with torch and drum.

Quiet as the Lowland was, the roof and curtains of leaves magnified the sound of her engine and the brush of her tires upon the road: and though her lights were dimmed, so thick was the darkness about us, the tunnel ahead seemed bathed in a blaze of light.

As we left the serpentine hill—

"How far are the cross roads?" said I.

"About two miles and a quarter from where we are now."

"No turning till then?"

"No."

"They're clear of the forest, you said?"

"Yes, they're in open country. We don't have to turn for Cruise, so I might be able to take them without any lights."

"Speed's more important," said I. "I don't want to loiter just there. But don't go too fast till then:

and tell me when we're approaching the end of these—beautiful woods."

I saw her nod.

By now I had a definite feeling that some sort of watch had been set. That we had slipped by that morning might well have been due to the fact that the enemy had not had time to post a sentinel. But, had I been in his place, I would have kept some watch on the Cardinal road. If I was right, we had this much in our favour—that whoever was there would not be expecting us to be coming *from* Cardinal ; for had the enemy dreamed that we had reached the castle, during the day he would have appeared at its gates.

Perhaps four minutes slid by. Then—

"We're nearly there," said Katharine. "We're coming to the last of the forest. You see it's lighter ahead."

I took a sudden decision.

"Then slow up and stop your engine and put out your lights."

She did as I said.

Straining our eyes and our ears, we sat very still. Then I opened the door by my side and let myself into the road.

I felt her hand on my arm.

"What are you doing, Esau ?"

"I'm going to reconnoitre. This place is made for an ambush : and I'm afraid to go on until I have looked at the cross roads and seen—what there is to be seen."

In a flash, she was out of the car.

"I'm coming with you," she breathed.

I bit my lip. Then—

"I trust you," I said, "to keep ten paces behind me—no less than that."

"Very well."

"And now tell me this. I think that's a bend ahead."

"That's right. It's the first of two bends, about fifty paces apart. That's the end of the forest, and there are the cross roads before you, two hundred paces away."

"I see. Keep directly behind me. I want to know where you are."

Our shoes were soled with rubber and made no sound, and though I was going short, my foot hardly hurt me at all. But I knew that, come what might, I should not be able to hasten for three or four days.

I was growing accustomed to the darkness, thick as it was, and I marked with satisfaction the definite glow that argued the starlight ahead; for if there was any-one there, since we were coming from darkness, we ought to be able to see him before he saw us. He might have heard the Lowland, the night was so still: but between the car and the cross roads a spur of the mountain ran down, and that should have been enough to blanket what sound we had made.

As I approached the first bend, I passed to the side of the way: then I stole round very slowly, to see the road empty before me, but now less dark than dim, while the second bend was outlined against the light of the stars. For any kind of ambush, this reach would have been ideal, and I had felt so strongly that danger lay in our path that I was almost surprised to see that the way was clear. (It would have been so easy to set a pole there on a trestle or leave a log in the road: and once the obstruction was there, anyone driving fast was simply bound to hit it, because, as their lights came round it would have been out of their beam: and if they had not been killed, when the car overturned, one sentinel could have completed the work which had been begun.) Still, though it seemed that my fancy was running away, I determined to view the cross roads before going back, and after a glance behind, which showed me nothing at all, I began to pad on more quickly towards the last of the bends.

I had very nearly made it before I was brought up sharp. My instinct had been right, after all. A fine wire cable, waist high, was across the road. This, which had been painted black, was quite invisible.

... ...

I was breathing in Katharine's ear.

"If there's anyone here, I think they'll be at the cross roads—I'll tell you why. They can see much more from there and they are expecting us to be going the opposite way, and if there should be a smash, they can be on the spot within fifty seconds of time: yet they won't be on the scene of the outrage—in case of accidents. I'm almost sure I'm right, because it's such common sense: but I'd like to be quite sure before I have a go at that cable—I don't suppose it's very hard to undo."

Together we rounded the bend. Then I bade her stay where she was, until I was once again ten paces ahead.

I could see where the cross roads were, but no more than that, for though I could see very well for forty or fifty yards, after that substance and shadow began to become confused and I could only discern the line of the road itself. Stretches of bracken had taken the place of the trees, and the ground on my right was far higher than that on my left, which showed that we were still on a mountainside, though the slope was much more gentle than it had been in the woods. Since the high ground made for darkness, I kept to the right of the road, with my lady moving behind me, but making no sound at all.

We had covered, perhaps, a hundred and seventy yards, and the actual cross of the roads was clear to be seen, when, without any warning at all, a figure strolled into my view from the road on my right.

For a moment he stood, I think, with his back towards me: then he struck a match and lighted a cigarette.

The sight of him made me so angry that, had I been ten paces nearer I would have chanced a pistol and laid him out with a weapon which could not miss: indeed, I was hesitating, whether or not to advance, when he settled the matter for me by sauntering on his way and out of my sight.

At once I turned back. . . .

Whilst Katharine watched, I fought with the cable until I could cast it loose. Then I coiled it up and dropped it into the ditch. And then we went back to the car and *I* took the wheel, for I meant to run the man down, if he gave me a chance.

"Put out the clutch for me."

She did as I said. . . .

I changed into second . . . between us, we changed into top. . . .

With our headlights on, we went for the cross roads at sixty—and gathering speed.

But I never saw the ghoul who was waiting to give us the *coup de grâce.* Perhaps he was safe in the bracken. After all, he was there to take life—not to lose it by playing the fool. And I had this consolation—that now he would report to his master that we had been going *away* from Cardinal. That accurate information would stand us in very good stead.

Katharine was speaking—with her eyes on the road behind.

"I take off my hat to you, Esau. You know how to use an instinct I've never had."

I shot her a glance ; for her words and her manner of speaking had taken me by surprise. But though I think she saw me, she gave no sign.

"I don't know about that," I said.

"I do. And it's done me good. I knew that you had no fear : but I saw no reason to think that you had resource."

"Can anything good come out of Crutched Friars ?"

"You never learned that there : it's your mother wit. Never mind. It's—helped me up. . . . Bear to the left in a minute and up and over a ridge."

As we swam over the crest, her head came round.

"All clear," she said. "D'you think that Laking will come?"

"He will," I said, "if he's in when the telephone goes."

"Mr. Laking—Formosa, one of The Shepherd's Crooks."

"My dear," I said, "he'll have to be told the truth."

"Of course. It doesn't matter—as long as he holds his tongue. You need an Achates badly—to-night's shown that. I'll pull my weight, and more: but I know where a girl gets off and I'm not going to cramp your style. But please never move without me—I may be able to help. I know my late confederates. I know their habits and outlook, and pretty ways they've got that you'd never guess. Judas, for instance, is left-handed—that's worth remembering."

"The relief," I said, "of hearing you talk like this."

Katharine laughed.

"Meet Formosa," she said. "I told you you'd done me good."

"Whom have I met till now?"

"Good, soppy fairy Katharine, who looks after little children who've lost their way."

We both of us laughed at that, and I put out a hand for hers.

My lady saw the movement and shook her head.

"Formosa's no time for that."

"My mistake," said I.

Katharine gave her short nod.

"I shouldn't make it again. Formosa can snap."

"So can good fairy Katharine. This morning——"

"That's not fair." Her hand came to rest on my arm. "You know very well that I never meant what I said."

"I know that now," said I. "Will you promise never again to say a thing to me which you do not mean?"

"I promise," she said quietly.

I took her hand in my right and put it up to my lips. As I let it go, I felt her curls on my cheek.

"Why are you so nice to me, Esau?"

"Because I love you," I said. "You know that as well as I."

"I wanted to hear you say it." She sat up there and shook her hair into place. "I told you Katharine was soppy. But I warn you, Formosa's a tough."

"I don't accept either description."

Her shoulders went up.

"Is George Laking like Sancho Panza?"

"At Oxford," said I, "he used to be called 'The Bull.'"

"Oh, dear. And what were you called?"

"If you must know, I was called 'Thunder'—because I made so much noise."

"You're quiet enough now," said Katharine.

"Much virtue in Crutched Friars."

"I'm glad you realize that. I was rather afraid the good fairy had led you astray. She never really meant more than that Crutched Friars should be the means to an end." Before I could deal with this statement, "And here is Cruise," she added. "First to the right, and then the third to the left. We're going to visit a plumber. His wife used to be our cook. They have the telephone, and I'd rather not try an hotel."

Two or three minutes later, we entered a builder's yard. . . .

My lady was warmly received, and Monsieur Legrand made haste to open his office and turn up George's address. Whilst we were awaiting the connection, a fine-looking youth appeared—to be introduced as a nephew, whose military service had ended a few days before.

"A little holiday, Madame, before he begins to seek work. He was to have been a footman. But now—what will you? His master-to-be is dead, and——"

Here the telephone-call came through.

Mercifully, George was at home.

"Yes, you're a good one," he said. "Rouen may have its charm, but——"

"Listen, George," I said. "I'm in a damned tight place."

"I'm glad to hear it," said George. "The heat at Rouen——"

"Damn Rouen," I said. "I couldn't help myself. Three days ago I wanted you very much. But now I damned well need you—in a matter of life and death."

"Not 'battle and murder'?" said George.

"As like as not. I mean it. And it's more than a one-man job."

"Where are you now?"

"I'm speaking from Cruise. That's ninety miles from Le Puy. Get leave somehow, George—on 'urgent private affairs.'"

"I've got it," cried George. "Six weeks. That's why I stayed on on Thursday—to clear things up."

I could hardly believe my ears.

"Fate again," I said, without thinking.

"What d'you mean?"

"Never mind. Can you come at once?"

"I imagine so," said George. "The special idea was to spend such leave as your guest."

Katharine was touching my arm.

"Hold on a minute," I said.

"Tell him to come to-morrow by the train that gets to Cruise at nine at night. Joseph, the nephew, will meet him and bring him here. And here a car will be waiting, to bring him on."

I passed the instructions on.

"O.K.," said George. "But let's be clear about this. I haven't got over Rouen. I shan't get over Rouen for years and years. And if, when I get to Cruise, Joseph, the nephew, is not there——"

"That'll do," said I. "I swear he'll be there."

"Very well. Till to-morrow evening. Leave someone for me to kill."

I put the receiver back and turned to Katharine.

"He's coming—to stay," I told her. "He's got his leave."

"Very good indeed."

I fingered my chin.

"I don't think we'd better meet him: you see, he

won't be suspect until he's been seen with us. But I'd like a man we can trust to drive him to Cardinal."

Katharine raised her eyebrows.

"To Cardinal? Not to Ousse?"

"To Cardinal," said I. "We opened the way to-night. They won't try that wheeze again, for they know we're wise. And Ousse must not be dreamed of—by anyone except us." I saw her nod. "And now, because of your father, I'd like to leave him a note."

Monsieur Legrand made me free of his writing-desk.

I kept the letter as short as ever I could. Then I gave it to Katharine to read.

"That's all right," she said. "Is there anything else?"

"One thing," I said. "I like the look of Joseph, the nephew. Why shouldn't he enter my service to-morrow night? He might be—valuable. And, if you could find room for him, he could spare your people the business of waiting on George and me."

"That's a good idea," said Katharine. "Of course he'll come. Would you like me to fix it up?"

"Yes, if you will."

Before five minutes were past, the deal was done.

Joseph was to enter my service the following night—for three months 'certain,' at one thousand francs a month. There and then I gave him money with which to fit himself out. And then I gave him his orders—with Katharine's help. These were to be at the station in plenty of time, to bring George back to the plumber's and there let him read my note, and then to come on with George, as fast as he could: but, above everything else, to hold his tongue.

As we returned to the Lowland—

"A taxi from the station," I said: "but a man he can trust to drive them to Cardinal."

Katharine translated my words, and Joseph inclined his head.

"It is understood, Madame."

We took our leave to a little blaze of goodwill. Uncle and aunt were effusive: their nephew was more reserved, as a servant should be: but his eyes were alight with pleasure and he could not keep the eagerness out of his voice.

Half an hour later we reached the village of Ousse. This, without incident. And a quarter of an hour after that, the Lowland was lodged in a barn of which I had the key. And then we took the path by the forest, to bring us to Cardinal.

Tired and lame as I was, that walk was over too soon.

The moon was rising now, and our way was not pitch dark, as had been the Cardinal road: and, because we were not in the Lowland, the silence was absolute. The grandeur of the timber about us, the perfume of cool, rich earth, a shaft of moonlight badging a glade of bracken, a star that hung like a jewel between two shadowy spires—these things and all they stood for were better than meat and drink. For the first time since leaving Rouen, I felt at peace—for here was sanctuary such as no castle could give. The slight figure moving before me might have belonged to some dream, in which ill will and unkindness had no place: and I found myself wildly wishing that we could renounce The Shepherd and all his works and take to the kindly greenwood for good and all. Then Reason touched my shoulder, and Katharine looked back over hers and waited for me to come up.

"Poor Esau, with his game leg. You've had a hard day."

"I've had a great day," said I. "And what about you."

"Formosa's herself again."

"I'm mad about her," said I. "Will you give her my love?"

She made no answer to that, and I stepped by her side in silence, till we saw the bulk of the castle looming ahead.

"There's Conrad's light," she said. "If we throw a pebble up, he'll come to the other window and let us in."

I found a small piece of wood. Then I pitched this into the pantry and stood with my eyes on the room.

"Formosa's a fool," said a voice: "but she—asked me to give hers back."

... ...

Twenty-four hours had gone by.

My ankle was very much better, in spite of my two-mile walk, and Katharine looked quite different after a good night's rest.

As I had expected it would, the day had passed

quietly enough, and so far as we saw, no stranger had entered Cardinal's gates. And now the evening was over and night had come in—with a mutter of thunder rolling over the hills and summer lightning playing over the topless trees.

My lady and I were sitting upon the terrace, watching the gap in the woods for the headlights of George's car.

Sir Valentine had retired.

"I think it better," he said, "that you should greet Laking alone. Make my excuses, of course: but we don't want to overwhelm an innocent man. He's been more or less pitchforked here, and I want him to feel at home. So I'll make his acquaintance to-morrow. I'm sure I'm right."

This most understanding outlook suited us down to the ground; for now we had nothing to fear, but George could be primed at leisure by Katharine as well as by me.

And so a cold meal had been set in the vaulted dining-room, and Katharine and I were waiting for the flash of his lights in the woods.

"I'm getting nervous," said Katharine. "You and I jumped in together, and that was that. But to strip your soul in cold blood to a man that you've never seen . . ."

"George will love you," I said. "And when he hears your tale, he'll go up in the air."

"For the look of the thing—perhaps. After all, I'm his hostess: he can't get away from that. But if he stays, he'll stay for your sake, Esau, and not for your point of view. You are in love with me, and so you ignore the fact that I have broken our caste's most sacred law. But he won't lose sight of that. Damn it. I've carried stuff that may have belonged to his friends."

"George," said I, "is no fool. He'll——"

"Fool or no, he's coming." She raised an arm and pointed. "Look at the gap."

On the opposite side of the valley, the break in the trees was full of a curious radiance which rapidly grew more bright. Then it went suddenly out, and all that was left was an intermittent flicker, which might have been that of a rocket slowly sinking slantwise down to the meadows below. Three minutes later, a car crawled over the bridge. . . .

We greeted George in the courtyard. Then we led him into the house, and Conrad took charge of Joseph and sent the driver away.

"The position is this," said Katharine. "You have not dined; but we have: and we have a tale to tell. So you shall eat and listen, and we will talk."

"And drink," said George. "You know. For the look of the thing."

So it fell out.

Behind closed doors and over the old oak table, I told him what had occurred and we had things out. I will not repeat what we said: but we did not leave anything out and Katharine told him plainly what she had been and why.

When she had finished, George looked from her to me.

"There's a brave lady," he said. "How simple it

would have been to tell me the tale. But no. No false pretences. She's bound to fly her flag. It may be The Jolly Roger, but what of that? If I'm to come in with her, I've got to be told the truth." He stood up and lifted his glass. "Miss Scrope," he said, "your most obedient servant, who thanks you very much for letting him be your guest."

Katharine coloured with pleasure.

"What did I tell you?" I said.

"Formosa is touched," said Katharine. "I can't put it higher than that."

Then she gave us her hands to kiss, and told him to call her Katharine and called him George: and we all three drank together to the doom of a man we knew.

"And now," said George, sitting down, "for a nasty jar. You've got me here, and I mean to pull my weight. *But I've brought the enemy with me as far as Cruise, for a wallah I noticed at Rouen got out of the Paris train."*

CHAPTER VI

A TEMPEST raged that night. For hours the wind blew and the rain fell down: but while the wrath of the gale passed over the castle's head, the long roar of the forests, bearing the brunt of the onslaught, was unforgettable. And then, when I woke the next morning, the heaven was blue again, and the sun was out, and a dripping world was gleaming with green and silver and smelling sweeter than any perfumer's shop.

But though this transfiguration was truly magical, it was not that that brought me on to the ramparts by seven o'clock. I wished to observe the village: for unless I was much mistaken, the enemy's coming was now but a matter of hours.

This was, of course, our own fault: and Katharine had blamed herself hotly for failing to make me warn George to cover his tracks.

"I'm losing my mind, or something. George was the clearest link. Where was the Lowland that night, when we beat them to Pont-de-l'Arche? Outside an hotel. Well, the obvious thing to do was to ask the hotel for your name. Before they've finished asking, in comes George red-hot and plasters his engagement with you all over the place. Laking is looking for Solon, who can't be found. All within earshot know this—including, of course, the 'wallah,' who's much obliged. And when George leaves Rouen for Paris, the 'wallah' goes, too. Damn it, the thing's too easy . . . I can't remember when I've left such a knot untied."

But if I am to tell the truth, I was not altogether sorry for what had occurred. The report from the ghoul at the cross roads might well have gained us a respite of several days: but it would have been very trying to wait and watch for trouble which did not come, and I felt that, now George was with us, the sooner we came to grips, the better for all concerned.

As I looked at the village below, one thing was immediately clear. And that was this. That unless, between us, we kept a continual look-out, the enemy could be upon us before we knew he was there. In a way, this would not matter, for, though he came up to the castle, he could not walk in; yet no one likes being surprised, and when I was joined by Katharine and then by George, it was plain that their peace of mind was just as exacting as mine. So, after a little discussion, Conrad and Joseph were summoned and told a part of the truth, and before they left, it was settled that Conrad should arrange with the landlord of Cardinal's only inn to send his boy up to the castle if any stranger appeared. Since the inn stood beside the bridge and five francs meant a good deal to the son of the house, we should thus be given the notice we wished to have, yet be spared the great inconvenience of keeping the watch ourselves.

Except that it failed me if ever I tried to run, my

ankle was well again; but, for what it was worth, I rested it all that morning, while my host showed George the castle and Katharine studied the files which the butler kept.

I had plenty to think about: but what concerned me most was the tale which would have to be told to Sir Valentine Scrope.

The position was odious.

Here was a great-hearted man, with the faith of a little child. That he had lost his fortune was not to be wondered at: he knew as much about business as I did of Barbary apes. He took his world for granted, and was content. His love for and pride in his daughter was touching to see. His sense of beauty was such as I had never conceived—he would sit by the hour by the fountain which played in the cool courtyard, listening to the lisp of the water and the whisper of the leaves overhead: and when a bird came to drink, he would hear it come and would bid it on to his shoulder and be obeyed. He walked and talked with Nature, as once Enoch walked with God. He was most generous-minded: and his honesty burned like a flame.

To lie to such a being cost one one's self-respect: to tell him the truth would be to commit a crime: that he should suspect for one instant that he was being deceived was quite unthinkable.

The more I considered the case, the more desperate I felt: yet now it seemed to me that something would have to be done.

For one thing, it was not decent that his guests should conceal from Sir Valentine matters so grave, yet actually use his servants to help them to their desires. For another, it soon would be hopeless to try to hide the fact that we were about some business of which he had not been told ; for, once things had come to a head, God only knew what hours we should have to keep, what sudden calls upon us the enemy's movements might make, and upon what goings and comings success or failure might hang.

On the face of it, it would not be hard to invent some tale or other which would account for the storm about to arise : but, once you depart from the truth, you stand in constant danger of making some bad mistake and I did not feel at all certain that, if I was really harassed I should be able to keep this danger at bay. Still, that risk I would have taken and have hoped for the best. What I could not conceive how to deal with was the line which our host would take the moment he knew that violence was to be used. He would, of course, declare that we must call in the police : and I could not for the life of me see how we could decline to do so, without arousing suspicions which only the truth could lay.

After a lot of reflection, I put the matter aside, in the hope that something would happen to give us a lead, for I could not face the prospect of destroying a work of art, which a gallant lady had sold her soul to preserve.

... ...

As the day wore on, but the enemy never appeared, I became more and more convinced that he had been misled by our sortie on Monday night. (Later I was to learn that this was actually so, and that he had left the district before he received the report that George was at Cardinal.) If I was right, he would return full tilt, when he learned the truth, because his one idea would be to stop the mouth of our earth. I, therefore, decided to take a leaf out of his book and to use the excellent post which the cross roads made.

I had no thought of an ambush, because he would, of course, be more than ready for that: then again the fellows were armed. But if, when we saw them go by, we followed them up, we stood a very fair chance of taking them unawares, for their eyes would be upon the castle and it would not enter their heads to look behind.

"That's very wily," said George. "Very wily indeed. We go on foot, of course."

"Yes," said I, "there's a path. I want us to leave by the window and give the village a miss. Then no one outside the castle will know that we're not at home."

"Oh, the Napoleon," said George. "Do we touch the Cardinal road?"

"We cross it—that's all. We cross it close to the gap." I pointed to the break in the woods. "It's really a continuation of the path from Ousse: and it runs up over that shoulder, while the road, of course, has to go round."

"I see. We take the path, while the enemy keeps to the road. How shall we know that he hasn't passed us *en route*?"

"I've thought of that," said I. "When we come

to the road, we go to the gap and look back. If Conrad is still on the ramparts, we know that all's clear so far, and so we go on. But Joseph remains behind, to keep an eye on the road. It will take us twenty minutes to get to the cross roads : so Joseph waits half an hour before coming on."

"You won't be beat, will you?" said George. "And now resolve a problem that's getting me under the ribs. How and what do we tell Sir Valentine Scrope?"

I covered my eyes.

"Don't," said I. "I can't bear it. I spent two hours this morning, thinking of nothing else. And for all the good I did, I might have been teaching French."

"It's grim," said George. "You can't get away from that. To deceive him makes my gorge rise : and yet to undeceive him would be the unforgivable sin. Well, that's all right. One chooses the lesser evil. One fools this magnificent hermit, who knows no wrong. But the hour is approaching, Thunder, when we cannot maintain our deceit. You can't break off an action, because, if you don't, you may be late for lunch."

"We must wait till it comes," said I. "I'd pave the way, if I could ; but I can't see where to begin."

"I expect you're right," said George. "But it's like riding out to war, with the lady you hope to save on your saddle-bow." He got to his feet. "Are you strolling the meadows this evening? Apparently that's his wont : so I said I'd go, too."

"No," said I. "My foot can keep me here. But you might keep an eye on me. If I don't like the look of the weather, I'll hoist a flag."

"The storm cone," said George. "All right. But somehow or other I don't think they'll come to-day."

He was perfectly right: and the sun went down in splendour on a peace that was not of this world.

That night we dined in state, and I shall remember for ever the quiet hour and a quarter for which we sat to the board.

The dining-room was vaulted and was panelled in old, black oak, and four five-candled sconces were shedding a steady light. Silver and glass and wood were giving this back in their immemorial way, and the fare was plain and old-fashioned as fare should be. George told me afterwards that the wine was extremely rare—no doubt by Sir Valentine's orders, for he seemed delighted to honour his two young guests: but I had no need of wine, for father and daughter together went to my head. I will not say much of the latter, except that she looked so lovely that I could hardly believe that she cared for me. She had chosen to put on black, which showed to perfection the exquisite skin she had; and her high-backed chair made a setting fit for a queen: her grace was so compelling and her address was so fine that I sometimes had the feeling that I had been translated into another age, and when I turned to look at her father, this strange illusion was only magnified. There sat the embodiment of chivalry. Strong and gentle, as his daughter herself had said; proud, though he did not know it; as natural as the day; thinking ill of no man; more than content with his lot—these qualities stood out of that strikingly handsome face, and since he had a great presence and held himself as a man of half his age, he fully upheld the standard his beautiful daughter set. The two were worshipful—I can think of no other word. Between Conrad and Joseph, the service was very good, and George's conversation was very gay: indeed, I confess with shame that I alone contributed nothing at all to a meal which beat any banquet to which I have ever sat down.

... ...

By seven o'clock the next morning, Katharine and George and I were nearing the edge of the forest which hung above the cross roads.

As I have shown, the timber gave way to bracken about two hundred yards from the cross itself, while the spur upon which we were moving ran down and came to an end at that very spot. It follows that on leaving the woods, we should have a commanding view not only of where the roads met, but of their approach; and since the bracken was tall and immensely thick, unless we were very careless, we could not be seen.

It seemed unlikely that there would be a sentinel there, but in case there was I bade the other two wait at the edge of the trees and then crawled on alone to where there seemed to be a dip in the ground.

This was well down the slope: and when at last I reached it, I found it more convenient than I had hoped; for here the descent was checked by a random ridge, after which, to make up for this check, the ground fell away more sharply for ten or twelve feet, before resuming the gradient which had prevailed above. Lying behind this ridge and peering between the stems which grew on its crest, I was able to look clean over the bracken which grew below, and yet a man six feet off would never have known I was there. But the cross roads were fifty yards distant, and more than that.

Here perhaps I should say that there was no finger-post and nothing to tell a stranger which road was the one he sought; so that all he could do was to chance it and read the first milestone he came to, to see if he had guessed right.

After a careful survey, I made my way back to the forest, to bring the others along, to find George up in an oak-tree with my field-glasses up to his eyes. From there he could see the Cruise and the Danders roads and could follow the line they took for two or three miles, so since the fork he was in made a very fair seat, we decided to put Joseph there as soon as he came. As he was not due for some time, Katharine and I went down to take charge of the ridge, while George stayed up in his oak until his relief should arrive.

As I gained the ridge, I looked round and beckoned my lady up. She made her way to my side and knelt very still for a moment, regarding the scene.

Then—

"You've an eye to country, Esau."

I smiled.

"I don't know about that. But I'm probably better than The Shepherd at this sort of game."

"You mean him to play it, don't you?"

"That, my darling, is at the back of my mind. I'm well aware that he may have other ideas. Still, as long as we stick to the country, if he really wants to get us, he'll have to stick to it, too."

She regarded me thoughtfully.

"Somehow or other I can't see him doing that."

"You think he'll try and lure us on to his ground?"

"I don't know what to think. But he is that masterful type that never pays the piper, but always calls the tune."

"I know," said I; "but this is clean out of his line."

"It isn't exactly in yours."

I laughed.

"I'll give Formosa that. Still, it does make the odds more even—you can't get away from that."

She turned and looked at me—with the softest look in her eyes.

"I can, my dear; but I won't. Do you remember our walk at Newhaven—one summer night?"

"Yes, my sweet. I remember it very well."

"And how I ventured to hint that the world should be your oyster—not Crutched Friars?"

"I do," said I.

"Good fairy Katharine, advising a nice young man. That's less than a week ago. And now Formosa is sitting at Esau's feet."

"I never asked that of her."

"I know. But isn't it strange?"

"It would be strange," I said, "if it happened to be the truth. And now please tell me this. When we met at Newhaven, I think you were carrying stuff."

"That's right. The Rochester diamonds."

"My God," said I.

"It's true. The port was stiff with police, and I didn't like the look in their eyes: and so I suggested that walk. I thought if I gave them a chance to go through the stuff in the car, they might wash out little Katharine and think about somebody else."

"Which proves my case," said I. "It was Formosa—not Katharine—with whom I went for a walk: and it is Katharine—not Formosa—who is kneeling here by my side. You're no more a crook than I am: you never were. For three years you've played Formosa—against your will: but though you've played her damned well, the moment you leave the stage you revert to type. Formosa, who knows her world, advises a callow youth: but Katharine and Jeremy Solon are just a girl and a man; and as there's a rough house coming, the girl very naturally does as the man suggests."

"You won't believe ill of me, will you?"

I took her precious hand and held it close to my heart, while a lorry came up from Danders and turned to the right for Cruise.

Then—

"Wouldn't you be hurt, if I did?"

"I don't think so," she said slowly. "I'd be terribly sorry, of course. But I wouldn't have the right to be hurt."

"You've no illusions, have you?"

She shook her head.

"That's your prerogative, Esau."

I put her hand to my lips. Then I slewed myself round and sat up, and she sat back on her heels.

"I love you," I said. "I love you body and soul. And no power in Heaven or earth will make me give you up."

The gentlest smile stole into her lovely face.

"It is written, 'Your young men shall see visions.'"

"I see one now. I'm looking into her eyes."

"You came here to look at the cross roads."

"I know. But there's nobody there. And George will be here very soon. And later on . . ."

"Ah, later on," she breathed, and the light went out of her eyes.

I knelt beside her and gathered her into my arms.

"We love each other," I said: "and love can break anything down."

A warm arm slid round my neck.

"It's broken me down, my darling. I thought I could stand anything. But my resolution has crumbled before the look in your face. And now I must tell you something, before George comes. I've made up my mind at last to tell my father the truth."

I started at that: but before I could speak she went on.

"He's got to be told something—I think that's clear. And I'm simply not prepared to lie to him any more. I don't believe I could do it. The fountain of lies has dried up. And so to-night, my darling, I'm going to tell him the truth."

I moistened my lips.

"Won't you wait a little?" I said.

She shook her head.

"I'm going to do it to-night. It's bound to hit him hard: but that is my fault. I've turned it over and over and round and round and round: but that was all waste of time, for I knew before I began that at last the time had come when I'd got to tell him the truth."

I swallowed desperately.

"I'm so afraid," I said, "It'll shock him more than you think. George and I are modern: we're ferro-concrete pillars that nothing can shake. But he is—of different stuff: and his life has been so sheltered, and his outlook is so—so rare that——"

"I know, my blessed, I know. But if I do not tell him—and tell him at once—he will surely stumble on something which will show him that things are happening of which he is unaware. And that *would* break him, Esau. He'd know there was something wrong: and yet, because he is blind, he wouldn't be able to look for the truth in my eyes."

"Yes, I see that," I said. "But I think it's clear, my sweet, that we're nearing the end of the course. And if we get home—as we shall—there will be no reason why he should ever know. I mean, it seems so awful, when you have done all you have, to—to render unto Caesar the things that are God's."

"It's the lesser evil, Esau. I know I'm right. It's better that he should be told the unsavoury truth than that it should enter his head that his daughter would turn his blindness to her account. As you said the other day, I might have known that some time or other the end was bound to come. Well, now it's here, my dear: and you know, it might have been worse."

"You mean, if you had been taken carrying stuff?"

"Yes, I mean that. At least, I've been spared that—that agony. And I shall be rid of a nightmare that's put five years on my age."

There was a little silence—whilst I went frantically over the ground I had covered already again and again.

It was, of course, quite hopeless. We were already skating on ice that was far too thin. To give one example only, Sir Valentine had no idea that the Lowland, when not in use, was without the castle's wall. Any moment he might discover this pregnant fact. And how were we to explain it? Who keeps his car two miles off, when the coach-house is ready and waiting to serve his turn?

At length—

"This is my fault," I said. "If I had gone, as you wished——"

"I didn't wish it. How could I? I thought it was better so. But I daresay I was mistaken, and you were right. And I am so thankful to have you. You see, I'd run out of courage. But now, with your arms about me, it's coming back."

I kissed her lips for that. Then I held her off and met the smile in her eyes.

"When you run out of courage," I said, "the world

will come to an end. But we both of us know you were carrying too much weight."

"Havoc's ahead," she said, "and yet I can smile. That's you, my darling. You've taught me. You've unlocked something inside me that I didn't know was there."

"And what have you done to me, you beautiful child?"

"Well, I haven't fooled you," she said. "But I think I've done everything else."

... ...

Between the ridge and the forest we spent the heat of that day: but though the hours went by, the enemy did not come.

As I had thought, there was no sentinel: this fact and Joseph's devotion gave us an easy time, for, once he was up in the oak, the latter could hardly be persuaded to leave his post. I think he coveted the honour of being the first to descry the enemy's car: so, though more than once I simply ordered him down for an odd half-hour, for the most part he did our duty with all his might. He gave the alarm by whistling, after the note of some bird—once for a van or a lorry and twice for a private car. Then we sat up and took notice and watched it go by: but when it had passed, we relaxed, talking and musing and dozing, and generally taking our ease.

The traffic was very slight, and more than once a full half-hour would go by in which nothing would pass.

Except for two bullock-waggons, nothing at all had taken the Cardinal road.

The afternoon was waning, when I saw George glance at his wrist.

"Ten minutes to four," he said. "I somehow feel that the gents aren't coming to-day."

"If they don't," said I, "it shows that their staff-work's bad. Of course we misled them badly on Sunday night."

"Ah," said George, "that cable across the road. I cannot get over that. It argues a ruthlessness which I had thought was extinct. I mean, it's a public road—not a private drive."

"That," said Katharine, "is The Shepherd. It was waiting for us, of course. But if somebody else had been killed, he would have cursed their soul for spoiling the trap he had set."

"How," said George, "does such a monster survive?"

"By fear," said Katharine. "A great many people would like to give him away. But they are afraid to do it, because, unless he went down for a proper stretch, they would only pay with their lives for what they had done. And he's not the sort of man who goes down. Information's not evidence."

"Well, I don't know," said George. "I've always heard——"

And there Joseph whistled twice, and we turned to the ridge.

For more than a minute we waited, before the drone of an engine came to our ears. It was very faint and it faded almost at once, by which we knew that the car was coming from Cruise and was taking a dip in the road a mile and a quarter away.

The drone flared up again, louder. In an instant now the car would sail into our view.

We lay still as death, with our eyes on the distant curve ; for the car was a powerful car and was travelling fast.

As we saw her rounding the bend—

" She's gray," I breathed. " She melts right into the road."

I heard Katharine catch her breath.

Then—

" It's them all right," she said quietly. " No doubt about that."

The car swooped into a hollow four hundred yards off. Then she spurted out of the dip and scudded directly towards us, up to the four cross roads.

As though to consult our convenience, she stopped just short of the cross, and The Shepherd and Judas together regarded some map, while the tough in the dickey behind stared dully before him, as though he were sick of life.

It was a glorious moment.

The two for whom they were searching were fifty yards off, calmly surveying their efforts and only waiting to see which road they decided to take : and they, unaware of such attention, were making no secret of their discomfiture, for Judas pushed back his hat and wiped the sweat from his face and The Shepherd struck at an insect and hit his hand on the screen. I fancy it needed but this to set his impatience alight, for he snatched the map from Judas and pitched it out of the car. Then with a shaking finger, he pointed to the Cardinal road, and when Judas attempted to argue, he shouted him down.

Looking more black than ever, Judas let in his clutch and the car went off with a bang down the Cardinal road, and all that was left was the map, lying on the edge of the tarmac, where two ways met.

As we leapt to our feet—

"We're off," said I. "George, get off with Joseph as quick as ever you can. For God's sake be careful where the path comes down to the road. If you go farther than that, you'd better leave Joseph there, to say where you've gone." I turned to Katharine. "You and I will come on together: but first will you get that map?"

Without a word, my lady set off through the bracken to do as I said.

By the time she had caught me up, the others were out of sight.

... ...

I made the best pace I could, but twenty minutes went by before I saw Joseph ahead. He was crouching behind a beech and was looking over his shoulder, finger to lip. Fifty feet beyond and below him was lying the Cardinal road.

At once I perceived the truth, and my heart leaped up.

The 'racing Merk' had stopped at the gap in the trees.

I had felt this might possibly happen. Had I been in the enemy's place, I should have stopped at that view-point—from which I could see so much without being seen. But few men think alike, and I had scarce dared to hope that they would not wait there a moment and then go on.

With Katharine directly behind me, I stole to where Joseph was. . . .

And then indeed I praised God, for The Shepherd had gone one better and had left the car, with his servant, just short of the gap and had plainly walked on with Judas, to enter the village on foot.

I turned to Katharine.

"Stay here with Joseph," I whispered.

As I made to go on, I felt her hand on my wrist.

"Esau," she breathed, "that's Satan. Please remember that he has earned his name."

"Maybe," said I. "But he made a dent on my car."

I crept on down to George, who was lying behind some brambles, six feet from the road itself.

"The position is this," he whispered. "I got here just in time to see the two Willies marking the castle's bulwarks and telling her elegant towers. Their backs were, of course, towards me, so I couldn't hear what they said. But twice I caught the word 'postern,' and I think The Shepherd said 'trap.' All their bad temper was gone: wickedness and vice had kissed each other. And two minutes after I'd come, they sauntered off down the hill, like a couple of chorus boys on a Saturday night. Their unattractive accomplice is going to stay where he is until they signal to him to bring down the car. There you are, you see. 'He's getting his glasses out."

Peering between the briers, I saw Satan take a binocular out of the car. Then he walked up to the gap and, after some slight adjustment, he put it up to his eyes.

I breathed in George's ear.

"Now's our chance," I said. "His name is Satan, and I commit him to you. Beat him down under your feet. Put your heel in the small of his back and help him over the edge."

"What, now ?" said George.

"Right away. As quick as you can. And put him down good and proper. I've got quite a lot to do before he comes back."

The Assyrian may have come down as the wolf on the fold, but George's descent upon Satan was better than that. Of course, it was easy money. Satan stood full in the gap, with his thickset back towards us and the glasses up to his eyes, intent upon watching his master and, naturally, never dreaming that danger of any sort could threaten his rear : and George was wearing rubber-soled shoes, so that he gave no warning of his approach.

In less time than it takes to record, he had gained the road and was standing behind his victim, judging his distance exactly as though the man were a ball and both were upon some field. And then he kicked the fellow—but not in the small of the back: and as George played full-back for Oxford, I could not help feeling that Satan had paid his debt.

Be that as it may, the latter rose up in the air with a startled screech and then crashed down the mountain, which here was extremely steep, while George slipped behind a bush to the side of the gap and stood peering through its cover, to watch how his victim did.

That was as much as I saw, for I was in the Mercedes and was searching her pockets and hood. I found two automatics and pocketed both: one was in each of the pouches that graced the doors. In the hood lay two or three maps and a bottle of mineral water, but nothing else.

"Go through the dickey," said George. "You've time to burn. Satan has only just stopped, and he's fully sixty feet down."

But the dickey bore no fruit.

I went through the pockets again and found a spare clip I had missed. I slid this into my pocket: and then I turned the key which was still in the switch.

True to type, the car started—the contact was more than enough.

I stepped down into the roadway.

Then I leaned forward and took the hand-brake off. . . .

I confess that it went to my heart to see the car gathering speed. She was too fair a production to send to her doom. But some things have to be done. We had the Lowland, and that was enough for us.

Her engine steadily idling, she flung down that

break-neck hill . . . failed, of course, to take the first of the bends . . . and met a gigantic fir-tree not quite head on.

Between them, her weight and her impetus carried her round and over on to her side: and because her engine was running she burst into flames at once.

I touched George's arm.

"Back into cover," I said. "We've done our job."

As I rejoined my lady, who was kneeling behind a bush—

"My God, Esau," she breathed, "your score's mounting up. That car was the very apple of Judas' eye."

"I'm glad of that," said I. "Did you see George kick into touch?"

Katharine sighed.

"You're hopeless," she said. Then, "I'm thankful you've got those guns; but remember they're only spares. They may leave their car about: but never their—magic wands."

A full minute must have gone by before we saw Satan's head appear at the foot of the gap.

It was not an agreeable vision. His face was scratched and filthy, his hat was gone, and I never saw fury so rampant in all my life. His mouth was working, his eyes were rolling with rage; and as he looked cautiously round, I confess I was more than glad to be out of his sight. A bullet might have stopped him, if he had set eyes on his prey; but I do not believe that he would have stood for a pistol, so blind was his wrath.

Indeed, he was so intent on discovering his assailant that two or three moments went by before he observed that his charge was no longer there. In fact he had hauled himself up and on to the road and was standing, crouching and peering, ready to rush, when I saw him start and stare at the spot where the car had stood. Then he looked down the hill and let out a yell.

The next instant he was running like a madman towards the flames.

"Now's our chance," I said. "Over the road, and down to the valley below."

It was really too easy, for Satan never looked back, and we all had crossed over the roadway before he had come to a standstill before the scene of the crash.

Three minutes later we reached the meadows below.

"I'm sorry," said I, "that we can't be in at the death. But Joseph must represent us. As soon as we're over the water, he will stroll into the village and, when he learns what has happened, will make his way over the bridge and help to swell the crowd which will be regarding the crash. As a late-comer, he will naturally ask for details and note the answers he gets, and if he uses his eyes as well as his mouth and his ears, he ought to be able to learn what The Shepherd and Master Judas are now proposing to do."

George translated my orders—which Joseph received with a pleasure he could not conceal: and then we skirted the village as fast as ever we could.

When we had used a foot-bridge to cross the stream, Joseph made for a lane which led to the little *place*; but we went on up to the castle and round to the stern-faced window from which we had made our exit ten hours before.

As though he was anxious to see us, Conrad was waiting there, and when he had lowered the bar, I lifted Katharine up and he helped her in.

As I set a knee on the sill—

"Two strangers are here, sir," said Conrad. "The inkeeper's boy came up twenty minutes ago."

"Conrad," said I, "our news is later than that."

"What's that, sir?"—eagerly.

"Joseph will tell you," I said. "He's coming back by the postern: he shouldn't be long."

For what it was worth, we all made straight for the ramparts to see what we could: but the hamlet seemed to be deserted, and all that rewarded our gaze was a sinister wisp of smoke which was rising out of the forest above and beyond the roofs.

"Oh, I can't bear it," said George, and covered his eyes. "We ought to have stayed on, Thunder, and witnessed the epilogue. I do hope they let Satan explain before he died."

"I'm sorry," I said. "But I think we were wise to withdraw. You see, they'll be all eyes for the next two hours. But as soon as the dusk comes in, I think we might try again. It really all depends on what Joseph says."

"You think they'll stay on?" said Katharine.

"I'm inclined to think," said I, "that they'll send for a car. Well, that won't be here for ages. What would be best of all . . ."

The sentence was never finished.

Someone was running . . . stumbling . . . making his way to the ramparts as fast as ever he could.

As we all swung about, Joseph burst out of a turret, with Conrad close on his heels.

The former was breathing most hard and was streaming with sweat. When at first he endeavoured to speak, the words would not come.

"What is it?" cried George. "What's the matter?"

Somehow Joseph made answer, between his sobs.

"I did . . . as Monsieur bade me. I went . . . to the scene of the fire. But I did not stay . . . *because Madame's father was there.* He was . . . in talk with the strangers. I think . . . but I cannot be sure . . . that he has invited them here . . . until a car can be fetched to take them to Cruise."

CHAPTER VII

TO say that I felt sick at heart means nothing at all. Never was budding tactician so hoist with his own petard. I had taken charge, and the others had let me do so: and now I had let us all in and had fairly lifted the enemy on to our back.

Still, something had to be done. . . .

In ten minutes' time we were ready—to do what we could.

Two staircase-turrets rose out of the small courtyard. These were lit by embrasures, from which a man could see, though he could not be seen. One turret made an observatory for Katharine and me: and George and Joseph stood on the other's stair. Conrad stood to the wicket which hung in one of the leaves of the castle's door, watching the road of approach through the wrought-iron grille.

Though George and I were both armed with the enemy's arms, we were not to use them, except in the last resort: and I think we both of us hoped that it would not come to that; for, for one thing, a pistol can kill, and, for another, neither of us had ever employed one before. It was easy enough, of course, to see how they worked: but I knew enough about firearms to know that a weapon with which you are not familiar may prove a broken reed, when it comes to the pinch.

We had next to no plan of action, except to conceal our presence and overhear all we could. But Conrad had been instructed to try to lure Sir Valentine away from his dangerous guests. I doubted that they would permit this. . . . In fact, the plain truth is that on what they said and did was depending what action we took.

So the five of us stood there waiting—four with their eyes upon Conrad, and Conrad with his eyes on the road.

I shot a glance at my lady, whose face was four inches from mine. Though all she had was at stake, I never saw her look cooler, more self-possessed. Her eye was not excited; she was not breathing quickly; her hand on the jamb of the embrasure was as steady as was the stone against which it was laid.

Feeling my glance upon her, she turned and smiled.

"What are you thinking, Esau?"

"I—admire your *sang froid,* my darling. The palms of my hands are wet."

"That's only practice," she said. "If you had done my job, you'd be just the same. The more you've got at stake, the cooler you get. But you must know where you are. For nearly a week I've never known what to expect: but now—well, there's no doubt left. We're in the ring all right: and the seconds are out."

"Thanks to me," said I. "Yet you throw no stones."

"Why should I? You've done your best. And

your best was terribly good. Who could have dreamed that my father would go to the fire? He must have heard some outcry and have gone to see what it meant. It's Fate again, Esau—not you. Fate has a way of taking matters out of one's hands. And now stand by, my darling. Conrad has seen them coming, so pull up your socks."

Perhaps three minutes went by—no doubt Sir Valentine walked slowly, because the men beside him were not accustomed to climbing a hill so steep. Then Conrad threw open the wicket and The Shepherd, followed by Judas, stepped carefully over the threshold and into the cool courtyard.

Though the former appeared at his ease, the latter did not. That is putting it mildly. While The Shepherd looked casually round, Judas' behaviour was that of a startled snake. His left hand fast in his pocket, he darted his venomous glances from side to side, as though seeking a chance of striking before he himself was struck. Then again the fellow was raging—the fact stood out: but The Shepherd betrayed no emotion, but only took out an eye-glass and screwed it into his eye.

Sir Valentine passed through the wicket behind his guests.

"Has Miss Katharine returned?" he said.

"Not yet, sir," Conrad replied—with the Shepherd's eyes on his face.

"Beg her to join us, as soon as she does come in. And bring some refreshment, Conrad."

"To the dining-room, sir?"

"No. The terrace." He addressed himself to his guests. "Let's go on up there, shall we? I'll lead the way."

The Shepherd hung on his heel.

"I find this charming," he said. "An antique jewel-case: a strong-box—by Benvenuto Cellini of Brobdingnag . . . some very beautiful lady should be enshrined and cherished within these walls. Is there only this one way in?"

"No," said his host. "There's a postern. That's on the other side."

The Shepherd regarded the turrets: I know that I held my breath as I met the flame in his eyes.

"But once within," he drawled, "ways without number, of course. Those turrets give to the ramparts?"

"To the terrace, too. But I shouldn't advise that way."

"No, no. I was marking your bulwarks." He moved towards Sir Valentine, who was standing with a foot on the step of the great front door. "And I like the grille in the wicket. Everything as it's laid down in the fairy-tales."

He threw another look round. Then he and Judas followed Sir Valentine in and out of our sight.

It was clear from The Shepherd's words that he was by no means certain that Katharine had not returned and that all he had said was really directed to Judas, that the latter might observe and consider the manifold chances of surveillance afforded by such a place. And there he can hardly be blamed, for we were commanding the terrace before the three stepped on to its sunlit flags.

George and Joseph were still in their staircase-turret: but Katharine and I were in Sir Valentine's study—a very private room, which I had not entered before. This had a miniature oriel, hanging over the terrace, a little way up: and anyone kneeling there could hear—and see, if he pleased—what happened below.

We heard them coming, of course, before they appeared. Sir Valentine and Judas were silent: but The Shepherd was still commending all that he saw.

Their entrance was interesting.

Sir Valentine's brow was clouded, and a hand was up to his beard. Perhaps because he was blind, his instinct was keener than that of another man. But I was ready to swear that he was regretting the impulse on which he had offered his hospitality. The Shepherd looked deliberately round and fingered his chin. And Judas darted his glances to right and left and then whipped to the balustrade, to stand searching the scene before him—in the hope, no doubt, of descrying our unsuspecting approach.

"Ideal," murmured The Shepherd, and let himself into a chair. "From every point of view, entirely ideal."

Sir Valentine answered shortly.

"It makes a pleasant retreat."

"A belvedere," said the other, "commanding all ways of approach. I take it that break in the woods is the gap by which we ventured to leave our car."

"From what you have told me, that's so. It's just below the crest of the hill."

"Quite so. I take it the postern you mentioned is down on the left."

I saw Judas' head come round.

"That's right," said Sir Valentine. "A flight of seventy steps leads down to the village below."

"And an oriel-window, too—most beautifully placed. And then our old friends, the turrets—embrasures and all. Most entertaining. We shall hold you to your promise to show us the rest of the house."

Sir Valentine frowned.

"Did I say that?" he said quietly. "Oh well, if you care to see it . . . before you go. . . ."

There was a little silence, which would have been awkward for any ordinary guests. But Judas ignored the others, only taking his eyes from the landscape to strike a match, and The Shepherd sat back, smiling, as though contemplating with pleasure the excellent hand which he held.

His complacency made me feel desperate. It rammed home the bitter truth that he had us—*and knew that he had us* where we belonged. With Sir Valentine at his mercy, he could dictate his terms.

It may be argued that George and I were both armed. But the brutal answer is this—that so were The Shepherd and Judas: and though we could have called upon them to put up their hands, it goes, I think, without saying that neither would have obeyed, unless the mouth of a pistol had been actually touching his throat.

I began to regret very much that we had not taken

our chance and closed with the two as they came in at the gate.

As though aware of my thoughts, The Shepherd lifted his voice.

"I think I'm right in saying that one of your guests has a car. I was told as much in the village, before you appeared."

Sir Valentine nodded.

"He has."

"Perhaps he could be persuaded to be so kind as to give us a lift back to Cruise."

"I'm afraid he's abroad at the moment."

"Quite so," purred The Shepherd. "Quite so. But when he comes in. It's only a suggestion, of course. And my servant has gone for a car. . . . But he's not very good on his feet, and a twelve-mile walk will take him some time to do." He glanced at his watch. "He ought to be back in five hours : but I can't help feeling that we oughtn't to stay quite so long."

Sir Valentine moistened his lips.

"In those circumstances, I think we may count upon him."

With the tail of my eye, I saw Katharine bite her lip. The Shepherd could afford to be artistic. Having been shown the way, Sir Valentine would invoke my assistance to speed the lingering guest.

Conrad appeared with refreshment—wine and water and cake, and fruit in a lordly dish.

"Delicious," drawled The Shepherd. "The kindly fruits of the earth."

Sir Valentine looked away. That the other grated

upon him was perfectly clear. Such fulsome appreciation would have made anyone sick.

Conrad served The Shepherd and then stepped to Judas' side.

The latter stared at the tray.

"Have you got any whiskey?" he snapped.

"I'm sorry," said Sir Valentine, quickly. "There's none in the house. If you would like some brandy . . ."

"Brandy will do."

Conrad left the terrace, to reappear with the spirit and serve the man. Then he poured some wine for his master and set the decanter down.

"Excuse me, sir," he said quietly, "but Poey is waiting to see you about the headstone for Madame Poey's grave."

Judas swung about, staring, and Sir Valentine set down his glass and rose to his feet.

Then he addressed The Shepherd, half out of his chair.

"I must ask you to excuse me," he said, "for five or ten minutes—no more. This poor man——"

"Pray let us come with you," said The Shepherd, exchanging glances with Judas, two paces away.

Sir Valentine stood very still.

"That," he said, "I cannot invite you to do. It's a very personal matter. The man worked with me on this house: and I promised to allow him to copy——"

"Perhaps," said The Shepherd, slowly, "perhaps he could call again."

Sir Valentine drew himself up.

"I must beg you," he said, "to excuse me. I——"

"And that," said the other, "I must decline to do."

Sir Valentine measured the man, as though he could see.

"But this is unheard of."

"The fact remains," said The Shepherd, and left it there.

There was an electric silence—which the rapid slam of my heart seemed likely to break.

The four men stood still as death—Judas with his hand in his pocket, The Shepherd regarding his nails, Conrad with his eyes on his master, and the latter with a face like a mask.

Then Sir Valentine gave a short laugh.

"Perhaps you're right," he said, resuming his seat. "Tell him to call again, Conrad: and when Miss Katharine returns, request her not to disturb me—say I'm engaged."

"Very good, sir," said Conrad quietly.

He bowed and withdrew.

The Shepherd sat down, smiling, and Judas turned again to the balustrade.

I could not think what to do. Our only card had been trumped, and the only good we had done was to force The Shepherd to show his unpleasant hand. Had George been with me, I would have taken some action without any further delay: but I dared not move without him and dared not leave my post to go to his side. I have never felt so helpless. Not to do something was intolerable: but The Shepherd had us by the short hairs: whatever move we made was certain to lose us the game. I could, of course, have shot him. Unused as I was to a pistol, from where I was I could have shot the man dead. But before I could shoot again, Judas would surely have taken Sir Valentine's life.

The Shepherd cleared his throat.

"I should like to have met your daughter."

"She is hardly accustomed to such an exacting guest."

The Shepherd raised his eyebrows.

"Oh, well. Perhaps later on. Is this the wine of the country? I find it extremely good."

Sir Valentine smiled.

"It is of the country," he said. "We don't ask much hereabouts, and we keep some things to ourselves."

"I felicitate you," said The Shepherd. "If I may venture to say so, you've done remarkably well to keep the secret of Cardinal all this time."

"I have no secrets to keep. I live and let live, and, though you may not believe it, I am content with my lot."

"A perfect existence," mused The Shepherd, "in an imperfect world. Still, talking of secrets, I think that the world believes that Sir Valentine Scrope is dead. I mean, if one looked at Burke, I think one would read that the title was now extinct."

"That may or may not be so. I know that four years ago the papers announced my death. Whence the mistake arose, I have no idea. But I never corrected a statement which you have found to be wrong."

"A curious outlook," drawled The Shepherd. "'The

world forgetting, by the world forgot.' Of course it's very convenient . . . from some points of view."

"It has saved a blind man correspondence, if that's what you mean."

"No," said The Shepherd, "I wasn't thinking of that."

As though to disappoint him, Sir Valentine made no reply.

There was another silence. . . .

Judas was getting restless. Although he had not spoken, the man had heard all that was said: and the falseness of the position was playing hell with his nerves. He had left the balustrade now and was standing, regarding Sir Valentine with a malevolent stare.

I understood how he felt. The Shepherd had lighted the fuse five minutes ago: yet no explosion had occurred. The suspense was intolerable.

Sir Valentine forced his hand.

"Yes," he said quietly. "What is it?"

Judas started. He had not dreamed that the blind man could see with his ears.

Then—

"I'm sick of this," he blurted. "Let's have a look at the house."

Sir Valentine crossed his legs.

"Perhaps later on," he replied. "If your servant's so bad on his feet, we've plenty of time."

The Shepherd was regarding him straitly.

"I'm inclined to think," he drawled, "that it might be a good idea." He rose to his feet. "I, er, hate to be so insistent, but if you would lead the way . . ."

Sir Valentine hesitated. Then he laughed and stood up.

"You have the advantage of me. Which way shall we go?"

"Supposing we began with the ramparts. . . ."

My lady knew the castle so well that, though we were not able to keep in touch all the time, we always knew where the three were and were able to pick them up and sometimes to be in position before they appeared.

As before, The Shepherd did the talking, while Judas, who brought up the rear, missed nothing at all. Such was his energy that I would have given a lot to know that George and Joseph were standing their ground, for if they attempted to play my lady's game, they would, I was sure, be discovered before the tour was done. As for Sir Valentine, his pride of possession gradually took control and, though at first he said little but 'Yes' and 'No,' by the time they had reached the chapel he was directing attention to some of the beauty they passed.

"I think that's the smallest wheel-window you've ever seen. . . . And that is a double pulpit. There may be another somewhere: if it is, it's not in the books."

"A 'double pulpit'?" said The Shepherd.

"Yes. Its back is really a panel which disappears into the wall. Draw that aside, and you step into an open-air pulpit, commanding the courtyard you saw."

As they left the chapel—

"And where does that lead?" said The Shepherd.

"Are you pointing to a passage on the left?"

"I am. It seems to end in a winding stair."

"I don't think that would interest you. If we go straight on——"

"I think it might," said The Shepherd. "Where does it lead?"

"It only leads to the guard-room commanding the postern-door."

Judas' and The Shepherd's eyes met.

Then—

"Is that all? Never mind. I want to see everything."

With obvious reluctance, Sir Valentine turned to the left. . . .

Katharine touched my arm, and I followed her out of a bathroom and down a gallery . . . under an archway and past two sudden stairs . . . and into a panelled chamber with an enormous hearth.

"Shut the shutters," she breathed, and went down on her knees.

When I had done as she said, the room was dark: but a little rectangular slit, six inches by two, was admitting a little daylight close to the floor.

Katharine caught my wrist and pulled me down to my knees.

"Look through, and you'll see the guard-room. I thought I heard them coming a moment ago."

With my head against hers, I peered through the aperture. . . .

Twenty odd feet below me, I saw a fair-sized chamber, whose walls and floor were of stone. Two windows, high up and barred, were admitting light: mid-way between these was the postern-door itself. In the opposite wall, a second door, now open, gave to the house and made the chamber into a vestibule. One of the other walls I could not see, for we were kneeling above it and so it was out of our view: but sunk in the one I could see was a little flight of worn steps which rose very sharply and seemed to bear to the right. The sun, which was low, was slanting through the two windows and planting patches of light on the cold, gray stone.

(I afterwards found that the room in which we were kneeling was that which used to belong to the officer commanding the guard. In fact we were using his peep-hole, by which, whenever he pleased, he could survey his command and see that its duty was being faithfully done.)

We certainly heard them coming, before they appeared, for Sir Valentine's voice was raised, as though to give audible warning of their approach. Remembering his obvious reluctance to bring The Shepherd this way, I guessed that he was afraid of encountering Katharine and us: and that both his guests shared this view was perfectly clear, for, when they came into our sight, the two were right up on their toes and The Shepherd's casual demeanour was a thing of the past.

Their host preceded them in; but, as he stopped, they passed him, one upon either side. Each had a hand in his pocket, ready to fire.

"As I told you," said Sir Valentine slowly, "there's little enough to be seen. The traces of——"

"Is that the postern?" said The Shepherd.

Sir Valentine nodded.

"That's right. We use it now as a——"

"Never mind how you use it. Where does that stairway go?"

"It's only six steps long, and——"

"I asked where it went."

"It goes to the watchman's seat, commanding the seventy steps and the village below."

I saw Judas glance at The Shepherd, who nodded his head: then the former flashed to the stairway, bent his head to the lintel and passed up and out of our sight.

Sir Valentine lifted an arm.

"To the left of the fire-place," he said, "there's a peep-hole. . . ."

The word was more than enough.

As The Shepherd whipped round, to look up, Sir Valentine's hand shot out. . . .

The mighty fist caught the man square at the base of the shoulder-blades—to send him flying and reeling out of our sight.

In that same instant, Sir Valentine leaped for the doorway through which they had come and, catching its edge as he passed, brought the oak to behind him with an almighty crash.

There was the roar of a pistol. . . .

But The Shepherd had fired too late. Five inches of iron-studded oak were barring the bullet's way.

... ...

Katharine was gone.

I never heard her go, but that was not surprising, for the roar of the automatic had made me deaf.

My job, however, was plainly to stay where I was and to do my best to continue the really brilliant work which her father had done.

Until he had struck The Shepherd, it had not entered my head that he had been playing a part, but now I realized his apparent reluctance had been assumed in order to lure the enemy out of the house: for now, of course, they had only one way to take.

But I did not mean them to take it.

If we could only manage to hold the postern-door, the two would be our prisoners—a shining thought. Though I could not see how we could do it, I felt that somehow or other it must be done; for never again should we have such a glorious chance of smashing for good and all the power of the dog.

I drew my pistol and slid back the safety-catch—and prayed with all my might that George or someone would come, for I dared not leave my post, but the postern had to be held if we were to win the trick.

At the time when he fired, The Shepherd was out of my sight, but as Judas flung into the guard-room, he reappeared, pistol in hand, with his eyes on the door which Sir Valentine Scrope had shut. Though he must have been inwardly raging, he showed no sign of wrath, but only stood still while Judas, for what it was worth, laid hands on the door. This was, of course, locked or bolted: and when he saw Judas turn, The Shepherd put up his pistol and took his eye-glass out. He polished this carefully. Then he put it back in his eye and took a look round.

I afterwards found that except, when the sun was

high and the guard-room was full of light, the officer's squint or peep-hole could not be seen from below, so though the man looked straight at me, his glance passed on. I watched him survey the postern and then the stair which led to the watchman's seat. Then he made a sign to Judas, who stepped to his side.

For a moment they spoke together. Then Judas turned and made once more for the stair.

It was easy to see what was coming.

The two were about to leave : and Judas had gone to make sure that the seventy steps were clear.

Cautiously I levelled my pistol, aiming for all I was worth at the latch of the postern-door.

I saw Judas reappear and I saw him nod.

At once The Shepherd stepped to the postern, and I let fly. . . .

I shall always believe that the bullet went by the man's ear, for he clapped a hand to that member and started aside. And then, without more ado, he leaped for the watchman's stair, to take it two steps at a time, with Judas right on his heels.

A precipitate exit is seldom dignified, but theirs would have made the fortune of any camera-man ; for, fast as The Shepherd moved, he did not move fast enough for Judas, coming behind. Because the stair was so narrow, the latter could not go by, but could only press on, with the happy result that he trod on The Shepherd's heel. This brought the two of them down—The Shepherd halfway up and Judas full on his back, and, deaf as I was, I heard the screech of fury the former let out. Still, they were up in an instant and round and out of my sight, though, to tell the truth, they might have taken their time, for I was too weak with laughter to fire again.

And then I saw how to deny them the postern-door.

We could not do this from without, for the watchman's window was commanding the postern steps. But if we could force the two blackguards to stay in the watchman's seat, the job could be done from within with the acme of ease.

There was very little risk—provided that they did not suspect that we should make the attempt. The great key was there, in the lock. And if George took over my post and fired at the stairway the instant he saw their feet, they would not dare to come down: meanwhile, I could enter the guard-room, steal to the postern, and draw the key from its lock, and then whip back into safety before our friends were aware of what had been done. To make assurance quite sure, Joseph could demonstrate at the foot of the seventy steps, displaying a hammer and timber as though we were actually thinking of barring the door from without. Distracted by his activity and only waiting for him to arrive at the door, the two would stay where they were, and George would have no occasion to open fire.

At least, that was how I saw it. But what I also saw was that if we were to succeed, we must act at once. Delay was dangerous. Some cloud had obscured the sun and every minute now the guard-room was growing more dim; and since The Shepherd's brain was very much finer than mine, he might any moment conceive and take some action which would put a spoke in our wheel.

I glanced at the door of the chamber in which I knelt. This was as good as shut: but had it been open, I should have been no better off. I dared not leave my peep-hole: I dared not shout: I could only stay still where I was, until somebody came. And God knew when that would be. For the others, the danger was past; and I had no doubt at all that Katharine and George were listening to Sir Valentine's story and doing the latter the honour he richly deserved, while Joseph was telling Conrad how George and I between us had sent the car to her doom. And whilst they were thus engaged, the chance of a lifetime was fading. . . .

At last I could bear it no longer.

I was, in fact, in the very act of rising, in order to gain the passage and shout for George, when the postern-door was opened and two little maids appeared, bearing between them the milk-can which they had lugged up from below.

When he had let Joseph in, Conrad had failed to re-lock the postern-door.

Of such is the luck of battles. . . .

To make matters worse, The Shepherd had seen the children mounting the steps: but I was completely surprised and so unready to deal with their invasion.

I heard him speaking in French from the watchman's stair, and I saw and heard the coins which he pitched to the foot of the steps. I saw the children approach, and I saw him come down with Judas and the two of them stoop and speak with their little friends. And then the four together made for the postern-door.

I did not see them leave, for I was out of my chamber before they had gained the steps. The chance of a lifetime was gone; but the two were twelve miles from their base and they had no car. If the village was roused against them . . .

And there I heard George calling.

"Thunder, where are you? Thunder!"

He was trying to make me hear, without raising his voice.

"Where have you been?" I cried. "We'd got them cold, and you and Conrad, between you . . ."

With that, I swung round some corner, to see him three paces away.

"Hush," he said, raising a hand. "Sir Valentine's dead."

CHAPTER VIII

SIR VALENTINE had died of angina pectoris.

Katharine had fled to his side, because she had feared the result of the energy which he had shown. Her fear had been justified. Somehow her father had managed to bolt the guard-room door and had then succumbed to a savage attack of pain. This had been so relentless that when it had passed, the giant was a dying man ; and though he survived to whisper that all was well and to smile at the way in which he had sped his guests, one minute later he died in his daughter's arms.

And there I will leave a matter which I would give much to forget, for though I have come to see that I cannot fairly be charged with Sir Valentine's death, at the time I felt wholly to blame for that calamity.

Indeed, I had no more heart for the fight which we had begun and was only thankful to think that The Shepherd and Judas were gone. I supposed that they would return—eventually : but George's terrible news had thrust them into the background, as nothing else could have done. The head of the corner had fallen. The man was dead for whose sake his gallant daughter had sowed the wind : and now she must reap the whirlwind, although her objective was gone.

It was well for us that the enemy made no move for the next three days, for, if we still took precautions, we took a good many risks : but I was ready to swear that they would take their time before they returned to the charge and, since our hands were full, we did what had to be done and hoped for the best.

Three times, on Katharine's business, George and I visited Cruise, and when the funeral took place on the second day, no one, I think, would have dreamed that two of the principal mourners were themselves in danger of death.

The service was held in the chapel of which its faithful master had been so proud, and from there he was taken down to the little churchyard and laid to rest in the shade of an English oak. Every man and woman of Cardinal shared in this simple rite, and most of them were in tears, because they had seen the last of a saint who had been their friend.

Except for this hour and a half, I had hardly set eyes upon Katharine since she had risen and fled from the officer's room ; for she had all her meals by herself and saw no one at all but Conrad, and, once or twice, George. Neither did she appear the following day. She spent some time, I know, in Sir Valentine's private rooms and she walked on the ramparts that evening, when dusk came in : but, though she sent us word that she was perfectly well and that we were to give the servants what orders we pleased, she did not ask to see us, and we, of course, took care to respect her privacy.

But each night, though she did not know it, I slept across her door, with a pistol close to my side.

So three full days went by, while Katharine mourned in secret and the enemy left us alone.

... ...

Though I had been fast asleep, the creak of an opening door was more than enough.

In a flash I was up on an elbow and ready to act.

And then I saw that the door that had moved was my lady's. . . .

As I got to my feet, it swung open, and she was standing there, and the beam of the torch in her hand was falling full on the mattress on which I had lain.

"I'm not in your way," I said quickly, and stood back against the wall.

She put out the torch and stood framed in the little doorway against the gentle glow of some light in her room—a slight, pyjama-clad figure, swathed in a dressing-gown.

"I couldn't sleep," she said slowly. "D'you do this every night?"

"I've done it lately," I said.

"And I never knew. It's very sweet of you, Esau: but I'm in no danger here."

I swallowed.

"I like," I said, "to have you under my hand."

"Don't stand on the stone," she said. "Have you no slippers here that you can put on?"

I stooped and put on my slippers and then my dressing-gown.

"That's better." She turned on her heel. "Come

and sit by the fire—and we'll talk, if you're not too tired."

Without a word, I followed her into her room.

I could not see this well, for the walls were dark, and the only light there was that of a shaded lamp which was burning beside her bed ; but a slow wood-fire was glowing upon a spacious hearth, beside which a deep arm-chair was taking important shape. The windows being wide open, the room was fairly alive with the cool, night air, but the fire just tempered a freshness which would have made a girl shiver who was not abed.

" You sit in the chair," said Katharine. " I'd rather sit on the rug."

With that, she took her seat on the fleece in front of the hearth and, after a moment's hesitation, I let myself into the chair.

" I'm still rather dazed," she said, looking into the fire ; " but I know that somehow I've got to get going again. In a day or so, perhaps. At the moment my battery's down, and I cannot start. You see, life seems so pointless, now that he's dead. I can't help you and I have no longer a reason for helping myself. Formosa's occupation's gone. He was her *raison d'être*, and now he is dead."

" He saved the game," I said. " I think he would turn in his grave, if after his sacrifice we went and threw it away."

Katharine pushed back her hair.

" Perhaps. I don't know. I find it so very hard to care any more. Don't think I don't love you, my blessed, because I do. But I don't seem very successful in things that I undertake, and——"

"You can say that of me," I said, "but not of yourself. You added three years to his life—three happy, care-free years. But I—didn't add: I only took away."

Her head was round in a flash.

"What nonsense, Esau! How can you say such a thing? My dearest boy, you were only a cog in the wheel. I don't even blame The Shepherd for—for what occurred. Which brings me back to the point, for I didn't bring you in here to talk about him. I'm not too good for the moment, as you can guess. Besides, I've lawyers to see and I've got to mop up. But I'd like to know what is happening. I've been hit over the heart, and that member is numb: but, as I said once before, I don't want you to be hurt."

"Nothing is happening," I said, "so far as I know. And I've learned my lesson all right. I'm not forcing any more issues. I've done enough harm."

I felt her eyes on my face. Then a hand came to rest on my knee, and I took it in mine.

"It seems," she said, "that we're sick of the same malaise. That's very dangerous, Esau. We've had a breather just when we needed it most: but we must get going again, or we shall go down. For the moment, I can't. I might, if there was some action which I could take. But I can't just stand by and hang on. If I tried, I should let you down: so I'm better out of the way. But I feel that you should do something, because I am so sure that they are not sitting still. I don't know what to advise—my brain's a mess. But don't let up, my darling, because they are out of sight."

I drew in my breath.

"My lady," I said, "because I sit still, don't think that I'm letting up. But I don't want to leave you just now. If I did, I should be so worried that I should make some mistake. The last time we drove to Cruise, I was beside myself until we got back."

"But, Esau, I'm safe enough here."

"I think you are, my sweet: but—I like you under my hand."

"You mustn't be foolish, my darling. God knows I don't want you to buy it: but I've seen enough to know that you're safe in the woods. And I don't want you to get stuck. In a sense, this place is a trap: and if they can shut its mouth—well, you will be done. As I said just now, I don't know what to advise: but I think that your forte is movement, and I feel, when you're sitting still, that you're playing their game."

There was a little silence.

She was right, of course: and I knew it. The line I had taken before was the line to take now. We were at home in the country: but the enemy was not—The Shepherd crawling through bracken would have been matter for mirth. And Judas belonged to the gutter—not to the ditch. And so it was perfectly safe for us to go out to see—and to strike, if occasion offered, as we had done before. And yet . . .

I did not want to leave Katharine, and that is the whole of the truth. When she was out of my ken, I was worried to death. On the face of it, this was absurd, for Cardinal was a stronghold which could not be forced. And yet I feared to leave her. I felt I must be within call.

"I feel," I said, "I feel we should keep together, you and I. I can't tell you why, my darling: but I do not like the idea of splitting our force."

"But I'm not a force, Esau. I doubt if I ever was: but now I'm a broken reed. If The Shepherd walked into this room, I shouldn't get up. We've been through so much together that now, when I'm not with you, you imagine vain things. But you mustn't do that, my darling. They really are vain, you know. With Conrad here and everything shut and barred——"

"I know," I said, "I know. But sooner or later, my lady, The Shepherd is coming back. And if you're to be in when he calls—well, I don't want to be out."

"But he can't get in, Esau."

"Possibly not, my darling. The thing is this—that Cardinal is his objective. His eyes are fixed on this house. If, therefore, I go away, you will be sitting alone at the danger-point. And he is—no fool. . . . You may be safe, because he may fail to get in. But I do not like leaving you at the spot at which such a man is doing his best to arrive."

There was another silence.

Then—

"I can't argue with you," said Katharine. "I can only repeat that I think that you're playing his game. I'm sure he's doing something: and I think you should make an attempt to find out what it is."

"I'll talk to George," I said. "Perhaps, if he stayed with you——"

"No, no. You can't do that. To go out alone would be madness."

"I can take Joseph," I said.

"Who can't talk a word of English. My darling, be reasonable. I don't want to force your hand or to make you promise something against your will. But please consider the point which I've tried to make."

"To-morrow morning—*this* morning I'll have it all out with George."

She sighed, as though with relief.

"That's right," she said. And then, "If only things were different, I'd ask you to take me away for a three-weeks' change. I think that's what I need to lug me out of the slough. I wish I could explain how I feel. Everything is an effort, because nothing is worth while. The mantle of Utter Futility weighs me down. And I can't put it off, Esau. I want to go to sleep and never wake up any more. But if I could go away, with you to look after me, I think in a little I'd be myself again."

I was down on my knees and was holding her hand to my heart.

"Why don't you do it, my darling? Leave for Marseilles to-morrow and there take ship? We can go to Colombo or somewhere, and The Shepherd can go to hell."

Her gaze was fast on the fire.

"Ah, if we could, my blessed. But that's no good, because, if we got away, we should have to come back.

And when we came back—well, he would be waiting for us. And one day you would go out—and never come in."

"Let's chance it, Katharine. Joseph can stay here with Conrad, and George will clean everything up. If we disappear——"

"Esau, do realize this—that we can't disappear. The Shepherd means to have us, and in less than twenty-four hours, he'd be on our trail."

"If we leave by night, my darling, no one outside the castle need know that we've gone. Least of all, The Shepherd. There is no reason why——"

"My dear, I can only assure you that we should be hunted down. It is his job to know things. Accurate information is just the breath of his life. And he pays damned well—by results. And so it comes in."

"I don't care. Let's go, my beauty. The future can shift for itself. We can do nothing worth doing until you're yourself again. So surely the thing to do is to get you fit. I mean, it stands to reason. How can I put up a show, when I know, if I call upon you that you can't respond?"

Very slowly she shook her head.

"Don't tempt me, Esau," she said. "I'm not fair game. Our only chance now—you know it—is to stand where we are and fight. Any compromise is out of the question: things have gone much too far. And to run would be to discard the only card that we hold. And that is the very one which I begged you just now to play. Touch. When you are in touch with these people, you've always a chance. You can see more or less what's coming. But once lose touch, my dear, and life would be simply a nightmare until it ended in death." She shrugged her shoulders there, and a hand went up to her head. "I suppose we do still hold it. The card, I mean. But it's more than three days since they went: and The Shepherd may have decided to bide his time. He's bound to win, if he does. . . . In fact, as I see it, he's bound to win any way. You and I are—well, outranged, Esau. A motor-boat can't take on a battle-fleet."

I put my arms about her and held her close.

"Courage, darling," I whispered. "The boat holds two."

"But one's no good, Esau. What is it like to be loved by someone who's short of a heart?"

Her head came to rest on my shoulder, and, after a little, I found that she was asleep.

... ...

Twenty-five hours had gone by, and George and I were crouching close to the cross roads and using our eyes and ears.

We had left the castle at nightfall, after a peaceful day. Myself I had seen that the gate and the postern-door were locked and barred, and Conrad and Joseph were doing night-watchmen's duty until we got back. One was patrolling the castle and paying special attention to Katharine's whereabouts, while the other was resting in the pantry, ready to let us in whenever we should return. I had not dared leave them a pistol;

but each was armed with a hammer, which he was to use at sight. And Katharine had promised not to go out of doors, but to stay in Sir Valentine's study until she retired.

Rain had fallen gently the whole of the day, to cease when dusk had come in ; and when we had started out, a clean-cut moon was shedding a powerful light. This stood us in excellent stead, for while we kept to the shadows, we could observe our surroundings almost as though it were day.

We had been out for six hours, but though we had covered the whole of the ground we knew, we had seen or heard no sign of the men we sought.

First we had gone to Ousse.

As I have said before, after Sir Valentine's death we had driven three times to Cruise, and though I was ready to swear that we were never followed on leaving that town, I could not possibly say that we had not been seen. If we had been seen and the Cardinal road was watched, The Shepherd must be aware that the car was without the castle when not in use : and not only without the castle, but garaged somewhere at hand, yet clear of the Cardinal road. Once he possessed this knowledge, his discovery of the Lowland would be but a matter of hours. And that would be serious ; for if the car was a prize, the path from Ousse to the castle would presently be in his hands.

It follows that, making for Ousse, we used the greatest caution the whole of the way : but when at last we got there, the padlock which kept our barn was fast to its chain and when I put a torch to a crevice, I saw my faithful car standing silent inside.

This was a vast relief. And when I remembered how we had gone forth in broad daylight, to spend, on one occasion, an hour in the market-town in which The Shepherd was lodged, I felt that his 'secret service' left something to be desired. Be that as it may, we had got away with the risks which we had to take and the secret which meant so much was still inviolate.

Thereafter we lost no time in returning to Cardinal. Since we could answer for Ousse, we meant to go on; but, as we must go by the castle to gain the valley below, for my sake we stopped for a moment, to make sure that all was well.

We had given our usual signal and one minute later Conrad had lowered the bar. He had said that all was quiet, that Joseph was on patrol, that my lady was still at work in Sir Valentine's room.

With this for comfort, I had led the way down to the valley, over the moonlit meadows and up through the hanging woods. . . .

And now the dawn was coming, and still, it seemed. we had the world to ourselves.

"There's nobody here," breathed George. "I'll lay to that. No man born of woman can stay without moving a muscle for twenty minutes of time."

I fingered my chin.

"They may have withdrawn," I said. "But in that case I cannot believe that they have left no one at all to see what we do."

"We may have missed him," said George. "They may have a post closer in."

"The gap in the woods," said I, "is the only place. And I'll swear by fire and water there's nobody there."

"And the woods behind the castle?"

I shook my head.

"There's only the path to Ousse, and we've accounted for that. A man posted there could see nothing. There's nothing to see."

"Except," said George, "our private way in and out."

"That's quite true," said I. "But if a post had been there, I should have been—well, disposed of exactly six hours ago."

George drew in his breath.

"I'm glad to know," he said, "that you realize that. I've taken some plunges to date, but leaving that casement to-night made my blood run cold."

"I was glad to get it over," I said. "I'll give you that. And I didn't like our ramble to Ousse. Katharine's perfectly right. When you're dealing with people like this, it's a damned unpleasant position to be out of touch."

George shrugged his shoulders.

"It looks as though we'd got to endure that state. If you want my private opinion, The Shepherd's sheered off."

"What, bag and baggage?" said I.

"Bag and baggage," said George. "I don't say he won't come back, but I think your tactics showed him that he was out of his depth. The loss of his car was the very hell of a jar, and—I don't know how far he walked, but I'll lay he was sick of life when he rolled into Cruise that night. And then, again, he'd fired on a *grand seigneur*. . . . A sewer-rat can do his stuff in the place to which he belongs ; but let him loose in the country and even a terrier-puppy can show him where he gets off."

"Well, I don't know," I sighed. "All I can say is this—that if I were in his place, I would have Cardinal watched. And now we'd better get back. I think next time we'd better go out by day."

"Yes, but not by that window," said George. "It's bad enough by night, with Joseph squirting his torch all over the place. But by day—no thank you, Thunder."

"You don't seem to fancy that spot."

"I'll say you're right," said George. "And I'll tell you why. Because it is one of those places which favour the early bird. A little sward, entirely surrounded by foliage except for the castle wall. The spot to shoot a spy in, at break of day."

"You're making me uneasy," said I, and glanced at the east. "Come on. Let's get back." We turned. "And before we go in, we'll comb that surrounding foliage for early birds. The light ought to be just right an hour from now."

So it was.

As we made our way over the meadows, the castle above us might have been drawn in pencil and colour was creeping into the topless woods.

Because it was sunk in the trees, the path which led

up from the meadows was still something dim, but the light there was more than enough to tell me whose body was lying six paces ahead.

Conrad had fallen face downward, full in the way.

... ...

As I turned the butler over, he cried out and opened his eyes.

" My leg, sir. It's broken. I slipped and fell. I was going to rouse the village. The blackguards are in."

" God Almighty," I cried. " And Joseph ? "

" I think he's dead, sir. He's lying outside the window. I didn't stop to see."

A thing like a wave was rising within my head. My senses were quailing before it, my heart standing still.

Somehow I framed my next question—just two words long.

" Miss Katharine ? "

"God knows, sir. I know they were with her—I heard The Shepherd speaking. That's how I knew they were in."

The wave curled over and broke.

I remember shaking my head, as a man who has come to some surface and wishes to shake the water out of his eyes and ears.

" But how did they enter ? By the window ? "

" I think so now, sir. I can't see no other way. They must have given your signal. . . ."

As I started up, George Laking caught my arm.

"Steady, Thunder," he said. "If you rush in, you'll buy it—*just as they mean you to.*"

"But——"

"Hear his tale first," said George. "I'll watch while he puts you wise."

With that, he drew his pistol and moved to a bend in the path a short distance ahead.

"When did this happen ?" said I.

"Just after midnight, sir. Joseph was in the pantry, and I'd been down to the courtyard, to look at the gate. I came back by way of the terrace, under Sir Valentine's room. And then I heard him speaking. . . . 'I should like to see the butler,' he said. 'D'you think he'd come if we rang ?' 'He happens to be out,' said Miss Katharine. 'Oh no, he isn't' said The Shepherd. 'Messrs. Solon and Laking are out—we saw them go. And we saw them return—from Ousse . . . *and have a word with the butler*, before they went on.' Well, I knew I could do no good, sir, if they were looking for me ; so I thought I'd best make for the village and give the alarm : an' I thought that Joseph was somewhere—until I got out. An' then I tripped over his body, down in the grass. So, though they'd put the bar back, they must have come in that way. But I hadn't hardly got on to the path itself, when I slipped in the wet and come down on the root of a tree. That was way back, that was. I've crawled as far as this. I ought to have stayed, of course. I can see that now. But I didn't run out of fear, sir. I thought if I raised the village . . ."

"That's all right," I said somehow. "You'll have to stay here for the moment."

With that, I went on up to George.

As I took my pistol out—

"They came in by the window," I said. "They gave our signal and entered just after twelve. I'm going up to see if the bar is in place."

"If it is——"

"We can't get in," said I, and heard myself laugh.

"Steady, Thunder," said George.

"Why did I leave her?" said I. "Can you tell me that? My instinct told me not to—it's told me not to for days."

"If the window's open," said George, with his hand on my arm. . . .

"I'm going in," said I. "You'll stand by and cover my entrance, as well as you can."

Perhaps two minutes went by before I could see the sward and, beside it, the castle wall. And then I saw Joseph's body, asprawl on the dripping turf.

Two more cautious steps. . . .

Then I saw that the window was open—that the movable bar had been dropped.

George never covered my entrance—he had no time. I was up and had entered the passage before he could think. My one idea was to reach Sir Valentine's room.

I think I tried to go quietly—I cannot remember well. But the corners and bends were so many that I could have been shot dead a score of times. Yet no one fired upon me, and after what seemed a lifetime I came to the elegant doorway, to see that the oak was shut.

For an instant I listened at the keyhole, but heard no sound. Then I lifted the latch, flung the door wide open and leaped to one side.

The precaution was needless, for nobody was within. The crimson curtains were drawn and the lights were on, and a huddle of ash still glowed where a log had been.

For a moment I stood looking round. Then, because the windows were open, the breeze of dawn fluttered in and out of the chamber, to set the curtains swaying and carry a sheet of notepaper down to my feet.

Dear Mr. Solon,

Charming as I find these surroundings, I decided some days ago that, for the settlement of our dispute, a city was really the most appropriate place. That you will approve this decision is too much to hope but I have prevailed upon Miss Scrope to return with me to the scene of our misunderstanding some ten days ago.

Youth is naturally impulsive: age alone sees the value of holding its hand. But you made me feel young this evening, more than once. It would have been so easy to—have things out. But, you know, I think I was right. I nearly always am.

Miss Scrope is really sailing for South America this time—probably one day this week.

... ...

Three frantic hours had gone by, before George and I were ready to leave for Ousse.

Joseph, who had been drugged, was almost himself

again. The man had nothing to tell, except that our signal had been given and, when he had lowered the bar, a cloth of sorts had been clapped over his face. He must, I think, have leaned out, when I did not appear: but that he could not remember, and so I must leave it there.

We had got Conrad in and had sent for the village doctor to set his leg. And, then putting Joseph in charge, we had thrown a few things together and taken some bread and cheese with us, to eat as we went.

Either because I was tired, or else because my brain no longer deserved that name, it never entered my head that the Lowland might no longer be standing where I had seen her last.

In fact she was—what was left of my faithful car. And that was not worth taking up. The flames which had destroyed her had also destroyed the barn. The roof had, of course, fallen in, and she was more or less buried beneath a welter of slates.

I cannot remember returning to Cardinal.

I think George had hold of my arm, and a peasant was stumbling behind us, raving that he was ruined and reciting the fabulous offers which he had refused for some building which now had no value at all.

CHAPTER IX

ROUEN was hotter than ever, when George and I climbed out of the Gournay 'bus.

It was the hour of sundown, after a sweltering day, and we had not bathed or shaved for forty-eight hours. This, of design. We hoped to escape recognition. It was our only chance.

Our overalls were filthy, our shoes would have been rejected by any tramp, our hands were engrained with grease and our hair was clipped to the scalp. If we had been followed to Paris, I think that in that city we must have been lost; for we parted company there, and each devoted two hours to seeking to cover his tracks. We had travelled by different trains to Gournay-en-Bray, and from there taken 'bus to Rouen, a matter of thirty miles. I cannot think what I looked like: but few, I think, would have dreamed that George was not what he seemed—a cheerful, French mechanic who thought himself lucky if he had enough to eat.

Our object, of course, was to find out where Katharine was lodged, and we hoped to do this by picking up one of the gang and trailing him home. Approach *The Wet Flag* we dared not, for all its environs were sure to be closely watched, and though I felt pretty sure that we could pass in a crowd, we could not, I think, have survived a deliberate scrutiny.

How slight was our chance of success, we were well aware. Yet no other course was open, for I had been led to Rouen just as a beast is led to the *abattoir*. Cardinal was not convenient—one does not slaughter a beast on the lawn of a country house: but Rouen, with its slums and its river, was almost ideal: a man could disappear there—be 'sunk without trace.' And since, to save Katharine, I must preserve my life, I could only endeavour to see before I was seen.

Of seeing The Shepherd or Judas, we had but slight hope, for they were not likely to favour the places to which we could go: but both of us knew Satan, and George would know the 'wallah' who had followed him down to Cruise.

So, using the meaner streets, we made our way down to the quay and, when the light was failing, we entered a low-class bar. . . .

It was the first of many.

For the next four hours we passed from bar to café and café to bar. Sometimes we sat out of doors, just clear of the glare of some light, observing the passers-by as well as such as entered and left the house: and sometimes we sat indoors, with our backs to a wall, always watching the door and listening to conversations conducted by the scum of the earth. Tears and laughter and gambling, furtive communications and sudden brawls, reasonless spurts of temper and maudlin charity, treacherous advances, blackmail and sometimes a rough goodwill—all these things we witnessed that sultry night: and we saw a thief sell two watches which he had stolen that day and two women empty the pockets of a man who was lolling between them, the worse for drink.

I wish to do Rouen no injustice. The lees of any great city are always vile. That we saw as much good as evil is probably true: but I remember the evil, because that night I was looking for evil men.

Supposed to be German-Swiss, I spoke only with George: but George spoke with all and sundry, if ever it seemed convenient for him to open his mouth. I seldom understood what he said, but five times out of six he made those who heard him laugh, which proves, I think, the perfection with which he played out his part. Indeed, he carried the whole of our sordid performance from first to last; and I only mowed and grunted and did as he said. He spat and picked his teeth and rolled his own cigarettes; and when I would have bought some, because I had not mastered the art, he would not let me do so, but gave me some gum to chew.

It was half-past one the next morning before we threw in our hand; and since we could not endure to sleep in the only quarters which would have become our estate, we made our way out of the city and lay down beneath a hedgerow till half-past six.

If George slept, I cannot tell; but though I certainly rested, I never closed my eyes. I saw the stars in their courses and a clear moon's leisurely progress over a velvet sky: I saw the heaven paling before the dawn and marked the ageless flourish proclaiming the rise of sun : but to me the pageant was only a sluggard clock, to tell me when Rouen would wake and her streets would be busy enough to let us tread them again..

To tell the truth, I was desperate : and when I thought of my darling, I was possessed. I could have moved mountains, if mountains had stood in my way : I would have jumped at murder, if that would have served my turn : but all my strength was useless, my resolution futile, my eagerness vain : the strong man armed could do nothing to save his soul. Sometimes I saw her locked in some shuttered room, with Satan to bring her food and leer at the lovely ghost that sat so still : sometimes I saw her free of some vile apartment that knew no air, with The Shepherd discoursing of the folly of kicking against the pricks : and sometimes I saw her in a cabin, whose port-holes would not open, whose bell was answered by a negro. . . .

There the old, black wave would seem to rise in my brain, and when it had curled and broken, and I could think straight again, my muscles were taut and cracking and the sweat was out on my face.

There was nothing to be done—*nothing.* I could only keep my distance—because if I was taken, then she would be left to her doom.

'My darling from the power of the dog.'

... ...

That day we tramped the streets until it was noon, ceaselessly watching for one of the men we sought :

but if they were out and about, we never saw them, and though we paid special attention to the hotel I had used, no one that we could see was watching that house.

After breaking our fast at a café which hardly deserved that name, we walked along the quays, because, to tell the truth, I could not sit still. Here we were presently offered a few hours' work—the job, in fact, of helping to coal some ship; and since I had little hope of finding our men by day and anything was better than waiting for night to fall, I nodded to George to take it and then began to wonder if I had made a mistake.

In fact, the work did us good, and when we came for our money at six o'clock, the ganger offered to take us on for a month. George thanked the fellow, but said we were going to sea and were hoping to work our passage to Buenos Ayres, for that I had a brother there in the motor-car trade, who had promised, if we could get there, to set us both up. Then he asked for the name of some vessel bound for that port, but the ganger shrugged his shoulders up to his ears, said he had coaled such ships when working at St. Nazaire and remarked that a bird in the hand was worth two in the bush.

So once again we drew blank.

But one thing we had achieved: and that was such a disguise that had I accosted The Shepherd and clapped him upon the back, I cannot believe that he would have known who I was. We wiped some dust from our faces and rinsed our hands, because, if we had not done so, we should have been turned away from the lowest bar ; but the stain of the coal remained, and when I saw myself in a mirror, I thought it was somebody else.

Perhaps because they were not by the waterside, the bars we frequented that night were not so crowded or noisy as those of the night before. They were smaller, less blatant haunts, where men put their heads together and some looked over their shoulders before they spoke. This made me feel that we were on promising ground, but the rooms were so poorly lighted —perhaps, of design—that sometimes we could not be sure of a man sitting back in the shadows, until he got up. It follows that our progress was slow, and midnight was striking before we had got very far.

In fact, at that very hour we were badly held up. The bar we were using was narrow and shaped like the letter L, and since the angle tables were all of them occupied, we were forced to put up with a place from which one arm of the L was wholly out of our sight. If, therefore, we were to answer for the customers out of our view, we could only sit still where we were until they came out ; for we were not far from the door and they would have to file by us to reach the dark, cobbled alley in which the establishment stood. And this, after consultation, we had decided to do, because we both of us felt that the farther end of this bar afforded the very seclusion which our men were likely to choose. We had, of course, made our way up there when we had entered the house, but a waiter had met us to say that that end was full : and that had made us wonder whether we had not stumbled upon a cheap edition of *The Wet Flag* itself.

We sat there for fifty minutes and might very well have sat there till closing time, if a drunken Frenchman had not put a spoke in our wheel.

We had hardly been accosted that evening, until he appeared from nowhere and asked for a light: that was well enough, but when we had given him one, he sat himself down at our table and called for wine. Since drunken men are touchy, we drank with him; but though George spoke him politely, he only stared in reply and then began to talk to himself.

This would not have mattered, if he had not raised his voice, but, after a little, heads began to come round and people began to smile, and before five minutes had passed our table was the cynosure of every eye.

So far as I could make out, his talk was all of women whom he had known and the memories seemed to afford him more pleasure than pain, for more than once he laughed till he spilled his wine: then he would pull himself up and look defiantly round, as though not he, but some other, had found his reminiscence matter for mirth.

At last I could bear it no longer and glanced at George: but when we got to our feet, as though he belonged to our party, the drunkard rose too, and we all passed out together into the ill-lighted alley of which I have spoken before.

Though George and I walked briskly, we could not shake the man off, for when he found we were gaining, he broke into a shambling trot. This made me ripe for assault, for so long as the brute was with us, we could not possibly enter another bar; yet take to our heels we dared not, because a running man is bound to attract the attention of anyone there to see; and though the alley was deserted, the street at its end was not. Indeed, I had just decided that we must round on the fellow and have things out, when to my complete amazement, he spoke in excellent English, using the following words.

"Don't look round, you two: but when you come to the corner, turn to the left: then carry straight on, till you see the cathedral ahead. I'll join you there, in the *place*, five minutes from now: that'll give you time to clear out, if you don't want to see me again: but since we're all three English, we might be able to help one another along."

With that, I think he fell back, but in any event at the corner he turned to the right, and we walked on alone till we saw the cathedral ahead.

"What about it, Thunder?" said George.

"We stay," said I. "We wait and see this fellow who's found us out. God knows what he's doing or who he is, but he doesn't sound like a policeman and he doesn't talk like a crook: and if he can solve a problem as well as he plays a part . . ."

"And there you're right," said George. "I could have sworn that he came out of Marseilles. He had a trick of speaking. . . ."

"It shows what we're fit for," I sighed. "But the point is this. He's probably purely curious: and when he hears what I tell him, he'll give us a tip or two and leave it at that. But he *might* be willing to help."

"What shall you tell him?" said George.

"I'm not sure yet. We'll have to see how he shapes, before we open our hearts."

A moment later we reached the cathedral *place*—a shadowy waste of pavement, where, with one minute's law, a man could have dodged a picket that knew he was there.

"He's a gent," said George, looking round. "He's giving us every chance of fading away. In fact, unless you want to, we'd better stand under that light."

The *place* appeared to be empty. Only the lights of two cafés which stood on its edge suggested life or movement of any kind. Indeed, the effect was eerie, for the moon, which was up, was masked by the great cathedral, so that we were in comparative darkness, while all the world about us was bathed in light: and though we did as George said and crossed to a lonely lamp, this did its work so badly that we might as well have stayed where we were.

The minutes went slowly by, and I was beginning to think that our friend had either missed us or changed his mind, when a figure slouched out of the shadows to where we stood.

Then the same voice spoke very quietly.

"Well, that's all right. But let's get out of this glare." He moved towards the cathedral, with us behind. "This'll do for the moment. I don't want to stay here long. And now—my name is Mansel, and I may as well say right out that you interest me. You see, I know nothing about you, and yet you seem to be doing the same as me. Looking out for some person or persons whom you are anxious to spot before they spot you. Then, again, you mean business—as I do. I mean, I think you're both armed. That we're after the same misdemeanant, I can't believe: I want a German called Rudy—a most undesirable man. And here let me say that I've nothing to do with the police. I'm not—unknown to them: but I never work for them: I work for myself. You see, I can do rough justice: and that is a thing which the police can never do. Yet very, very often justice, unless it is rough, can never be done. But perhaps I'm telling you."

"Indeed, you're not," said I. "We're a couple of raw recruits: but—well, we're out to do rough justice, because we can't go to the police."

Mansel regarded me straightly.

"Rough justice," he said, "is sometimes a two-edged sword. I mean, it can't be explained in a court of law."

"I know," I said. "That's a risk I'm ready to take. But I've not got as far as that. I've still got to find my man."

"Sure he's in Rouen?" said Mansel.

"No doubt about that," said I. "He gave me an invitation to come to this town and be killed."

The other nodded.

"It's quite a good place," he said, "in which to bump a man off. May I ask why he's done you this honour?"

"Because I know who he is."

Mansel fingered his chin.

"Don't you think the police know?"

I shook my head.

"I happen to know that they don't. I really can prove what I say. He belongs to a very good club, but less than a fortnight ago he received the Rochester diamonds—here in this town."

For fully a quarter of a minute Mansel stood still as death.

Then—

"I'm almost afraid," he said, "to ask you his name. In fact, I'd rather not hear it spoken aloud. But if it's the name which I think it may possibly be, Rudy can go to hell and I'll come in with you."

I breathed the name in his ear. . . .

I saw him moisten his lips.

Then—

"That's right," he said quietly. "By God, my son, I don't wonder he wants your life. The men I have tried to bribe. . . . But I've yet to meet the crook that will give him away."

... ...

Then Mansel led us out of the city to where his car was waiting to pick him up, and in little less than an hour we three were sitting back in a fine Rolls-Royce and Carson, Mansel's servant, was whipping us over the roads to a lonely farm.

Since the strain had now been taken, I fell asleep in the car and can only dimly remember that I was led into a bedroom and shown a bed, upon which, because of my state, I tried to refuse to lie down. And Mansel was giving orders, and George was saying "He hasn't slept for four days," and the draught between the door and the windows was lifting the little curtains, on which some fable of Aesop was printed in red.

I never woke till noon: but when at last I sat up, George was sitting, smoking, on the foot of my bed.

Before I could ask a question, he lifted a hand.

"It's quite all right," he said. "I've had a bath and breakfast, and you're going to have the same. We've got a day off, my boy, and Captain Jonathan Mansel is doing our job."

"But——"

"I've put him wise," said George. "He knows the whole of our story from first to last. We talked for two hours last night, and he left at five this morning to get to work. We are to meet him this evening at nine o'clock. And then we shall hear what he's done and what he proposes to do.

"And now get hold of this, Thunder. Our luck has come in with a bang. First and foremost, not only is Mansel an expert at what we've been trying to do, but his astounding efficiency hits you between the eyes. I'll give you a little example. . . .

"Last night I asked him this question. 'How,' I said, 'did you penetrate our disguise?' 'I never should have,' he said. 'When first I saw you, I thought you were what you seemed. But I've studied lip language a bit; so when you were speaking together, I saw what you said. I tell you it shook me up.

French stokers don't use the King's English under their breath.' "

"That's good enough," said I. "I'll say he's the man we want."

"Secondly," said George, "for years it has been his ambition to find The Shepherd out: but he's never been able to place him—nobody has. He knows *The Wet Flag*—he's been there, but not for the last few years. 'Too dangerous,' he said. 'I should never have come out alive.' 'Why isn't it closed?' I asked. 'The police must know.' 'Of course they do,' says he. 'It's a case of Live and Let Live. Hornets will always be, so where's the sense of routing them out of their nest?' "

"And thirdly?" said I.

"Thirdly—the best of all. D'you remember last night he said he was after a man?"

I nodded.

"A German, called Rudy. He didn't say what he'd done."

George leaned forward, bright-eyed.

"Rudy's a pillar of the White Slave Traffic, Thunder. It follows that Mansel's aware of how that traffic is run. For the last three weeks he's been studying nothing else. All, of course, from Rouen. And though he's yet to meet Rudy, he knows a hell of a lot of what he himself described as 'about the closest borough I've ever tried to survey.' "

I took a deep breath.

To say I was thankful means nothing. Despair had been changed into hope—almost into confidence. The awful weight I had carried was suddenly lifted and gone, and though I was not such a fool as to think that the danger was past, I knew that the odds were now even, instead of being so fearful as scarce to be worth setting down.

" My darling from the power of the dog.'

Two or three moments went by, before I could trust my voice. Then—

" What's Mansel doing now ? "

" Locating a vessel," said George. " He knows that white slaves are taken by tender to Havre and that there they are put on board some South American ship. It's that tender he's out to find : and she's what he calls ' slippery.' She's always moving about—on perfectly lawful occasions, most of the time. This is because of the efforts made to suppress her true trade."

" A blind," said I.

" Exactly. Nobody knows she's a couple of padded cells. But Mansel does : and he knows her name and her shape. He makes it all look very easy. ' Once we've found her,' he said, ' we're practically home—always provided The Shepherd fulfils his threat. And I'm perfectly certain he will. Crooks fight shy of taking a girl for a ride : yet he *must* be rid of her, in case she opens her mouth.' "

" ' Practically home ? ' " said I, with a hand to my head.

" My very words," said George ; " and he smiled in my face. ' The tender,' he said, ' is the hall through which my lady must pass. Very well. We wait in the hall. If The Shepherd sees her off, I make his acquaintance there. If he doesn't, we take her away—and I make his acquaintance later, thanks to the information which she can give.' "

There was one dreadful question I had to put.

" Supposing . . . she's gone ? "

" She can't have. No slaver has touched at Havre for more than a week."

So died the last of my terrors, and though George went on talking, I hardly heard what he said.

After a little, he got to his feet and stretched.

" It's like a Greek play," he yawned, " and Mansel's the god in the car. I tell you, Thunder, I never met such a man. He's an answer for everything: and the moment you hear it, you see that the answer's right. That, of course, is greatness. With it all, he's most unassuming and begged me to tell you you'd put up a splendid show. 'It was Katharine Scrope,' he said, 'that weighted him out of the race. But for her weight, he would never have taken his toss. I mean, that goes without saying. But now the tables are turned, and she's round The Shepherd's neck. And her weight will bring *him* down. . . . But if things go as they should, he'll never get up any more.' "

... ...

At five minutes to nine that evening the Rolls was stealing down a shadowy lane, when Mansel rose out of some bushes ten paces ahead. As I made to leave the car, he motioned me back: then he spoke a word to Carson and whipped inside.

"Good news," he said quickly. "The tender is down the river—thirty odd miles by water, but very much less by road. She's moored this side of Caudebec—that's where we're going now. All cats are gray in the dark, but the moon will rise in three hours, and very soon after that I hope we shall pick her up. Now she's loading at Rouen on Monday—you'll never guess what. French mustard. Well, that made me think at once; for the Argentine is a *gourmet*—he knows how to live. Sure enough, the S.S. ——, *for Buenos Ayres*, will touch at Havre on Tuesday, that is, in four days' time.

"Now what we cannot tell is when and where the tender will take on her special freight, or, in plainer terms, Miss Katharine Scrope will embark. It will certainly be by night and probably not at Rouen, because for the last two years those who run these cargoes have had to pull up their socks. It is now, in fact, an extremely dangerous game, and the river police at Rouen are not too bad. Everything points to Monday—to Monday night. The tender loads her mustard and pushes off from Rouen, as soon as the sun is low. Havre is eighty miles off and would take her about six hours. If she likes to stop on the way, it's easy enough. . . . But we cannot *bank* on Monday because, with two sound-proof cabins which do not appear, she could easily tie up at Rouen with Katharine Scrope on board."

I tried to steady my voice.

"She may be on board at this moment?"

"She may. I don't think it's very likely, but still

she may. So what we have to do is perfectly clear. First, we have to make sure that the lady is not on board. Then, having made sure of that, we must never lose sight of the tender until the ship she is serving is under way."

There was a little silence.

Then—

"Pass," said George, quietly, and Mansel laughed.

"Not so hard as it looks," he said. "And I'll tell you another thing. That 'Fortune favours the bold' is perfectly true. I've proved it again and again. If you ride straight for your point, the jade will lead you over the worst of the jumps."

There was another silence.

Then I moistened my lips.

"I'd got a speech ready," I said, "for when I saw you again: but now I can only say that if ever in days to come I can be of service to you—well, you've only to let me know it and I'll be there."

A hand came to rest on my shoulder.

"Thank you," said Mansel, simply. "No man can ask more than that. But you mustn't get the idea that you're in my debt. I'm entirely delighted to help you to save such a gallant girl: but you are affording me a chance for which Scotland Yard would pay out five thousand pounds—a chance of taking a dean of the underworld."

A quarter of an hour went by before Carson slowed up, and we left the car where three ways met in a wood.

"I shall want you, Carson," said Mansel. "Put the

Rolls in the thicket we used to use and then come on to the footbridge over the sluice."

At once the Rolls moved off, and Mansel led us due south and then took a path on the right.

"We are now," he said, "on a salient or tongue of land, with the river running all round it, except across its neck where we left the Rolls. Carson and I know it well, for we wasted a week round here on a clue which proved to be false. Now the tender is moored off the western side of this tongue, under the lee of the forest to which we shall very soon come. That is as much as I know, and the tongue is five miles long: which means that we're bound to find her within two hours. But it's no good our looking about till the moon is up, so, as soon as Carson comes, I'll send him to get us some food at a place I know, and then we'll have a picnic down by the riverside."

And so it fell out.

Under the trees of the forest which graced that reach of the Seine, we ate and drank the fare which Carson had brought, as though we were pleasure-seekers, eating their supper abroad: the perfection of our surroundings needed a poet's pen, and when it came into my head that on that flawless evening thousands of people in France were certainly doing as we, it seemed almost absurd that the four who had chosen this most romantic spot should not be seeking pleasure, but be engaged upon matters of life and death.

When we had finished our meal, George and I sat smoking, whilst Mansel slept; for we, of course, were rested, but he had been up and about for twenty-four hours. Carson roused him, as soon as the moon was up, and five minutes later our search for the tender began.

We were moving up stream and we must have gone more than three miles, when Mansel, moving before me, stood still and lifted his head.

For a moment he listened intently.

Then—

"There's a car in the forest," he said. "Pass the word to Carson and follow me."

With that, he began to run, not looking any more at the river, but glancing now and again at the trees on his left.

Naturally, I did the same, and after a moment or two I saw a long way off a moving flicker of light.

A car, with its head-lamps dimmed, was coming up at an angle as though to cross our front: this, because of the river, it could not do: it was bound to stop at some point on the river's edge. . . .

And there I realized that it was for this very point that Mansel was running so hard. He wanted to get there first—to be in position there before the car had arrived.

Somehow or other we did it, with forty seconds to spare: the going was in our favour—the towing-path we were using was smooth enough, but the car was going slowly because, as I afterwards found, the track upon which it was moving was in a terrible state.

Be that as it may, when a small saloon stole cautiously out of the track, to come to rest on an apron which gave to a landing-stage; George and Carson were crouching behind the briers on its right, and Mansel and I were kneeling behind the ruinous shed which rose on its left.

Somebody stopped her engine and put out her lights. Then a door was opened and somebody left the car.

For a moment or two there was silence, as though whoever it was was using his ears.

Then—

"Curse this moonlight," said Judas, and shut the door. "Get back into the forest and wait for me there. An' don't lose this —— car. 'Please, sir, a Willie pushed me' won't work again."

CHAPTER X

SATAN made no reply. Perhaps his heart was too full. But he took it out on his gears, as he went about, and Judas cursed him wildly for making 'that —— row.'

Then the car swung off the apron and into the forest again, while Judas stood full in the moonlight, watching her go.

For more than a hundred paces, she held on her way: then I heard her engine stop and I saw her lights go out: so did Judas, standing with a hand to his chin: then he turned on his heel and made for the landing-stage.

Mansel breathed in my ear.

"D'you recognize him?"

"It's Judas," I said. "The other man's A.D.C."

Mansel nodded.

Then—

"That is the tender—there. He's going aboard. We'll do the same, if we can, and see what's what."

Now, since the tide was low, the tender's deck was below the landing-stage, and though I could see her funnel and part of her stern, I could not see any more of the craft herself: and I should have lost sight of Judas, if he had not taken a torch to guide his steps, for baulks of mouldering timber stood up on either side of the landing-stage, and since we were well to the left, the baulks and their shadows combined to conceal the man. As it was, I was able to watch the beam of the torch, till at last it fell on the funnel and then disappeared.

Mansel touched my arm.

"Remember," he said, "no violence. We're out to see and to hear. However great the temptation, we must not touch him to-night."

"I know," I said. "I promise. Do—do you think she's on board?"

"I don't think so," said Mansel. "And now let's go. Keep three paces behind me and do as I do."

With that, he whipped back to the trees and, when we were out of the moonlight, across the track. At once he turned back to the apron, and as he passed George and Carson, he told them to stay where they were.

"If there should be trouble," he said, "Judas' one idea will be to get to the car. You will see that he doesn't do it. But if there is no trouble, you are to let him go by."

Then we skirted the little apron, keeping within the wood, and one minute later we stood on the water's edge.

The landing-stage was now between us and the moon, and the shadow its bulk was casting was only some ten feet off, but Mansel went down on his stomach and wriggled across the gap, and I, of course, did likewise—I fear in some impatience, because I was so anxious to get aboard.

Now the landing-stage was a very rude affair and

must have been built a great many years ago. Had it been kept in repair, it would, I think, have stood any kind of shock, for its piles were like so many tree-trunks and these were tied together with so many beams. Three rows of beams there were, which ran the length of the stage—I suppose, to act as fenders against the thrust of some ship: but they made things easy for us, for we walked along upon one and held to the one above us, in case we slipped.

So we came to the tender, which looked like a miniature tramp and seemed to be in darkness, except for the light of the moon.

I saw Mansel searching her deck. . . . Then he stepped over her rail and glided into the shadow of her companion-hatch.

I saw him peer down the stairway. Then he turned his head and motioned to me to come up.

"Keep one pace behind me now."

I nodded my head.

Below a light was burning and men were in talk. I could hear the murmur of voices and then a laugh.

Mansel passed down the companion, with me on his heels. . . .

The companion led directly into a small saloon: no light was burning here, and yet we could see our way, for a light was burning somewhere behind our backs.

I confess that my heart was beating as never before, but Mansel never wavered or so much as poked his head. Indeed, he seemed to sense the lie of the land and to know that, thanks to this, we had nothing to fear.

That he was perfectly right, I saw for myself—as soon as I had descended and turned about.

Standing at the foot of the stairway, with our backs to the dingy saloon, we found ourselves facing two gangways, one upon either side of the stairway itself. Doors were hung in these gangways, and that on the right was shut : but the door on the left was open, and lights were burning beyond.

Looking through the doorway, I saw that the gangways curled inwards and almost at once became one, out of which doors gave to cabins on either side. Light was shed by a lamp which was burning behind the companion, just where the gangways met, and the door of a cabin was open and men were speaking within.

At once Mansel proved the gangway whose door was shut ; for this, being round the corner, was very dark. Then he stepped back to my side and spoke very low.

"We can't hear there," he said. "We'll have to go on. But we must be ready to clear, if somebody moves. The instant you feel me touch you, whip down the saloon. A man coming out of the light won't notice us there."

Then he turned to the other gangway and stole to the open door, and, after listening a moment, stepped over the sill. Directly I did the same, the voices of those who were talking became very clear—not so much because we were closer, as because we had passed the obstruction the stairway made ; for the cabin in which they were speaking was upon the same side as we, and, having to turn two corners, the sound was spent before it had come to our ears.

"Rumour says it's Formosa," said a man, with an accent I could not place.

"Well, Rumour's wrong," spat Judas. "It's a girl of the name of Scrope."

"Maybe that's Formosa's name. I guess she wasn't christened Formosa, no more than Bermuda was."

"It's not Formosa," said Judas. "Formosa's down in the country. She's stuck herself in a castle an' won't come out. I don't mind saying we want her—an' want her bad. But we're not such —— fools as to turn her off. You don't kill golden geese—they're a sight too rare."

"I've known it done—when they won't lay no more eggs."

"Who says she won't lay any more? She's fallen foul of his nibs because of a Willie's health. I'll say he was sore to start with, but——"

"Rumour says it's Formosa," said the other.

Judas expired.

"I've told you it isn't," he said, "but let that go. If you like to call her Formosa, that's your affair. There's the six photographs of her—name and age on the back."

"Now listen here," said the other, and cleared his throat. "I know what I know about this, an' I'm not coming in. Ordinary stuff I will ship: but I'm not going to sign for Formosa, and that's God's truth."

"You're out of your mind," said Judas. "Why ever not?"

"'Cause I don't choose to," said the other. "An' I'm my boss."

"Look at that face," said Judas. "There's a full five hundred there."

"I won't say there isn't," said the other.

"An' you can afford to drop one fifth o' that?"

"That's my affair."

"One hundred quid?" said Judas. "An' the franc where it is?"

"Put it away," said the other. "You can't bend me."

"I wonder," said Judas, softly. . . .

There was a moment's silence: then somebody poured some liquor into a glass.

"Good weather for grapes," said the other. "My brother down at Bordeaux——"

"Quite so," said Judas. "How's Daisy?"

"Doing well," said the other. "She's maiding in San Francisco, and likes it fine."

"Nursemaid again?" said Judas.

"Housemaid now. Lives like a —— queen, an' she's got a half-share in a car."

"There now," said Judas. "Some people have all the luck. An' Choker Kay——"

"What's that to do with Daise? She wasn't in on that job."

"In or out, she wouldn't have stood a chance. Not after Choker Kay had opened his mouth."

"He lied," said the other, calmly. "An' a lot of good it done him, the rotten swine."

"Say he lied," said Judas. "The child was dead."

The other smote upon some table, so that the glasses rang.

"What if it was? My girl was up in Paris. Until she read the paper, she'd——"

"I know, I know," said Judas. "That's why she did a trot. An' now she's in San Francisco, an' doing well. An' the poor dam police still hoping. . . ."

The other laughed—a very unpleasant laugh.

"I'll see you, Jew Boy," he said.

"Will you?" said Judas. "Right. Daisy is now at Lyons. She works at a sweet-stuff shop in the Rue Laval. She calls herself Ella Bohn, and she says she's Swiss. And she is engaged to be married to one of the *gardes mobiles*."

I thought the silence that followed would never end: and when at last it did, the other man's voice was changed.

"What . . . then?" he said very thickly.

"This," said Judas, sharply. "You'll load our cargo, Mangey—load it next Tuesday morning at one o'clock . . . *unless you want Daisy taken on Tuesday night*."

There was another silence, almost as long as before.

At length—

"You've . . . got me down," said Mangey. "How did you know?"

"Rumour," said Judas, lightly. "But that's by the way. If we bring her down on Tuesday, an' you're not here——"

"Lose it," said Mangey, hoarsely. "I've said I'm down."

"Then sign for her now."

"But——"

"Sign for her *now*, you ——. I've had enough from you. And here's a bit of advice. *Don't ever sin against us*, 'cause we shall know if you do. An' we shan't come an' argue, Mangey. *We shall post a little letter* . . . with Daisy's name and address. An' then we shall just write 'Paid' against your name in our books."

If the other made any answer, I do not know, for here Mansel touched my arm, and I turned at once and made for the dark saloon.

We reached its depths together, and turned about. Then Mansel set a hand on my shoulder and spoke in my ear.

"There's trouble coming to Judas. He's gone too far. There was danger in Mangey's tone, and that last threat will push him over the edge."

That was as much as he said, and the two of us stood like statues, watching the little gangway and the frame of the door within it—a thin rectangle of light.

Nearly a minute went by before Judas appeared—I saw the light on his face, as he came to the sill. The other, I thought, was behind him; but the gangway was so narrow that Judas' body filled it, to block my view.

I saw him stoop for the lintel and then stand up, and since he was taller than the doorway, he looked like some headless figure, standing against the light.

Then two things happened together.

Somebody let out a sob—the sob of a man who has made some physical effort with all his might: and Judas hollowed his back and threw up his head.

He made no sound that I heard, but he seemed to be

trying to turn. And then his body fell forward, flat on its face—to show us the man who had killed him, standing framed in the doorway, with a hand upon either jamb.

A rat of the underworld had put a spoke in our wheel.

... ...

One may feel ripe for murder; but when one sees murder done, it hits you over the heart. At least, that is my experience. I will not say that my head was going round, but I could not focus clearly and I felt that I must have air. So, for less than a moment—although it seemed longer than that. And then I was trembling all over, and Mansel was standing behind me, with a hand on each of my arms.

Mangey was still in the doorway: but almost at once he turned and passed out of our sight.

"All right now?" breathed Mansel.

"Yes, thanks," I whispered. "I'm sorry. But what on earth can we do? We'd got the game in our hands: and now he's torn everything up."

"It's quite all right," said Mansel. "We'll save it yet. Mangey is badly placed, and I think he'll do as I say."

"Is—is Judas dead?"

"Dead, or as good as dead. He's got a knife in his back. And now let's go and see Mangey. Time's getting on."

We were just halfway to the gangway, when Mangey appeared in the doorway, with something over his arm.

(I afterwards found that this was the tick of a mattress, which he, of course, was proposing to use as a shroud.) Mansel stopped when he saw him, and let him come on: but the fellow never saw us, but peered at the corpse for a moment and then went down on his knees.

In fact, he had a hand in the pocket of Judas' coat, when he found himself bathed in the light of Mansel's torch.

I think I shall always see the look on his face.

He was a man of sixty, or thereabouts: his hair was iron-gray and his nose was blue and his face was weather-beaten, as sailors' are. But now his mouth was open, his eyes screwed up, and he wore the exact expression of a baby about to cry. The effect was so unnatural that I averted my eyes, and I think it shook even Mansel, for when I looked again, he had lowered the beam of his torch.

"Put up your hands," he snapped. "And do as I say."

I saw Mangey's hands go up. In one was the photograph of Katharine, which he had signed.

Mansel went close to the man.

"Stand up and turn round."

"Who's you?" said Mangey, hoarsely.

"Never mind who I am. I've a rod. Stand up and turn round."

Mangey obeyed slowly, and the barrel of Mansel's pistol rose to his shoulder-blades.

Mansel passed me the torch.

"Put the beam on the body," he said: "and watch your step. We're going into the cabin to have a talk."

I did as he said—to see the hilt of a knife sticking out of the back of the corpse. The coat was stained for three inches about the hilt: but I saw no blood on the floor, perhaps because the knife had not been withdrawn.

"Into the cabin," said Mansel.

Mangey began to go forward, and Mansel stepped over the corpse. . . .

The cabin was very tiny and short of air. A locker beneath a port-hole served for a seat, and before this was fixed a table, on which were wine and whiskey and the glasses the men had used. And there were five photographs of Katharine, passport size.

By Mansel's direction, Mangey passed to the locker and there sat down, placing his hands upon the table and thereby adding a picture to those that were there. Now he was round, his eyes were like two gimlets and fast upon Mansel's face. The man could not think where he stood. All his shrewdness had failed him: his cunning had broken down.

Mansel was speaking to me.

"I want the others aboard. Post them by the companion, and say that if Satan should come, he is not to descend."

Be sure I wasted no time. . . . Indeed, if George and Carson had cared to complain, they could with justice have done so, for I gave them Mansel's orders and stated that Judas was dead and then whipped back to the cabin as fast as ever I could.

"Provided," Mansel was saying, "provided you play my game. Satan's easy money. He'll never call your bluff. But the other one will, Mangey. You know what chance you stand against a man like his nibs."

"—— all," said Mangey, and put his head in his hands.

"Less," said Mansel. "He'll smell the doings before you can open your mouth. And that'll be that, my friend. And Daisy——"

"That's why I done it," said Mangey. "To save my girl. I don't know whether you 'eard what that —— said."

"I heard," said Mansel. "But this won't save her, you know. You don't save people by putting the rope round their neck. But I *can* save her—if you like to do as I say. Look sharp an' make up your mind. Satan's back in the woods. I don't know how long he'll wait, but he'll come to look for the Jew Boy, before he goes."

Mangey leaned forward.

"You can't have it both ways," he said. "I 'eard you send for the others . . . to stop him from comin' down."

"What a fool you are," said Mansel. "D'you think I want him here while I'm talking to you? When I go, they go with me . . . and Satan's free to come down . . . and to help you sink that carrion, for all I care."

The other blinked at him.

"What are you? A —— policeman?"

"No, I'm not," snapped Mansel. "If I was a policeman, you wouldn't be sitting there. An' while we're talking of policemen, just drink this down—that I can talk to the police, because they have nothing on me.

And if you were to double-cross me, by God I'd open their eyes."

"Sez you," said Mangey.

Grimly Mansel surveyed him.

"Don't get me wrong," he said. "D'you think I care if a water-rat misses stays? But I heard you jib at taking Formosa on. And *in return for that,* if you like to do as I say, I'll see you out of this jam."

"That's queer," said the other slowly. "I never seen Formosa: but near two years ago she was very good to my girl. Sick of a fever, she was: an' Formosa took her off and put her in her own bed. An' nursed her well: an' slep' on the floor herself."

There was a moment's silence.

Then—

"Take it or leave it," said Mansel. "It's up to you."

His eyes on the table, the other spoke to himself.

"Well, I ain't got nothing to lose." His head went up. "All right, mister. I'll see you. What d'you know?"

Mansel spoke over his shoulder.

"Come into the cabin, will you?"

I came right in.

Mansel addressed Mangey.

"Look well at this man," he said.

Mangey studied me carefully, head to foot.

"Yes," he said, "I guess I'd know him again."

Mansel returned to me.

"Ask George to come down a moment."

I did as he said, and George was surveyed in his turn.

Then George was returned to his duty: but I stayed on—to hear the explicit instructions which Mansel gave.

I will not set these down, because I am going to tell how Mangey carried them out: but when it is remembered that, except while dealing with Mangey, Mansel had had no chance to think anything out—unless you count the few moments succeeding Judas' death—I think it must be admitted that he had a very rare brain: for his plan was subtle enough, but, what is more to the point, he had every tiny detail cut and dried, and the moment Mangey said that he would come in, Mansel dictated his orders, as though from some sheet and had an answer all ready for every one of the questions which Mangey asked.

At length he stood up.

"Well, there you are," he said. "Go on and get to it now. I may say I'm coming with you. Satan will not see me, but I shall be there. And I shall hear all that is said. So I shouldn't make any mistakes—if I were you."

"You don't trust me far," said Mangey, and got to his feet.

"Why the devil should I?" said Mansel.

"You're a one," said Mangey, and let out a laugh. His spirits had certainly risen, for as he left the gangway, he kicked the corpse in the stomach and laughed again.

One minute later he left the landing-stage and made for the wasted track, with Mansel close behind him and myself upon Mansel's heels.

... ...

Why The Shepherd employed him, I do not know. The fact remains that Satan was fast asleep.

When Mangey shook his shoulder, he started up with a whoop.

"Good God," he said, "it's Mangey. Where's Jew Boy gone?"

Mangey's answer was quite unprintable: but it found high favour with Satan, who had small use for Judas, as I have shown. I heard the blackguard chuckling, as he clambered out of the car.

"No, where is he reelly," he said, "you wicked ole man?"

"Gone down the river," said Mangey, "walkin' along o' the bank. I was to come an' tell you to take the car to the cross roads an' wait for him there."

"Walkin' along o' the bank? Whatever for?"

"Snoopin'," said Mangey, and spat. "I only hope he falls in and sucks his toobs full o' mud. Jus' because I can't do Tuesday——"

"Why can't you do Tuesday?" said Satan.

"'Cause o' the tide. I can't do Monday nor Tuesday—the tide don' fit. If I took her aboard on Monday, I couldn't get up to Rouen, to load my stuff: if I took her aboard on Tuesday, I couldn't get down to Havre till the afternoon. 'So it's got to be to-morrow,' I told him, 'or not at all.' You'd o' thought I'd stung him for sixpence, the way he talked. Called me a —— ——, an' said I was only fit to handle a punt in a sewer. An' I've been treading this river for forty-five years next March."

"Yes, but who's he snoopin'?" said Satan.

"I'm coming to that. At last he throws in his hand, with a mouthful o' threats—an' makes me sign for a girl what I've never seen. An' when I says 'That isn't business,' 'We don't do business,' he says, 'with filth like you.'"

And, with that, the old skipper let fly, condemning Judas in terms which I dare not set down and expressing such hopes for his future as, had the dead man been buried, must have made him writhe in his grave.

"Easy," said Satan, "easy. I know all that. I want to know who he's snoopin', you —— ole fool."

"He's snoopin' a couple o' Willies that——"

"A couple of *what* ?" screamed Satan.

"Willies," said Mangey. "They come aboard to-night and asked to be taken on."

But if Satan heard what he said, he made no reply ; instead, he darted glances to right and left, and then he prowled round the car, poking his head and peering and striving to probe the darkness in which we stood.

"You too ?" said Mangey. "That's what the Jew Boy done."

"I'll say it was," said Satan. "You —— wash-out, why didn't you tell me before ?"

Then he asked what 'the Willies' were like, and Mangey described me and George, and the things Satan said of us both were even more dreadful than Mangey's abuse of the Jew.

"What time was this ?" he demanded.

"I don't know," said Mangey. "I never looked at no clock. They hadn't been gone very long before Jew Boy came. First thing I knew, I heard them fallin' about; and so I come up an' out to see who it was. One of 'em talks in French: but it wasn't a French I knew, so I has them down to the cabin and into the light. Willies all right, they were, with four days' growth on their chins. They didn't look down an' out, but that's what they said they were, an' they asked to be taken on for the run o' their teeth. 'Taken on'—just like that. . . . And one of 'em wearin' a wrist-watch that looked like gold."

He spat contemptuously.

"Go on," said Satan, "go on. What 'appened next?"

"Well, I was all alone, so I couldn't do nothin' then—I wouldn't of minded one, but the two was over my weight. But I told 'em to come back this evening at half-past ten. 'Neither sooner nor later,' I said: 'for I shan't come aboard before ten, an' I sail at eleven o'clock. I promise you nothin',' I said: 'but I've got to load at Rouen'—I didn' say when—'an' if you like to work for your dinner, maybe I'll let you wipe the stevedores' eyes.'"

"Go on," said Satan. "What then?"

"Well, they swallowed that," said Mangey, "an' said they'd be back to time. Then they asked me the way to Caudebec and sheered off, goin' down stream."

Satan was biting his fingers.

"He'll never get 'em," he muttered. "He ought to have come for me. I'd find those ——, if they were abroad in Hell. But he wanted 'em all to himself: an' then to come back to his nibs an' say 'Look what I've done.'"

"You can 'ave them to-night," said Mangey. "What for d'you want them so?"

"Never you mind," blared Satan. "You get back to your hooker an' rake her decks." With that, he flung into the car and started her up. "Where did he say? The cross roads?"

"That's where he said," said Mangey.

"An' I'm to sit there with the car, while he turns them off?" He spouted a frightful oath. "But I'll lay he doesn't do it. He'll never run them down. He can wait behind a door with a rod in his fist; but he'd never come up with a heavy, unless he was fast asleep."

Then he let in his clutch with a bang, and the car went lurching over the broken road. . . .

As the sound of her engine faded—

"Windy," said Mangey, and spat.

"Easy money," said Mansel, "I told you so. And now you'd better get back and bury your dead."

... ...

Though the trap was now set and baited, it was by no means certain that The Shepherd was going to walk in. There was only, I think, one weak spot in Mangey's tale, and that was his excuse that, except on Sunday morning, the tide would not serve. (This could not be avoided: had Mangey agreed to a later date, The Shepherd might have walked in *and left Katharine behind*: but now he had the chance of killing two birds with one stone—that is to say of disposing of George and me between ten and eleven o'clock and putting Katharine aboard at half-past twelve.) But what was very much worse than any weak spot in the tale was the very awkward fact that Judas would not reappear. Still, this was not our fault. Mansel could do most things that a man can do ; but, as he put it himself, ' I've yet to master the art of raising the dead.'

We followed Mangey aboard and watched him below. Then Mansel called us together and spoke in our ears.

" I don't know how long Satan will wait at the cross roads : but I'm sure that in spite of his bluster he'll hesitate to let Judas down. So I think we can count on his waiting until it is light. And then he'll go home . . . to his master . . . as fast as ever he can.

" Well, we've got to try and follow—in case of accidents. I dare not leave the tender—I don't trust Mangey an inch. And Solon must stay with me. So Mr. Laking and Carson will now go back to the Rolls, take up some likely spot on the Rouen road, and fall in behind as soon as Satan goes by. I'll leave it there, for Carson's extremely clever at trailing a car : but I don't think you need be afraid of taking odd risks, for Satan's one idea will be to make his report and, as he's nobody with him, he won't be able to keep a look-out behind. You've got his number, Carson ? "

Carson repeated the number of the saloon—a thing which I must confess I could never have done.

" That's right. Now if you should run him to earth —and I hope to God you do—Carson will leave the car and Mr. Laking will then take over the wheel. Carson will know what to do : Mr. Laking will take the Rolls on and park her wherever he can, and will then come cautiously back to where he saw Carson last. As for communication, we'll have to hope for the best. Mr. Solon will be close to the apron most of the time.

" Has anyone any suggestions ? "

Nobody had.

" Very well. You two get off and do your bit. If you can get back before dark, I'd like you here. But things don't always fit in : and if you're doing good work, by all means stay where you are."

So George and Carson went off, to pick up the Rolls ; and presently Mansel went down, to see for himself that Mangey was duly performing the task which his folly had set. And so I was left alone on the deck of that sinister ship.

I will not relate my feelings, which may, I think, be imagined as well as described. But one thing I must record. And that is this. Whether because what had happened seemed still unreal, whether because Mangey's story had rung so uncommonly true, the curious fact remains that more than once I found my eyes on the tow-path, in case a man who was dead should come back that way.

I remember that very well, as also the moon upon the water and, very far in the distance, a spark of light—which made me think of my darling, and how, but for Judas' death, she must have been saved.

And then my musing ended, my ghost was laid, for a sudden, savage blow on the back of my head put me down and out.

CHAPTER XI

"HOW d'you feel ?" said Mansel.

I could not see him, but I was sitting down and his arm was about my shoulders, holding me up.

"Well, I'm still alive," I said, "but I've got the deuce of a head."

"That's hardly surprising," said Mansel. "You've been out for nearly three hours."

Slowly I looked about me, blinking my eyes. It must be broad daylight, if I had been out for three hours.

"I don't want to be silly," I said, "but I seem to have lost my sight."

"No, you haven't," said Mansel. "At first I thought the same. But we're in a dark room—that's all. That's why we can't see."

"My God," I said. "Don't say you bought it, too ?"

"I did, indeed," said Mansel. "And I'm greatly ashamed of myself. I never remember making so bad a mistake."

I sat very still.

"Can you tell me what's happened ?" I said. "I—I don't understand."

"What's the last thing that you remember ?"

I put a hand to my head, which was aching as never before.

" George and Carson," I said, " went off for the Rolls: and then you went down below to see how Mangey was getting on with his job."

" Very good," said Mansel. " And now I'll put you wise. The mistake which I made was this. *From first to last I assumed that Mangey was all alone.* Don't ask me why I did it, because I've no answer to give. The fact remains—I did it. And, as a result, you and I have gone down the drain. We shan't stay down, you know. To be beaten by Mangey is quite unthinkable. But at the present moment he's got us where we belong.

" What happened was this.

" When I let him go down alone, he went straight to another cabin and roused a pal: and since the cabins have port-holes, the two saw George and Carson going ashore. By the time I came down, the pal was ready and waiting, and whilst I was speaking to Mangey, he laid me out. Then one of them went on deck and dealt with you."

" But what's his object ? " said I. " The only chance he'd got was to stick to you."

" He means to do better than that. He knew that it was my intention to take The Shepherd on: but he didn't think I was up to The Shepherd's weight. I don't altogether blame him. The Shepherd's reputation passes belief. Now, if I took The Shepherd on, and The Shepherd won, Mangey's last state would be very much worse than his first; and so, if he could, he determined to turn his coat. And this, as we know, I gave him the chance to do.

"If and when The Shepherd appears, he's going to say we killed Judas and forced him (Mangey) to tell the tale which he did. And then he will hand us over—as proof of his devotion to The Shepherd and all his works."

"I'm all against that," said I.

"So," said Mansel, "am I. And as soon as you feel yourself, we'll have a look round. They've taken our pistols, of course: but they missed the torch. I'm not using it now, because I want to save it as much as I can."

"One moment," I said. "Has Mangey gone to the cross roads, to tell Satan what he's done?"

"Well, I hope he hasn't," said Mansel. "I daren't say more than that. Because, if he has, The Shepherd won't wait till to-night. But I think that perhaps he's not gone, because he's afraid of encountering Carson and George. Be careful when you stand up, or you'll hit your head."

With an effort, I got to my feet—to find the ceiling so low that I had to stoop.

"And now, where are we?" I said.

"Ah," said Mansel. "I wondered when that was coming. But I won't be beaten by Mangey. We're going to get out."

"Go on," I said. "Where are we?"

"In one of the padded cells."

... ...

The position was very ugly—we both knew that. And if Mangey had gone to the cross roads, we were as good as done. If he had not, we had perhaps fifteen hours in which to make our escape: but cells are not made to break out of and the life of the torch could hardly be more than three hours. Yet, if we failed to break out, the game was up, for The Shepherd would take no chances and neither of us was armed. In that case, Katharine's rescue would hang upon Carson and George—who would be greatly embarrassed in any efforts they made; for The Shepherd would know what had happened, but they would not. As like as not, trying to find us, the two would play into his hands . . . which meant that once again the monster would have his way and Katharine would sail on Tuesday 'to take up another job.'

Our greatest hope was this—that George or Carson or both would very soon return to make their report, and that when the day wore on, but neither of us appeared, they would become suspicious and come aboard. If they put the screw on Mangey, he might give in: but in any event they would know that things had gone wrong and so would be forewarned when The Shepherd appeared.

Meanwhile, it was up to us to do what we could to escape without any help and so to restore the position which Mansel had won. But when he had lighted the torch and I saw what our prison was like, I must confess that my heart sank down to my boots.

The cell was six feet square and five feet six inches high, and the whole was lined with sail-cloth, ceiling and walls and floor. There was no port-hole or grating or anything of the kind, but the door was plain to be seen, because of the cut in the sail-cloth, four feet by two. I need hardly say that it had no handle. There was no furniture and not so much as a bracket which we could tear from its fastenings, to use as a tool. The sail-cloth itself was neither strained nor slack, so that, while it would give to violence, it could not be taken hold of at any point: and though it was very dirty, it showed no sign of disorder or even of wear.

What, of course, I could not see, but afterwards found, was that there were four layers of sail-cloth all over the cell; that the walls were padded with sawdust, but not the roof: that the cloth was held to the walls by straps of iron, which were themselves padded and covered, so that they did not appear.

Now, though the heat was dreadful, there could be no doubt at all that somewhere or other there was an inlet for air: but though we tried to find this, by prodding the cloth all over, to see if it gave, the stuff was so harsh that we met with no success. This insignificant effort was more than enough to set us streaming with sweat, and before we did anything else we stripped to the waist.

"And now," said Mansel, "I'll tell you what I propose. In case we cannot get out before The Shepherd arrives, unless we are content to be butchered—and I am not—we had better make some preparation to put up some sort of fight. If we can detach the sail-cloth above our heads—detach it on every side except that of the door, it will then hang down like a curtain against the wall. Then, when they open the door, they will at least be prevented from seeing into the cell, and you can't brush sail-cloth aside as if it were silk. And once the stuff is down, there may be something above it which helps our case."

With that, to my great delight, he produced a three-bladed pen-knife out of a little pocket, sunk in the side of his coat, and whilst I held the torch, he made the first incision that sail-cloth had ever known.

He had to go carefully, for the sail-cloth was very tough, but after a minute or two he had slit the first layer across from side to side—this, right up in the angle which the ceiling made with the wall. Then, turning first right and then left, he slit it for two or three inches towards the door: and then we took hold of the tab which was now hanging down and, pulling together, ripped it the rest of the way.

With the other three layers of sail-cloth we did the same, so that soon all four were hanging down over the door: since all were held fast at the top and dragged on the floor, they made a more awkward obstruction than we had dared hope they would; and I think that we both felt better when this was done. At least, I know I did; for now we should have some warning of danger at hand, and the door could not open upon us before we knew where we were.

And something else we gained by what we had done, for we had uncovered two vents which gave to the open air. These holes were admitting no daylight, and to this day I do not know where they led: but by putting our faces against them, we, so to speak, drank from them, and though the liquor was tainted, I never felt more thankful in all my life.

The ceiling was built of hard wood and seemed to be stout, so we wasted no time upon that, but turned to the business of stripping the walls of the cell: but we did not touch the wall which was facing the door, because it seemed so likely that that was in fact the very side of the ship.

Here perhaps I should say that, whilst I was still unconscious, Mansel had done his utmost to force the door: but this he had found so fast that it might have been a part of the wall.

It took us just half an hour to strip the three walls, and for all the good that we did, we might have left them alone, for all their seams were caulked, and though they were built of timber, this was so tough that they might have been built of iron.

To strip the wall in which the door had been hung, we had to work under the curtain which we had made, and this was most exhausting, because we were there deprived of what air there was. Indeed, by the time we had done, our state was lamentable.

Our lungs were labouring—and were losing half their labour, much as a slipping clutch: the sweat was pouring off us and streaming into our eyes; and we were covered with sawdust from head to foot. Of this filth the chamber was full, and since our skins were so greasy, the stuff had only to touch them to stay where it was. It clung to our lips and our nostrils, so that we breathed it in, and, what was almost worse, it settled upon our eyelids and made its way into our eyes. What with this, and the lack of air and the savage pain in my head, I began to feel that I simply could not go on and that death itself would be better than striving against such odds. But Mansel ignored all the torment as though it did not exist, except that he once observed that, whenever we left the cell, we must remember to take our jackets and shirts, "for if we don't," he said, "we shall both catch cold: and if there's one thing I hate, it is a cold in the head." This put me to shame, as perhaps it was meant to do, and I turned again to the battle he seemed determined to win.

We then attacked the one remaining wall, that is to say the wall which was facing the door. When this was stripped, we found that it was not, as we had expected, the side of the ship itself, but was built of wood like the others, except that the wood was soft wood and none of the seams were caulked.

It was not match-boarding—it was stouter than that: but if we had had a cold chisel, we could, I was sure, have forced it without any fuss. But, of course, we had no chisel: and though we did our utmost to wrench from its fastenings one of the iron straps, we could not get our fingers behind it and so had to let it be.

But Mansel would not give in.

He chose a joint in the woodwork, more open than some, and began to make this wider by paring the edges away.

It was a very slow business; but by using his sharpest blade, he gradually widened the joint, until some grains of sawdust began to fall through.

"Good God," said I. "Do they use nothing else in this ship?"

Mansel pursed his lips.

"I rather think," he said, "it's a wall of the other cell."

Once again my heart sank down.

To have a faint hope of breaking out of prison is good: but when the only way out will bring you into another as strong as the one you are in, the hope is not so much dashed as made a mockery.

Mansel shook the sweat from his eyes and bade me put out the torch.

"D'you remember Jack Sheppard?" he said. "How he broke out of Newgate the second time? Well, this is the way he did it, passing from cell to cell. He was in 'The Castle,' you know; and he didn't like the look of the door: so he broke from 'The Castle' into 'The Red Room' and forced that door, instead. And that's what we're going to do. Stand by with that torch."

Working in turn, it took us more than an hour to pare away enough wood for a man to get his fingers behind a board, and though we did what we could to spare the knife, by the time we had done the business, its blades were growing blunt.

Now the slit we had managed to cut was three feet from the floor, so I went down on my knees, with my back to the wall, and Mansel took his seat on my shoulders, put his right hand into the hole and took a grip on the board. Then he planted his feet on the boards upon either side and bracing his wrist with his left hand, put forth his strength.

But the wood was just too thick. And when he threw in his hand, and I took his place, I could feel it bending before me, but that was all.

"Two grip-holes," said Mansel, quietly. "That's what we want. But, first, we'll make this one bigger, and try and have a look at that cell. At least, we've plenty of time, for if Mangey had gone to the cross roads, your friend would have been here by now."

"What time is it?" said I.

"Just half-past seven."

I have not mentioned two things which tried us extremely hard. One was the fact that we could not stand upright, but always had to be stooping, for fear of hitting our heads. This, as was only natural, we often did, and so piled Ossa on Pelion, because the headaches we had required no stimulant. But worse than this was the thirst, which the heat and our perspiration jointly induced. Indeed, we were dripping without and parched within, and when I thought of the liquor which I had consumed in two evenings, yet did not desire, I felt as a spendthrift does who has fallen on evil days. And I thought of the rich man in Hell, who pleaded that a beggar he knew might dip his finger in water and touch the tip of his tongue.

It did not take us so long to widen the hole enough to admit the torch: but it was a ticklish business cutting the canvas away—the sail-cloth, I mean, on the other side of the boards—for the sawdust kept falling down and we could not see what we were doing or what we had done. For fear of dropping the knife, we fastened it to a shoe-lace and tied this round the finger of whoever was doing the work : but in fact we never did drop it, because, though it was secured, to see it disappear would have shortened our lives.

When at last we had cut out three sides of a very small square, I put my forefinger through and held back the flap we had made, and Mansel put the torch through the opening and tried to look along it, between the torch and my hand : but before he could see at all, the sawdust closed in, and we had to spend ten good minutes raking out with our fingers what seemed to be a never-failing supply.

At last the source of this filth seemed to dwindle and presently fail, so again I held back the small flap and Mansel peered into the cell.

We had made the hole big enough for him to swivel the torch, and as he threw its beam round he reported what he could see.

" There's the door. It looks like ours, except that it's got a small cut. I see. That's for someone to look through, to see that the prisoner's all right. At least, we've been spared that attention. Hullo, there's a looking-glass, stuck up on a chair : with a couple of branches for candles—and candle-ends in them, by Jove. And there's a mattress and blankets. Solon, my boy, the place has been used as a bedroom. And there's a pair of girl's shoes. They must be Daisy's. That's right. After she'd run from Paris, this is where she lay up. I do hope the weather was cooler. Still, any port in a storm. Half a shake. There's something this side of the cell, but I can't quite see what it is. The mirror's reflecting it : but if I'm to see what it is, I must keep the beam off the glass: and if I keep the beam off the glass, I can't see the glass myself. . . . No, I can't do it. We'll have to try something else."

With that, he sat back on his heels, and I let the flap go.

Then he took the lace from the knife and tied it about the torch: the other end he tied to his finger, and whilst he was doing this he spoke very quietly, as though he were thinking aloud.

"There's something down on the floor, on the other side of this wall. Some gear of sorts. It may be worth nothing to us. And yet . . . I've a definite feeling that we should see what it is. So I'm going to push the torch through and let it hang down the wall. It's beam will fall on to this gear: and then I can look at the mirror and see what it is. And now I'm ready; so put your finger through and hold back that flap."

Now to lose the torch was as bad as losing the knife, and I must confess that while Mansel was guiding it through the hole we had cut and then releasing it gently, to let it hang down, I felt quite sick with fear lest we never should see it again.

Mansel had his eye to the hole. . . .

"Tools," he said quietly. "Try and believe me, Solon, for as we're alive, it's true. I believe it's a cracksman's outfit—I can see a brace and some bits. Yes it is. There's a jemmy, Solon. Leaning against the wall. A perfect beauty: the very thing that we want. And now, of course, I see. . . . This cell is Mangey's spare room. It's no more and no less than a harbour . . . where Mangey conceals odd friends who have got to lie low. And one of these was his daughter—I've seen her shoes. And another, my son, was a burglar . . . who's left his tools with Mangey, until he needs them again."

"But they're out of our reach," said I.

"They won't be for long," said Mansel. "The top of that jemmy's about a foot from our hole."

With that, he pulled up the torch and began to wheedle it backwards into the hole we had made, when, as though to spite us, a landslide of sawdust took place, altogether blocking the passage and cutting us off from the torch.

Though I worked as hard as I dared, it took me a quarter of an hour to clear this obstruction away, for, of course, as fast as I picked the stuff out of the hole, its place was taken by dust which was waiting to fall.

All this time the torch was burning and wasting its precious light: but we could do nothing about it, until the sawdust was gone.

And then at last, as before, the fall of sawdust gradually slackened and died, and one minute later Mansel had the torch in his hand.

I saw him glance at its lense. Then he peeled the shoe-lace off it and gave it to me.

As he picked up the knife—

"We must widen this hole," he said, "until we can get an arm through. Up to the elbow will do. And then we shall have that jemmy, and then, by God, we'll get out."

That was as much as he said, before falling to work:

but, since I had eyes in my head, I knew as well as did he that the torch was beginning to fail.

I had to hold it closer and closer, for him to see how best to pare the woodwork away. . . .

When its light was very dim, he stopped his cutting a moment, to draw a line on the wood with the point of a blade a roughly semi-circular line, containing the hole we had made : and then he cut a series of notches along this line, so that, though we had no light, we should know which way we were cutting and how far we had to go.

Then he handed the knife to me, while he took the torch. But before I had worked for two minutes, the light went out.

... ...

Many people may think that, since our task was so simple and only laborious, it could make but little difference whether or no we had the use of our eyes. I can only say in reply that the very simplest labour, to be performed in the dark, not only calls for a cunning which only the blind possess, but sometimes strains the nerves to the breaking-point.

For one thing alone, our progress was painfully slow. Our eyes would have told us the angle at which we must keep the blade : but this our touch could not do ; so the blade was constantly slipping or driving too deep. Our eyes would have not only told us where next to attack, but would have directed that attack, until the paring was off or the chip fell away : but now we had only our fingers to govern the line which we took, which meant that we first had to read *and then to remember* the clumsy reports which they made. What was, I think, as trying as anything else, neither could tell what the other was seeking to do, and explanations were useless, because we were short of our eyes.

There can be no doubt at all that we should have taken far longer, but for the series of notches which Mansel had had the foresight to cut on the wood ; for, whatever else went wrong, we always had these to work for, and they, of course, told us our progress as nothing else could have done.

Finally, let me say this—that it is my considered opinion—and Mansel agrees with me—that it took us three times as long to cut out that piece of wood as the job would have taken if we had had the light of the torch. And if anyone finds this strange, may I just say this ? That, so long as we had the torch, we had not broken a blade : but that I did break a blade, some twenty minutes after the torch had gone out. *And Mansel broke another* . . . but ten minutes after that. That left us with only one blade. And when you have one blade of a pen-knife, with which to do work which no pen-knife was meant to do, and when on that work are depending the lives of two men—and, probably, that of a lady like Katharine Scrope . . . then the man who is using that pen-knife watches his step. And if ever he feels it jar, the sweat on his body turns cold.

Four hours and a half it took us to cut that wood-work away. But it might have been one or twenty, for all I knew. I had lost all sense of time. And when at last Mansel breathed, "My arm will go through," I only said "Give it to me," and put out my hand for the knife.

And so I missed that great moment, when Mansel put in his arm and felt for and seized the jemmy which he had seen: and I was still waiting for the knife, when, instead, he put the jemmy into my hand.

I am ashamed to say that, when I found out what it was, I very near burst into tears: and since I dared not speak, I found Mansel's hand and shook it; and he clapped me upon the back.

"And now," he said, "I propose to break into the other cell. It may seem the long way round, because I'm perfectly sure that we can break out of this. But we cannot break out of this, without making the deuce of a noise. But the other cell has that shutter—that little trap in the door. We ought to be able to force that quietly enough: and then if we put out an arm, we may find a bar or a bolt which we can undo. Then again, if Mangey does come, we may as well both be armed. And we know there's a brace in there . . . I don't say a brace is handy, but it's better than nothing at all."

The jemmy was like a young crow-bar, and five minutes later we entered the other cell. . . .

Mansel was stooping beside me, and I heard the chink of steel. And then he put the jemmy into my hand.

"I've found another," he said; "rather lighter than this. It'll suit that shutter better, if I know anything."

I could not see how he worked, but he made very little

noise, and after two or three minutes, he led my hand up to where the shutter had hung.

At once I put out my arm, to feel for a bolt.

"Put your arm down," said Mansel. "I don't think these doors are bolted—I think they're barred. I don't think they've got any hinges. I think they are really panels, which you lift in and out of place."

God knows how he knew, but he was perfectly right.

Passing my hand down the door, I came to a flat iron bar, some three inches wide.

I told him what I had found.

"Can you get your fingers beneath it? One end is probably free, while the other turns on a pin."

He was right again. The bar was so fixed that, when its free end was lifted, it moved like the hand of a clock. I lifted the free end up, withdrawing my arm as it rose: and when it came to the peep-hole, I put in my other hand and swung it the rest of the way.

(I should, perhaps, have said that the darkness beyond the door was just as impenetrable as that in the cells: but there was a little more air, suggesting a draught.)

"I think the door's free," said I.

"Then hold it up by the peep-hole, and ease it out with your knees."

When I did as he said, the door began to give way, and almost at once I felt its weight on my hands. I let it gradually down, and after perhaps three inches it came to rest.

"Splendid," breathed Mansel. "Now lift it into the cell and prop it against the wall."

Again I did as he said.

"And now stand by. I'm going to have a look-round."

With that, he stepped over the sill. . . .

Nearly a minute went by. All the time I could hear him moving, quite close to the door.

Then I heard his voice again.

"Listen," he said. "This place is a square-shaped well, about seven feet deep. We are at the bottom of this: and directly in front of the door is a ladder of iron rungs. I can only assume that this leads to a trap of sorts. So I'm going up, to get my shoulders beneath it and see if it gives. Take these things"—he gave me our jackets and shirts—"and stay directly behind me, keeping a hand on my heel."

As Mansel turned to the ladder, I stepped over the sill: then I put out my hand, as arranged, to take hold of his heel. But I never got so far; for I was still groping, when the ceiling began to open and then to swing back and away, and there was the blessed daylight, to dazzle my thankful eyes.

I saw Mansel hanging above me and looking all round. Then he whipped up and off the ladder and helped me out of the trap . . . out of the trap—and into the dingy saloon.

... ...

In fact, the ladder ran up beneath one of the seats or divans, surrounding that seedy room. These were tilted backwards against the side of the ship. But a section of one of these sofas was made to rise up and fall forward away from the wall; and when Mansel put pressure upon it, standing below, that section immediately yielded, cushions and all.

Here, perhaps, I should say that the cell into which we were thrown was approached in a similar way; and that had we examined the seats on the opposite side of the saloon, we should have found a section, hidden and cut and hinged as was the one we had moved.

... ...

The saloon was empty, and we could hear no sound.

"Drop the clothes," breathed Mansel; "and you keep watch while I cover the man-hole up."

I stood with my eyes on the gangway, where Judas had died. . . .

After a moment or two—

"All right," breathed Mansel. "Get on your jacket and shirt."

I saw that he had his on; and when I glanced at the sofas against the wall, their cushions were all in order and there was nothing to show that they had been moved.

I fought my way into my things. . . .

Without taking his eyes from the gangway, Mansel crooked his finger, and at once I stepped to his side.

"It hurts to leave Mangey," he said: "but I'd like to get ashore, if we can, without his knowing we're gone. I don't want to disturb his arrangements—which, now that we're out of the bill, will suit us down to the socks.

And The Shepherd will probably kill him, when he finds that the cupboard is bare. And now tell me this—can you swim?"

I told him I could.

"Very well. I want to avoid that stage; for the cabins command that stage, and though we shall get ashore, we shall not be able to tell whether we have been seen. But if there is no one on deck and we slip into the river the other side, we can swim down stream a bit and then come ashore out of sight. Besides, I'd like a wash: and a plunge after all that sweating will close our pores."

So it fell out.

If there was someone on deck, we never saw him, and I am ready to swear that he never saw us. We let ourselves into the water with scarcely a sound, and ten minutes later we landed, just out of sight of the tender, some two hundred yards down stream.

I can never say how much I enjoyed that bathe—although I was bearing a jemmy which must have weighed fifteen pounds. After all the torture we had suffered, the lap of that lazy water did more than wash from our bodies the sawdust and sweat: and I know that I waded ashore, a different man. I must also confess that I drank as much as I could: and though, no doubt, it was tainted, I never felt any the worse.

Within the forest, we stripped and wrung out our clothes: then we put on our trousers again and began to make our way back to the edge of the apron which served the landing-stage.

"Laking will be there," said Mansel. "What d'you bet he doesn't curse us for not appearing before?"

"He won't dare curse you," said I.

"I'm not so sure. As like as not, he's been waiting about eight hours."

This was true. It was now a quarter past three—of a beautiful afternoon.

Two minutes later, George rose out of a bush.

He looked me up and down, with a hand to his chin. Then—

"Had a good bathe?" he said grimly, and Mansel began to laugh.

"I know," said George. "It's a scream. 'Mr. Solon will be close to the apron most of the time.' Well, I can prove that he hasn't for seven hours."

"He's a good excuse," said Mansel. "And now for your news."

"Oh, nothing much," said George. "We know where The Shepherd hangs out. And Carson has entered the house and located my lady's rooms."

CHAPTER XII

THE effect of the mind upon the body can be a remarkable thing. By every right in the world, Mansel and I should have been at the end of our tether—unable to take any action until we had rested or slept, for we had spent twelve hours in the padded cells: but our very escape restored the strength we had expanded, and George's wonderful news made me feel like a giant refreshed.

Mansel was dealing with it before I had taken it in.

"This changes everything. I believe The Shepherd will come here at ten o'clock: but I very much doubt if he'll bring Formosa along; for he had fixed 'Tuesday morning,' and I don't think he'll be disposed to let a rat like Mangey alter his date. But now this doesn't matter, for we shall be at his lodging when he moves off and we shall see for ourselves whether or no he takes Formosa along. If he does, we've only to follow. If he does not, we enter the lodging and free her and then sit down and wait for The Shepherd's return.

"And now for the Rolls and Rouen. We cannot spare the time now, but as soon as we're all in the car, we'll have Laking's tale."

"And what about yours?" said George.

"Ours can wait," said Mansel. "Suffice it that I

made a mistake—which caused us great inconvenience for several hours. And that is why Solon was late: so you mustn't blame him. I needn't ask if Carson is watching the house. . . ."

"He was," said George; "some eight and a half hours ago."

"Then he still will be," smiled Mansel. "Where did you leave the Rolls?"

"I ventured to bring her nearer. She's not very far from the cross roads—say two miles off."

"Good for you," said Mansel. . . .

Then he and I put on our shirts and our jackets—for the sake of any we met, as we went along: and he showed me how to carry a jemmy, between my arm-pit and knee. But he gave me the smaller one, and took the big one himself. And then we set out for the car as hard as we could, keeping at first to the trees, but later using the track, which seemed as deserted by day as it had been by night.

As soon as we reached the Rolls, Mansel opened a secret locker and took two pistols out: but when he offered me one, I said that, if it came to a scrap, I should do better work with a jemmy than anything else.

"I quite agree," said Mansel. "I think you would. But we are going after no ordinary man, and I think you should carry a firearm, in case of accidents."

"As you please," said I, and put the weapon away.

Then he took the driver's seat, whilst George and I sank down in the cushions behind.

As he started the engine—

" Out with it, Laking," he said. " Before we get to Rouen, I've got to know where I am."

... ...

" Satan left the cross roads," said George, " about five o'clock, and he passed us five minutes later, going all out. The roads were much more empty than Carson liked, but in fact this didn't matter, for, to judge from the way he drove, Satan's one idea was to make his report. He fairly beat Godolphin out of that small saloon—there were times when I thought she'd take off and go up in the air.

" Well, as soon as we got to Rouen, he switched to the left and led us north by east to a quarter I didn't know. Carson did terribly well, as you said he would : we were practically always the length of a street behind. We were soon among private houses—roads, not streets—and halfway along one of these the saloon began to slow down. Carson had stopped in a flash and was out of the Rolls, and I took over the wheel, as Satan swung into the drive of a house on the right.

" It seemed best to go on down the road : and as I went by the gateway, I saw Carson enter the drive.

" Well, I shoved the Rolls round a corner, a street or two off, and then I came back to the road, to have a look round.

" The house is one of a row, but it is detached. It stands well back from the road, as all of them do, with a high-walled garden in front and a garage in this garden, standing against the house."

Mansel put in his oar.

"If you were to stand in the gateway, what would you see?"

"An open, pebbled space, about fifty feet deep. After that, you come to the house, which is two storeys high. On the right of the pebbled space is a well-grown, ill-kept shrubbery, ten feet thick. This has grown up above the wall against which it stands, and since the house next door has a shrubbery, too, you can't see the garden wall from either side. On the left of the pebbled space, first you have bushes again, and then the garage begins about twenty-five feet from the house. It is a double garage, built against the house and the garden wall."

"Right," said Mansel. "Go on."

"Well, after I'd walked by once, I thought I'd hover about at the end of the road—it was only just half-past five, and so there was no one about. Apparently I did the right thing, for after about twenty minutes I saw Carson strolling towards me, as if he had time to burn. I turned and walked back to the Rolls, and he followed me up.

"This was his tale.

"He'd whipped inside the garage while Satan was leaving the car: and while Satan was lowering the curtain, Carson had entered the house—by a door which leads from the garage into a sort of hall."

"How many cars?" said Mansel.

"One besides the saloon—a good-looking sportsman's coupé, painted black."

"Right. And then?"

"Satan flung up some back stairs and then through a door, so Carson followed him up and stood just behind the door which Satan hadn't quite shut. He saw him knock at and enter a room six paces away: but he didn't shut that door, either: he stood with his hand on it, talking, and Carson heard the word 'Willies,' and a man inside letting fly. And then another door opened, and a woman put out her head. She stood there listening a moment: then she walked into the passage and up to where Satan was. She left her door wide open, and Carson could see that it gave to a little hall. Carson put her down as an athlete—coarsely handsome and plainly immensely strong. She elbowed Satan aside and went into his master's room: but before she could get a word out, she was cursed to hell and further *for leaving her charge.*

"Well, that was enough for Carson. . . . He made his way back to the garage, where he knew that the curtain was lowered, but was not locked into place. So he raised it enough to crawl out, and then shoved it down again. And then he came to find me.

"Now it seemed to us quite likely that, now that he'd made his report, Satan would return to the cross roads to see if Judas was there: and it seemed to us equally likely that, if he was going back, he would go back at once. We, therefore, decided that I should wait a while before pushing off, because our roads were the same and I didn't want him on my tail. Carson, of course, was to stay, in any event. In fact, he left at once—for the top of the garden wall. I waited till a quarter to seven, but as nothing had happened by then,

I took the Rolls and set off. And by eight o'clock I was by the edge of the apron as we had arranged.

"Well, that isn't quite all. When nearly two hours had gone by, but you didn't appear, I began to get uneasy and wonder if something was wrong. In fact, I was seriously thinking of going aboard, for the tender might have been an abandoned craft. And then a queer-looking fellow appeared on deck. I never saw where he came from, but suddenly there he was. He had the look of a Spaniard, and very soon it appeared he was one of the hands, for he gathered a mop and a bucket and started swabbing the decks.

"I watched him for twenty minutes and then I decided to act. I made my way into the forest and presently on to the tow-path a quarter of a mile up stream. Then I came sauntering down, and when I was nearing the apron, I hailed the tender in French. When the fellow appeared, I asked him where Mangey was. He asked what I wanted him for, and I said I'd got a message for Mangey himself. He offered to give it to him, but I wouldn't have that. 'You go and fetch Mangey,' I said. 'I know him by sight. But I've never seen you before, and I don't want to see you again.' He grinned at that, so I knew I was under his guard. 'Mangey's ashore,' he said. 'I don't know where he's gone, but he said he'd be back at five.' And so I sheered off up the towpath, the way I'd apparently come; for I knew that if Mangey was gone, then you were gone, too."

Mansel laughed.

Then—

"'For everywhere that *Mangey* went, The lambs *were* bound to go.'"

"Good God, was I wrong?" said George.

"I'm afraid the answer is 'yes': but that wasn't your fault. Nobody could have done better or more than you did. The scandalous truth is this—that Mangey got bored with his lambs. So he didn't take them with him, but shut them up in their pen before going ashore."

"Oh, I don't believe it," said George. "You're having me on."

"I wish I was," said Mansel. "And now here's Rouen coming. Tell me which way to go."

So we came to the district in which my darling was lodged. . . .

Since we were both known by sight to The Shepherd's gang, George and I stayed in the Rolls, while Mansel strolled past the house, to let Carson know we were there.

In five minutes' time he was back.

He put his head in at the window and spoke to George.

"Is this where you berthed this morning?"

"Yes," said George, wide-eyed.

"And Carson knows that?"

"Yes."

"Very good. We can only sit tight. Both cars are out of the garage, and Carson has gone from the wall."

... ...

This news was a terrible blow ; for all of us knew very well that Carson would never have left his post on the wall, unless my lady had been in one of the cars. That he had endeavoured to follow, we had no doubt : but how could a man on foot keep a car in sight ? The thing was out of the question. In traffic he might be able to trail it a little way : but in such a district as this a car would get a clear run. And there were no taxi-ranks.

That The Shepherd had left with Katharine could mean but one thing—that the man had changed his plans, because of Judas' failure to reappear. As I have shown, we had been afraid of this : but we had only feared that he might not fall into our trap : it had never entered our heads that he would leave his lodging and carry my lady with him, out of our ken. For that was what he had done. That he had not left for the tender was painfully clear ; for even now it was only half-past four, and had he been bound for the tender, he would not have left before dusk. But, apart from where he had gone, we could not think why he had gone ; for he could have no reason to think that we knew his address.

The truth is this—that we did not know what to think : and the more we went over the ground, the more uneasy we grew. . . .

There was one explanation—a very good explanation of why The Shepherd had gone : but though it occurred to us all, none of us put it forward and each of us tried to thrust it out of his mind. And that was this—that Carson had been discovered . . . up on the wall. And if this were so, we were done . . . and Carson was dead.

Sitting well back in the Rolls, I stared through the dusty windscreen and down the suburban road, cursing our bitter fortune and praying for Mangey's death.

We had picked up our pilot, Mansel, and he had steered us into the harbour's mouth : and there, in the moment of triumph, we had gone aground on a shoal which was not on the map. *Mangey*. When Mangey had murdered Judas, we had had the game in our hands : and by his murder of Judas, the game had been lost. And, after that, Mansel had saved it—snatched victory out of defeat. And once again Mangey had torn it . . . by putting us out of action during those vital hours : for if I had been 'close to the apron' when George had arrived, Carson would have been reinforced by a quarter to nine.

I put my head in my hands—and tried very hard to believe that we were not back where we had been two days before.

"Look at it this way," said George. "What were The Shepherd's reactions to Satan's report ? His first was sheer amazement that you and I should have got as far as we had. You and I, 'the Willies,' had actually spotted the tender and were making a clumsy effort to get aboard. His second was sharp annoyance that Judas had tried to find us instead of holding his hand until ten to-night. His third was a shrewd suspicion that we had got Judas down.

"Now, if I am right, he was forced to swallow this truth—that we were a sight more efficient than he had supposed and that if we could spot the tender and then get Judas down, it was well on the cards that we'd followed Satan home. 'Well, that doesn't matter,' he says. 'Let them come up here and meet it. I'll put them where they belong. But, if they don't, and I'm to go out to-night—well, I can't leave Formosa here. I'm not going to take her with me—I don't want her on in this act. So I'll take her away and shove her in some safe place, and then I'll go down to the tender at ten o'clock.' "

"You think he'll be there?" said I.

"Yes, I do," said George. "He'll be on the tips of his toes, but I think he'll be there. He'll never suspect the story which Mangey told. According to that, we shall be there at half-past ten. And he wants you worse than ever, in view of what has occurred."

"Well, I think you're wrong," said I, "but I hope you're right. All I want is a chance to twist his block from his trunk. And if anyone kills him first, I'll break their neck."

With that, I lifted my head, to look for the twentieth time at the clock in the dash; for, after the frantic action which I had taken that day, to have to sit still in a car, much as a paid companion whose mistress is paying a call, was straining my patience almost to breaking-point.

Of such poor stuff are we made. Three hours ago, I would have sold my soul to be sitting back in the Rolls, with the blessed air in my lungs and the sunlight filling my eyes: but now that was all forgotten, and I was chafing like a madman, because I was forced to sit still and to take my ease. Perhaps I may be forgiven. Three times in the last fifteen hours my hopes had been raised sky-high—and then dashed to hell. Such usage does not bring out the best in a man.

Once more I sat back, with my eyes on the sunlit road. . . .

Mansel was not to be seen. He was, presumably, moving between the house and the Rolls, and keeping them both in view, so far as he could. The district was unfrequented. One or two nursemaids with children had passed us by, and a van delivered some parcel three houses away: three times a car had swept the length of the road, and another was standing empty a little way off: and except for two or three cyclists, I think that was all. The world went very quietly in the Avenue Lannemezan.

I began to count the trees on the opposite side of the road. . . .

Another car appeared, coming in our direction and moving leisurely. Its appearance upset my counting, and I began again. One, two, three. . . .

And there I heard George catch his breath.

"God Almighty," he said. "It's the small saloon."

There was no time to warn Mansel.

All we could do was sit well back in the Rolls . . . and pray that whoever was driving saw nothing strange in the fact that *a Rolls-Royce with English numbers* was standing, waiting, two hundred yards from his house.

And then, to my consternation, the saloon began to turn in to our side of the road. I watched it coming nearer and nearer . . . drawing up to the pavement, a short six paces ahead. . . . But I could not see who was driving, for the flicker of sunlight and shadow upon the screen.

I slid my hand on to my pistol and pushed back the safety-catch. My tail had been twisted enough. Whoever looked into the Rolls would open his eyes in Hell.

And there the door was opened—*and Carson got out.*

He glanced up and down the pavement. Then he walked up to the Rolls and stood looking past the car, with a hand on its door.

I guessed that Mansel was coming, but I could not wait.

" Carson," I cried, " where is she ? What d'you know ? "

He never looked into the car, but I saw him smile.

" It's quite all right, sir," he said. " They're taking her down by water. We've plenty of time."

... ...

As we drove the way we had come, we listened to Carson's tale.

" The first thing I knew, sir, the garage curtain goes up. That was just about a quarter to four. At once I slips off the wall and into the bushes below. Looking between the leaves, I saw Satan get into the coupé—not the saloon. Then he backed her out an' round, and I saw there was four inside. He brought her slowly round, with her back to the house ; so from where I stood I could see right into the car. Beside him was sitting the woman I'd seen before; and a smooth-faced man with queer eyes was sitting behind with a lady—I couldn't see her very well, but I guessed who it was. As Satan stopped going back, he says something over his shoulder: and the man with the eyes says 'Go by the race-course, of course, you —— fool.' And then they went off.

"Well, they'd left the curtain up, and there was the saloon: and they'd told me the way they were going, so I didn't waste any time.

"I very soon picked them up, an' I followed them down to the river by roundabout ways. They stopped beyond the city—up river, I mean. Three miles up I should say, towards Pont-de-l'Arche. A strange-looking place—I couldn't make out what it was. An' then I saw the boat-houses, four or five. It was really a sort of garage for motor-boats. I could see that they were expected, for a launch was against the raft: they went straight down to this and I watched them aboard.

"This time I was able to see my lady plain. An' if you ask me, she was doped. The other had hold of her arm and was talking an' laughing and generally playing up: but she never spoke nor smiled, and I think she was dazed.

"They and the man with the eyes went into a sort of cabin, right up in the bows; and Satan went in with a suitcase and then came out and went aft. A fair-haired tough was there—he'd been holding the launch to the raft. An' Satan said something to him, and he started the engine up.

"An' then they went off down stream."

There was a little silence. The tale was done.

At the third attempt—

"Miss Katharine will thank you," I said, and felt ashamed of my voice.

"It was easy enough, sir," said Carson. "They played right into my hands."

... ...

Nearly five hours had gone by.

We had rested and broken our fast and made some purchases: the Rolls was berthed by the cros sroads, where George had concealed her before: and we were, all four, crouching beneath the landing-stage. We could not be seen from the tender, yet we could see the river both up and down; and since any craft which meant to run alongside would have to begin to sheer up some distance away, we could not possibly miss the approach of the launch.

Now we had with us fifty metres of very stout fishing-net; and it had been arranged that, as soon as the launch arrived, George and Carson should swim with this to her stern. And with this they would foul her screw. The deed could be done in silence, yet most effectually; for once the propeller was swathed with tackle like that, a dozen revolutions would bring her work to an end—which meant that the launch would be helpless and could not so much as be steered.

Whilst they were doing this, Mansel and I were to make our way on to the tender as best we could: this we expected to do without being seen, for though

Mangey or one of his people was almost certainly watching the landing-stage, the arrival of the launch would distract them and they would leave at once for the opposite side of the deck.

When they had done their business of fouling the screw, George and Carson would return to the landing-stage, but this time approach the tender, still moving beneath the foot-boards and so out of sight. In this way they would be able to look through the port-holes which served the dingy saloon, and on what they saw take place there, their action would then depend.

This was the best we could do ; for we had no idea at all what line The Shepherd would take, and though we should have preferred to be aboard the tender before the launch came alongside, we dared not risk being seen by the man who proposed to deliver us into The Shepherd's hands.

" In fact," said Mansel, " the time for taking risks is over and gone. That is a luxury which we cannot afford to-night. For one thing, Judas' disappearance has whetted The Shepherd's suspicion as nothing else could have done : and when such a man is suspicious, he fires at sight. Then again, before the night's out, I very much hope that he'll have his back to the wall : but when such a man perceives that he has his back to the wall—well, he's just about as safe as a viper that's short of her young."

That was as much as he said : but I think we all knew that he meant that we had our work cut out, if we were to make this omelet without the breaking of eggs.

Here perhaps I should say that we do not know to

this day whether The Shepherd was proposing to dispose of my lady that night or whether he had brought her merely because he desired to have her under his hand: but I think the truth is this—that he meant to put her aboard and have done with the thing, provided that he was first able to put George and me to death. The fact that he came down by water, instead of by road, proves, I think, that what Mansel said was true—that Judas' disappearance had shaken him up and that though he could not believe that two 'Willies' could stand against him, he was determined to take no chances at all.

Night had fallen by now, and the moon was not due to rise for another two hours; but craft could not move upon the river without their lights and these disclosed their position and sometimes more than that. Since the weather was fine and hot, more than one launch went by with a gramophone playing and a searchlight flooding its path, but though bigger vessels passed us, well out in the stream, the night was so dark that we could not see what they were. And then, at last, at about a quarter to ten, we saw twin green and red lights bearing very slowly towards us and moving down stream. They must have been still a hundred and fifty yards off, when a searchlight leaped out of the darkness, to rake the stage and the tender for less than three seconds of time: then all was dark again, and only the green light was left, to show where some craft was moving close to the bank. No engine was running. The launch which was approaching was drifting—drifting very slowly down to the tender's side.

I do not know who was steering, but he must have had eyes like a cat, and he must have been a nice helmsman, for the launch was moving so slowly that she could only just have had steerage-way. Be that as it may, he brought her very gently right alongside, and we saw her shape distinctly before she passed out of our sight—for, when she came to rest, the bulk of the tender concealed her from anyone still ashore.

Till this moment we had not been sure that anyone on the tender was looking out: but though we had never seen him, Mangey must have been sitting somewhere on deck, for we heard him start up and then call down the companion—no doubt to the Spaniard whom George had seen swabbing the decks.

"Stand by below," he said. "There's a craft alongside."

"Off you go," breathed Mansel, to Carson and George.

The two slipped into the water without a word.

(Perhaps I should have said that they were already stripped, but that, lest the white of their bodies should catch some inquisitive eye, they had wrapped the net about them from shoulder to toe. They had, therefore, nothing to do but to let the net slip from their bodies into the crook of their arms and then to enter the water and make for the launch.

"Come," breathed Mansel, to me. . . .

As we reached the side of the tender, I heard Mangey speak again.

"You, is it?" he said. "I thought——"

"—— your thoughts," said Satan. "Where's Jew Boy gone?"

"How should I know?" said Mangey. "I tole you——"

"I'll say you did," said Satan. "An' now you can tell his nibs. An' where's the Willies you promised, you —— murderer?"

There was a little silence.

Then—

"I'll tell his nibs," said Mangey, calmly enough.

As the two turned to the launch, Mansel and I whipped over the tender's rail and on to her deck. . . .

Now I had expected that Mangey would tell The Shepherd the truth—always excepting the truth about Judas' death. In other words, I had thought he would simply relate how he had been forced by Mansel to tell the tale that he did and how he had caught us both bending and thrown us into the cell. But, though he may have meant to, he decided to play for safety and tell The Shepherd a lie. I shall always think the truth is that Satan's epithet 'murderer' shook him up and made him afraid to confess that the tale he had told to Satan was all untrue. Be that as it may, he actually stuck to that tale, declaring with oath after oath that 'the Willies' had gone off down stream and the last he had seen of Judas was his 'slidin' off in their wake.'

All this he said kneeling down on the tender's deck, to bring his head down to The Shepherd's who stood in the launch below, while Satan squatted beside him, but held his tongue. The two did not lower their voices, which could not, of course, have been heard from the landing-stage: they could hardly be expected to know that Mansel and I were standing four paces away.

"You're lying, Mangey," said The Shepherd "You've seen the Willies all right: but they didn't put Judy out."

"I don't say they did," said Mangey: "but now you come to mention it, what made the Willies come back?"

"'The Willies come back'?" snapped The Shepherd. "What d'you mean?"

"What I say," said Mangey. "The two came back this morning at break o' day. I was jus' goin' ashore, when I see them down the tow-path, comin' up stream. Digs was aboard by then, so I slid below and told him to watch his step. I marked 'em through a port-hole, whispering together an' tipping along the stage. I guess they thought I'd turned in, and they meant to board the hooker an' stow away. Well, so they did—but not the way they intended. Talk about a fair cop. . . ."

"D'you mean," said The Shepherd, slowly, "d'you mean that you've got them here?"

"That's right, sir," said Mangey. "We got them down between us and shoved 'em in one o' the cells. We took their guns, an', what with no water this weather, they won't be up to much: so if you'd like to see them . . . I mean, perhaps they'll tell you where Jew Boy is."

Such was the tale Mangey told. It had one obvious flaw—that it was Mansel, not George, who had been rendered senseless and thrown with me into the cell. But Mangey could weather that, by saying the light was dim when we came aboard. But if it had one flaw, it had one shining virtue—from our point of view: for it did not disclose to The Shepherd that most important fact *that there were arrayed against him not two, but four.* Mangey knew this. For that very reason, this evening, he had been watching the shore. But now he could watch it no longer, because, if his tale was true, the only 'Willies' there were were down in the cell.

So Mangey betrayed The Shepherd—by seeking to save himself.

Before two minutes had passed, the launch had been made fast to the tender's side, and The Shepherd and *both* of his men had followed Mangey into the small saloon. And Digs was below already. Five rats in the self-same trap.

CHAPTER XIII

"GET the others aboard," said Mansel.

In less than thirty seconds, George and Carson were there.

"Mr. Solon and I," said Mansel, "are going aboard the launch. You two will watch the companion. Lay out whoever comes up. If you kill him, it doesn't matter: but try not to shoot."

Then we left them, armed with the jemmies, and boarded the launch.

Mansel entered the cabin and taking a torch from his pocket directed its beam to the floor.

Katharine was sitting upright, with her hands in her lap. She looked very pale and weary, and her air was that of one who has shot his bolt. She did not look desperate. She gave the impression that something within her was broken, that though her flesh was alive, her spirit was dead.

She did not move at our entrance, or shift her gaze, but sat staring straight before her, as though she were all alone: but the woman beside her started and let out a gasp.

"Well, Mabel," said Mansel, shortly. "Isn't that nice? And I thought you were working for Rudy. An' this is Formosa, is it? Well, well, she's had a good run, but it's our day out." He jerked his head at the tender. "Up you go, my girls. I've got a van in the woods."

Her eyes like saucers, the woman whom he had called Mabel opened her mouth.

"An English busy, by God."

"An English busy," said Mansel, "lent to the Rouen police. Come on, look sharp, you two. You're not the only peas in the pod to-night."

The woman got to her feet: but Katharine sat fast.

"An' none of the rough stuff, Mabel. I've got two plantinum bracelets, in case you feel like that."

Mabel's reply was unprintable, but Mansel only grinned. Then he turned to Katharine.

"Come on, Formosa," he said. He put his arm about her and raised her up. "She don't look too grand," he added, turning to me. "Take Mabel up. I'll bring Formosa along."

I fell in behind the woman, now in the cabin's mouth. . . .

As I bent my head to follow, she hit me full in the face, and, before I had got my balance, had leapt on to one of the seats and dived into the Seine.

"Glory be," said Mansel. "I prayed for that. On to the tender, my lad, and I'll hand you my lady up."

A moment later, Katharine was in my arms.

"Esau, Esau," she whispered.

I bent my head, to set my cheek against hers.

"My blessed Kate . . . my darling . . . from the power of the dog."

"Oh, Esau, I can't believe it."

"You've had a bad dream, my sweet: but now you're awake. Here's George, by your side, to tell you we're out of the wood."

Mansel was speaking again.

"Someone must take her into the forest at once. And stay there with her, till we've finished this business off. I can't spare Carson, so one of you two must go."

I gave my burden to George and took his jemmy away.

"It's up to you," I said. "I've someone to—see."

"Well, give him my love," said George. "You know what I mean."

"Here's her suitcase," said Mansel. . . .

"Esau, Esau."

My lady had hold of my coat.

"A little minute, my darling. We're almost through. You will sit in the forest with George, until I come."

"I know. I heard what was said. But for God's sake be careful, Esau. He knows that Judas is dead, and he's lost control. I've seen him angry before, but never like this."

As we moved to the tender's side—

"We have him cold, my darling. And George will tell you that Mansel is more than up to his weight."

I saw them over the rail and on to the landing-stage: and then I joined Mansel and Carson at the companion-hatch.

Mansel was flat on his face, peering down the stairway into the grim saloon. So I lay down beside him, to see and hear what I could.

The five had not got very far.

One hidden trap was open—the fellow to that by which Mansel and I had emerged ; and The Shepherd, Satan and Digs were standing round about it, as men stand round the lair of some beast which they hope to bolt. The Shepherd was holding a torch and throwing its beam on the ceiling, to light the scene. A glow of sorts was rising out of the trap, and, as we were soon to learn, the others were down below.

The Shepherd was growing impatient.

" Larry ! " he snapped.

A head appeared in the trap—the head of the man who had been driving the launch.

" What the devil's the matter ? " spat The Shepherd.

Larry shook the sweat from his eyes.

" There's a kind o' curtain," he said, " hangin' over the door. You can't get at it, to shift it, and——"

" ' Can't get at it ' ? " raved The Shepherd.

" No, sir. We've tried to pull it, but——"

The Shepherd stamped his foot.

" ' Pull it ' be damned. Cut it. Rip it, you —— lady's maid."

Larry's head disappeared.

The truth, of course, was this—that neither Mangey nor Larry fancied the job ; for whoever thrust by or under the very embarrassing curtain which Mansel and I had let down, would put himself at the mercy of a couple of desperate men. At least, that was their belief : and if Mansel and I had been there, it would have gone very hard with the first man to enter that cell.

Larry put up his head and spoke to Digs.

"You got a knife?" he said.

As Digs' hand went to his pocket—

"One moment," said The Shepherd, softly. And then, "*Where's . . . Mangey's . . . knife?*"

I despair of describing the significance with which he invested these words; and the silence which succeeded his question was that of death.

At length—

"Mangey," said The Shepherd, quietly.

The seconds passed, but Mangey made no reply.

"I called you, Mangey," said The Shepherd. "Come up . . . and speak to me here."

Larry's head disappeared, and after what seemed a long time another head took its place.

"Yes?" said Mangey, thickly.

"Come up and out," said The Shepherd.

Mangey came slowly up, but he did not climb out of the trap: he stayed where he was on the ladder, with a battered oil-lamp in his hand. He did not speak, but he made a helpless movement, as though to suggest that that was the best he could do, because he needed two hands to climb out of the trap.

"Give the lamp to Larry," said The Shepherd; "and do as I said."

Deliberately Mangey obeyed.

As he wrung the sweat from his forehead—

"Nice mess they've made," he said. "Torn the canvas down like——"

"Quite so," said The Shepherd, smoothly. "Where is your knife?"

"Ah," said Mangey, "that's what I'd like to know. I know I 'ad it this morning. It must of fell out of my pocket when——"

"Look in my eyes."

Very slowly the luckless skipper lifted his head. . . .

They say that murder will out. But that night I saw murder *dragged* out . . . wrenched by sheer force of will from the heart of a guilty man.

I saw Mangey cower away, with the back of a hand to his eyes.

"I never done it," he whimpered. "I never done Jew Boy in."

"Tell him I sent you," said The Shepherd—and shot him clean through the brain.

Anything more cold-blooded could hardly, I think, be conceived: but if anyone present was shaken, he gave no sign. The three men stood their ground, with Mangey's body before them, flat on its back. Then The Shepherd put up his pistol and turned to Digs.

Now this was the very first time that The Shepherd had looked our way, and when he did so, I felt my hair rise on my head. Dark as it was, I could see the flame in his eyes.

I had seen this once before—in a lighted street: but, as I have shown, the saloon was in semi-darkness, and so the dreadful effect was half as vivid again.

I can only suppose that they picked up the light from the ceiling and gave it back: but to see those two glinting orbs in the black of his face was a very unpleasant experience and one which I would give a a very great deal to forget.

I saw the man motion to Digs: if he spoke as well, I could not hear what he said, for my ears were still singing with the noise which his pistol had made.

But he jerked his head at the trap, and Digs stepped over the body and made his way down below. . . .

After perhaps a minute, we heard the rip of the sail-cloth, torn as we had torn it twelve hours before.

In the silence which followed The Shepherd stepped up to the trap.

"Well?"

"There's another layer," said Larry. "Another layer of canvas we'll have to get through."

At this The Shepherd let fly, and Larry appeared on the ladder—as much, I think, for some air, as to try to explain. But The Shepherd cursed his head off and drove him back.

"I don't care if there's twenty layers, you white-livered dog. I'll give you one more minute to fetch those two —— out."

There was no mistaking the dangerous note in his voice and Larry and Digs worked like madmen to rip the sail-cloth away. Indeed, there could be no doubt that if they had been afraid of encountering Mansel and me, they were now much more afraid of, so to speak, pushing The Shepherd over the edge. We could hear them cursing and grunting and tearing the canvas down, while The Shepherd stood fuming above them and tapping the floor with his toe.

Now the cell into which they were breaking was in a confusion which will hardly go into words. It was near a foot deep in sawdust and sail-cloth was hanging and sprawling all over the place. Since they had no torch, but only a mean oil-lamp, the picture which this revealed must have been so strange and unnatural that a man better placed than Larry would have found himself at a loss to describe what he saw: and since the time they had been given was more than up, but the men for whom they were looking were not to be seen it is my belief that the two went into the cell—as much to be out of range, as to think how best to report their unsavoury news.

But this is all speculation, because the next that we knew was that someone was screaming in terror and a flame like that of a beacon was flaring out of the trap.

What exactly had happened, no one will ever know. Perhaps the bottom fell out of the primitive lamp. But fire broke out somehow, and the sawdust and sailcloth went up in a sheet of flame.

The Shepherd started back. Then, quick as a flash, he did the unspeakable thing.

He caught the lid of the trap and slammed it back into place.

... ...

No one on earth could have helped those unfortunate men and I very much doubt if they could have helped themselves; for they were in the midst of a furnace and, the flames apart, they must have been asphyxiated almost at once. Still, to slam the furnace-door was to kill what chance they had, and only a very monster could have done such a terrible thing.

But worse was to come.

We could hear the dull roar of the fire, and wisps of smoke were rising from the edges of both the traps, when The Shepherd gave Satan an order that froze my blood.

"Fetch Formosa down here."

There could be but one explanation of such an order as that. The man had reason to think that George and I were now being burned to death: he proposed to have done with Formosa—by committing her, too, to the flames. From the point of view of a fiend, his decision was wise. The tender was doomed. Any minute now the flames would break out of the traps, and long before help could arrive the vessel would be blazing from stem to stern. If the ruins were ever examined, an odd bone or two might be found; but no one could tell whose they were and no one would care. Formosa, with five other beings, would have been 'sunk without trace.'

I was up on my feet now and was standing back from the hatch. I cannot remember rising: no doubt, mechanically, I had done as Mansel had done.

The latter was speaking quietly.

"Leave him to me. Carson, stand by to catch him. I don't want the fellow to fall."

But Satan did not appear.

He must, I think, have boggled at carrying out an order of such ferocity, for The Shepherd stamped his foot and raised his voice to a roar.

"I said 'Fetch Formosa down here.' Move, you —— wash-out. We've got to be clear of this hooker in two minutes' time."

So Satan came up the companion—to do his master's bidding and bring Miss Katharine Scrope to be burned alive. . . .

I did not see Mansel hit him but I heard the thud of the blow: and Satan seemed to lift himself up and then to collapse. But though his feet were trailing, he did not fall, for Carson was holding his body under the arms.

Mansel was speaking again.

"Lay him down there. . . . And now listen. I mean, if I can, to take The Shepherd alive. You two will stand out of sight upon either side of the hatch. I shall be up on its hood. And when I say 'Excuse me,' you will each of you seize one arm. But if I say anything else, you will both of you jump for cover as quick as ever you can."

Now the hatch was, as I have shown, a companion-hatch—that is to say a rectangular hole in the deck, with a flight of stairs running down: this hole was covered with a hood, and no one could reach the deck, except by its mouth: neither, as he came up, could he see to right or to left, but only straight before him, for what that was worth. And that was little enough, for the mouth of the hatch was less than three feet wide.

Disposed as we were, we could hardly have failed to capture nine men out of ten: but The Shepherd was the tenth man, as all three of us knew. Apart from what Katharine had said, we had seen for ourselves that the man was beside himself: and when Satan failed to return . . .

I shall never forget standing there, with my eyes upon Mansel's face: he was lying still as death on the top of the hood, leaning over and down, with his eyes on the stair. I could hear the roar of the fire, now more intense, and smoke was making its way from the mouth of the hood. And my teeth were chattering so, that, lest they should betray my presence, I had to thrust a finger between my jaws.

Out of so many big moments—for so they seemed—I think sometimes that this was the biggest of all. I was waiting to scotch the snake—the snake which had turned upon us because I had seen its spots, which had, for that indiscretion, passed sentence of death upon my lady and me. For more than a fortnight now, we had lived and moved in the shadow of sudden death, more truly captive than if we had lain behind bars: and for nearly a week of that time, each had suffered the awful torture of never knowing whether the snake had struck—whether to hope was hopeless, because the other was dead. But now all that was over, the gates of safety and freedom were open wide, and we were about to pass through them—by making our jailer prisoner, by scotching the snake.

Right up to the last I feared that The Shepherd's terrible instinct would teach him the reason why Satan did not return: and I think that it would have done so, if passion had not been blunting his finer faculties. The luck was against him that night. Had Mangey told him the truth, when first he arrived, I very much doubt if the man would have left the launch: and this would have made things very much harder for us, for, so long as he stayed on the launch, Katharine would have been lying directly under his hand. And had he not been ruled by impatience, he would have discovered that Mansel and I had escaped and would have had three men left to help him to fight the battle to which he was going alone. In a word, he had grounded upon the same shoal as had we. Mangey. The water-rat he had stamped on had let him down.

And there I saw Mansel nod. . . .

Almost at once the beam of a torch appeared. The Shepherd was on his way up.

I saw Mansel's hands go down. . . .

Then—

"Excuse me," he said, and took the man by the neck.

To seize his wrists was easy, because, mechanically, his hands had gone to this throat; and, once we had them, the fellow stood perfectly still. But when I told Mansel that we had him and Mansel had let him go, without any sort of warning The Shepherd threw himself back.

He was so heavy and rage had lent him such strength that, had the companion been wider, Carson and he and I must all have gone down: but the hood simply could not admit more than one at a time, and Carson and I were literally jammed in its mouth.

For a moment he strained like a madman, bracing his feet against a step and doing his very utmost to drag us down: then he seemed to see that it was hopeless and I felt his muscles go slack.

When we pulled him back to the deck, he did not

resist: but when he was up, he peered at Mansel and Carson, as though the two were unreal.

Then—

"I know Mr. Solon," he said. "But who are the other two?"

None of us made any answer; but Mansel ran his hands down him and took two pistols away.

Then—

"Put his hands behind him," he said.

A moment later The Shepherd was wearing gyves.

... ...

Five minutes—not more—had gone by, and the launch was drifting down stream. As before, she had five aboard; but only two of these belonged to her passenger-list: and one of those was unconscious, and one had cuffs on his wrists.

Carson was steering, and Mansel, our prisoner and I were sitting in the cabin, whose blinds were down. Satan was sprawling in the doorway. I glanced at him now and again for a sign of life.

Before we had left the tender, Carson had entered the water and taken the net from the screw: and I had found Katharine and George, told them that The Shepherd was taken and begged them to make for the Rolls and wait for us there. When I got back, the flames were in the saloon, so we used the launch's engine to get us away from the scene: but when we had rounded a point and the tender was out of our sight, we stopped the engine and switched the search-light on, for we wanted no one to think that we had something to hide.

The Shepherd regarded Mansel, who was himself perusing the contents of a note-case or wallet which he had taken out of The Shepherd's coat.

"You have the advantage of me."

"Clearly," said Mansel, shortly. He held up a visiting-card. "Your name . . . and address . . . and club ?"

The other raised his eyebrows.

"May I know by what right——"

"Not your club," said Mansel. "I might have known. I think the hall-porter of Walter's would——"

"I have been a member of Walter's for twenty-five years."

"Thank you," said Mansel. He passed a paper to me. "Just run your eye over that."

The paper was very old and the fine handwriting was faded, but easy to read.

This great ruby was given by King Henry the Seventh to Robert, Lord of Charing, for services rendered in 1506.

As I handed it back—

"One of the Mountjoy heirlooms," said Mansel. "Stolen from Castle Godfrey two years ago."

The Shepherd sighed.

"Would it interest you," he said slowly, "to know where those heirlooms are ?"

"Very much," said Mansel. "But it's fair that you should know this—that though it would interest me, it will not help you. Nothing can help you. You're going to lose your life in ten minutes' time."

The Shepherd smiled.

"Such frankness suggests that you've nothing to do with the police."

Mansel made no reply, but he held up a photograph of Katharine, exactly like those which Judas had given to Mangey the night before.

"Link after link," he said. "But there's one to come."

"Which is that?" said I.

"My, er, sobriquet," said The Shepherd. "Unless your friend can find that, no one will ever believe that it is my career he has ended and not that of somebody else. In the old days they cut off the head and put it into a sack—and later produced it to those of little faith. But that method is out of date. Besides——"

"This is much better," said Mansel, and held up a *ménu* card.

The Shepherd sat very still.

Then—

"I'd forgotten that," he said quietly. "One ought not to keep such things. But the trifle amused me—it's really admirably done."

This was less than the truth.

On the back of the *ménu* card was a fine pen-and-ink caricature. It was the man to the life, with his glass in his eye. He was smiling expansively—*and he was dressed as a shepherd . . . in the true Arcadian tradition . . . with breeches and stockings and ribbons, adorning his hat and his crook.*

Mansel laid the papers together and put them back in the case. As he slid this into his pocket—

"Good enough for my purpose," he said.

"Which is?" said The Shepherd.

"As you surmised," said Mansel, "to be able to prove who you—were."

The Shepherd nodded.

"Before we, er, part," he said, "may I ask a question or two?"

Mansel raised his eyebrows.

"I don't know that they will be answered. But you can always try."

The Shepherd inclined his head.

Then—

"Did you get at Mangey?" he said.

"I tried to," said Mansel: "but Mangey let me in."

"How did you get on to him?"

"I was after Rudy," said Mansel. "And Messrs. Solon and Laking were after you. So we pooled our information—with this result."

The Shepherd sighed.

"Always the same," he said. "*Cherchez la femme.* I assume you were watching the tender when Judas came down."

Mansel nodded.

"The rest followed on."

"Quite so. The details can wait—for ten minutes. . . . But why did Mangey kill Judas—and force your hand?"

(I think those four last words will show what a lightning brain The Shepherd possessed. After only three questions he had the truth in his hands.)

"*Cherchez la femme*," said Mansel. "He threatened to squeak about Daisy, if Mangey put a foot wrong."

"And then led the way out? Well, well. . . . Some people will never learn. Did Mangey know that you were four strong, and not two?"

"Yes," said Mansel.

"And, lest he should buy himself trouble, the fool suppressed that highly important fact." The Shepherd expired. "That is the kind of folly which has lost battles and wars. We read of Caesars and Napoleons; but it is the Mangeys of this world that have made its history."

There was a little silence.

Then—

"Anything else?" said Mansel.

"One thing more—I still have some minutes left. It is . . . with some diffidence . . . that I refer to Miss Scrope."

"That I can well believe."

"Naturally," said The Shepherd, and crossed his legs. "The trouble, of course, was this—that big business knows no law. I had hoped that she would see reason—that when Mr. Solon was dead, she would see the wisdom of, er, coming back to the fold. Such a course would have been without precedent: but then Miss Scrope is a very exceptional girl, and business being business, hers would have been the exception that proved the rule. That, then, was the position—I hoped for Sir Valentine's sake, that she would return to the fold. The lover might be dead, but the father remained. When all's said and done, it was business. Deprived of Cardinal, Sir Valentine would have fretted and pined away. If I could see that, so could she. And so I hoped *and believed* that she would come back. What is more, I know I was right. For her father's sake, Formosa would have picked up her bit. And then, to my great inconvenience, Sir Valentine died. . . .

"Well, that altered everything. The moment I heard the news, I knew that Formosa would never serve me again. More. With nothing to lose, she would certainly do her best to revenge Mr. Solon's death. In a word, from being invaluable, she had become most dangerous. I could not—make away with her. I defy any man alive to have made away with so lovely a work of art. Yet she had to be done with—somehow; because I could not afford to spare Mr. Solon's life. . . .

"I am not excusing myself—because such business as mine requires no excuse. For compassionate outlaws there is no room in nature. I am simply stating wherefore I did as I did. . . .

"And now, once again, the case is altered. Mr. Solon has been reprieved, and I am as good as dead. Only, Formosa remains."

There was another silence.

"'Formosa remains,'" said Mansel. "What do you mean by that?"

"I think you know what I mean. In the last three years Formosa has carried hundreds of thousands of pounds' worth of stolen gems. She's never been taken, of course: but for some years to come she will still be a valuable prize. And when my reign is over, and the many who know Formosa know that they have nothing to fear, I think that more than one will decide to better himself by pointing her out to the police.

"Now I cannot prevent that happening: neither can you. But, with your help, I might even now be able to, shall we say, spoil their game. You said just now that you would be interested to know where the Mountjoy heirlooms are. You were good enough to add that such information would not assist my case. Would it assist Formosa's?"

"It might," said Mansel, quietly.

The Shepherd leaned forward.

"I have upon me the key of a coffer I own. In a safe-deposit at Paris—the name's on the key. Lying in that coffer are some of the finest jewels that have been stolen in Europe during the last two years. Any big man will identify every one. I'll give you that key—tell you where to find it and let you take it yourself—if you will use those gewgaws to buy Formosa off. Give a list to the police, and say if they want them back, they can have them on one condition—that action is never taken against Miss Katharine Scrope." He threw himself back on his seat. "I believe it's called 'reparation': but nobody, high or low, will ever have made such reparation as that."

"D'you mean this?" said Mansel.

"I do. Will you do as I say? My time must be nearly up, so call it 'a last request.' After all, she is my protégé: and it would be distasteful to me in the highest degree that she should be, er, inconvenienced after my death." With that, he rounded on me. "Don't look so surprised, Mr. Solon. There's no inconsistency here. I'm doing this because I have nothing to lose. Half an hour ago, Formosa was only a pawn. But now my race is run. Business has ceased to be business, and I can *afford* to remember that before I took to stealing, I was a gentleman."

Mansel rose to his feet.

"You may take it from me," he said, "that Miss Scrope will never be troubled, provided your coffer in fact contains what you say it does. I can fix London *and* Paris—with such an argument."

The Shepherd nodded twice, with his eyes upon Mansel's face. Then he threw up his chin.

"If you care to unfasten my collar. . . . The key is attached to a chain which is round my neck. Don't try to undo it, but pass it over my head."

Thirty seconds later, a platinum chain and a key were lying in Mansel's hand.

He examined the key, and tested the strength of the chain. Then he slipped the latter over his head and tucked the two into his collar and out of sight.

The Shepherd was speaking again.

"At the risk of exceeding my time, I have one more statement to make and two more questions to ask."

"Well, please be quick," said Mansel. "The sooner Miss Scrope is in bed the better for her."

"Quite so. The statement is this. Five years ago I was warned to beware of Greece. A soothsayer uttered that warning—a very wise man. From that day on, I would never deal with a Greek." He shrugged his shoulders. "An idle precaution, of course, for Fate never shows her hand and oracles speak in riddles which few can solve. Well, we know that the warning was sound, for Mr. Solon bears a famous Athenian name." He turned to me. "I assume it's some sort of corruption."

"Yes," said I. "The original name was Soleyne."

"Quite so. But the point is this—that when a man is doomed, Fate takes no chances at all. Strange as I found your name, I never connected you with that downright prophecy. I could have killed you twice over that night at Cardinal: but because my eyes were blinded, I let you go. And then, when it was too late and I was back at Rouen, then I was allowed to remember that I must beware of Greece.

"And now for my questions. . . .

"First—" he returned to Mansel "—exactly how do we part?"

"We're going ashore," said Mansel; "but you will go down with the launch. I imagine you'd rather be drowned than be burned alive."

"Infinitely," said The Shepherd, blandly. "Indeed, I have always understood that death by drowning was unexceptionable."

"I propose to lay you out first."

"I beg," said The Shepherd, indignantly, "that you will do nothing of the kind." Mansel made no reply. "And now pray make your arrangements. I'll leave my second question right to the last."

"My arrangements are made. Ask it now."

" I stand corrected. May I know whom I have the pleasure of addressing—or would that be indiscreet ? "

Mansel looked down at his hands, as though uncertain whether or no to reply. Then he looked suddenly up.

" My name is Mansel," he said.

His eyes aflame, The Shepherd started up from his seat.

" Well I'm damned," he said hoarsely.

" No doubt about that," said Mansel—and flicked him under the chin.

I use the word ' flicked,' because he appeared to hit him no harder than that : I never knew till later that Mansel had been one of the finest boxers that ever stepped into a ring.

Be that as it may, The Shepherd's head went back and the fellow sat down and fell sideways on to his face.

" I'm sorry," said Mansel, quietly. " That was your job. But he is not out like Satan, and you shall pinion the fellow and send him down.

With that, he produced some cord, and I lashed The Shepherd's ankles together and then his wrists.

As Mansel removed the hand-cuffs—

" We must leave no trace," he said. " But that's not enough. Whenever the launch is found, I want them to look for Satan and not for us." He put his hand to a shelf and pulled a life-belt down. " Get Satan's jacket off and tie this on to his carcase as quick as ever you can."

Whilst I was doing this, he opened the cabin's port-holes, of which there were six. These were diminutive. Then he picked The Shepherd up and set him down on the floor, with his face to the cabin's mouth.

As he hung Satan's coat on a hook—

"Will you take the helm from Carson, and send him here? As soon as you've got your bearings, turn away from the shore and switch the search-light out. There's a craft a mile away, but I can't see anything else."

I did as he said—and never saw Satan again: for they heaved him overboard and Carson slipped into the river and towed him ashore. (In fact, the cold water revived that very unpleasant man: so, as soon as the two had landed, Carson took the precaution of laying him out again.)

Mansel came aft.

"There may be a cock somewhere: but, if there is, I can't find it, and so you must stave her in. Will you come and do the job, while I hold the torch? She's flimsily built, so it oughtn't to take very long."

With the aid of the heavy jemmy, it took me a very few moments to wrench a plank from its place, when the water burst in like a fountain and soaked us both.

As I stood back and away—

"'The glory of young men is their strength,'" said The Shepherd, agreeably.

I turned my head, to meet the flame in his eyes.

"I've no compunction," I said.

"Of course not. And Mr. Laking. Is he on duty to-night?"

"On other duty," said I, "to his great regret."

"Allow me to congratulate you on your auxiliaries."

"I'm much obliged."

"And on your engagement."

"Thank you."

"Will you tell her that I deeply regret——"

"—that you were prevented from burning Formosa alive?"

"That," said The Shepherd, "would not be strictly correct. I should, as we know, have preferred to dispose of you both: but, had my hand not been forced by the outbreak of fire, I should never have considered employing a method so crude. No. What I was going to say was how much I regret that considerations of business should have compelled me to, er, meddle with her private affairs. You, for instance, and Cardinal. It would have been great presumption, had I had less to lose. I'll give you this, Mr. Solon—as you came up to my table, that night at *The Wet Flag*, I saw from the set of your jaw that either you or I would have to be, er, written off before very long. I had reason to think it would be you. But, since it has not been you, you must try to believe that I do not grudge your success. The odds against you were stupendous. There were no odds. Yet, you are standing there free, whilst I am lying here bound. Now that is a great achievement, look at it how you will. And I attribute it largely to the fact that you declined to be daunted by a prospect which was as hopeless as it was formidable.

"Now lest these words should seem to you to smack of hypocrisy, let me say this—that, if, in response to some half-baked conception of magnanimity—which I'm sure Captain Mansel would do his best to correct—you were at this very last moment to set me free, I should take a leaf out of your book and should use my best endeavours, however hopeless it seemed, to destroy, first, Captain Mansel, and then Miss Scrope and yourself. That statement should answer for my sincerity."

"I'll say you know how to lose."

"That's instinct," said The Shepherd. "It's not experience."

The water, halfway to our knees, was nearly up to his chin.

I indicated the jemmy, still in my hand.

"Would you," I faltered, "would you like me to lay you out?"

"I can think of nothing," said The Shepherd, "that I should dislike so much."

All was very quiet now, for the water within the launch had risen above the gash which I had made in her side. Very far in the distance, I heard the drone of some car: but though I strained my ears, I could not hear the throb of a screw, and upon our reach of the river there was not a single light. The launch was now in mid-stream, and I could but just distinguish the banks upon either side, but when I looked back I could see the red glare of the fire, and the trees of the forest standing against the glow, and the water beyond the point reflecting the flames.

Mansel touched my shoulder.

"Any moment now," he said. "When the water

reaches the port-holes, she'll settle at once. Drop the jemmy overboard and stand by to swim."

The Shepherd's head was right back. His mouth was just clear, but the water was up to his ears.

As his eyes met mine, he smiled.

"I have always maintained," he said, "that death is a great adventure: and when I have had occasion to cut short another's life, I have always consoled myself with the reflection that, for all we knew, I was doing him a very good turn. In that spirit, I take my leave. Good night, Captain Mansel."

"Good night."

"It has been a very great pleasure to meet so distinguished a man. Good night, Mr. Solon."

"Good night," said I.

"May I say that I hope you'll be happy?"

"Thank you," said I. "I'll tell Miss Scrope you said that."

"That's very generous. One always values most highly the things which one least deserves."

I saw the water lipping a port-hole, and whilst I was watching and waiting for it to break, I heard a sudden plash on the opposite side. And then, before I could think, all six port-holes were discharging small bows of water, after the way of a mask through which some rill has been schooled to fall into a pond.

"Quick," said Mansel.

One after another, we mounted the seat and dived. . . .

I looked back now and again, as we made for the shore; for the cabin-lights were still burning, although the others were out: and though each time she seemed to be disappearing, the next time I turned to look, she was always just there.

I decided to swim ten strokes before turning again. . . .

As I came to the eighth—

"She's going," said Mansel.

I was just in time to see her go down by the head.

... ...

As we waded ashore—

"Well, that's that," said I.

"More than he deserved," said Mansel. "He was 'an hard man, reaping where *he had* not sown and gathering where *he had* not strawed.' Human life in his eyes was a chattel—a belonging: no more than that. As such, he took it away, and as such, he rendered it up five minutes ago. If you had to plead for him, Solon, what would you say?"

I answered at once.

"That, at least, he bore no malice."

"Exactly," said Mansel. "And that is a very rare trait in the underworld." His fingers went to his throat. "To that we owe this quite invaluable key. It's as good as the King's pardon for a certain lady we know."

CHAPTER XIV

NOW that the terror was laid, the thing that concerned us most was Katharine's health.

She showed no sign of sickness, but she was very quiet; and, remembering all she had suffered during the last ten days, we feared that any moment she would break down.

Arrived at the lonely farm, we roused the farmer's wife, to help her to bed, and then I knelt by her side, until, with her hand on my shoulder, she fell asleep. But I did not like leaving her: and Mansel and George agreed that, though we were all worn out, we must take it in turn to watch, that one of us might be at hand, in case she should wake.

It was then arranged that, if she was fit to travel, we should all leave for Southampton the following night, to spend ten days or a fortnight at Mansel's country home. When George and I protested that we could not presume so far, Mansel only smiled and clapped me upon the back.

"I'm not issuing an invitation—I'm issuing an order," he said. "And I expect you to obey it--I'm still in charge."

"If you put it like that," I said feebly. . . .

"I do," said Mansel. "Miss Scrope's condition

apart, it is of the utmost importance that we should leave this district as soon as may be and should repair to some harbour, where we can rest and refit. I needn't elaborate that: but it would be a thousand pities, if, when we have done so well, anything were to happen to spoil the show we've put up. Mabel and Satan won't dare to open their mouths: but the tender has been destroyed and the launch is gone, and, when the latter is found—as it almost certainly will be in two or three days—the police will get very busy: and though it doesn't follow that they will get very far, I should very much prefer that we were not only hulled down, but well out of range. Then, again, as you know, I have a trust to discharge; and the sooner that that is done, the better for all concerned. Finally, my little sister will be very good for Miss Scrope: and the place is very restful—life goes very quietly there—yet it will remind her of nothing, because I am sure she's never been there before."

To our great relief, my lady slept very well, and she stayed in bed the next day until after tea: but, though she was plainly better and glad to listen and talk, she never referred to her abduction or to the days she had spent in Mabel's company.

As I knelt again by her side, she touched my cheek.

"Poor Esau—with his beard. It was strictly correct, of course: but you must have been so thankful to take it off. Was that why you didn't kiss me?"

"No," I said. "You looked too tired to be kissed. But you're different to day."

"I feel very different. I—hadn't been sleeping well."

I stooped to kiss her lips, and she slid an arm round my neck.

"That day in the bracken," she whispered. "When you made love to me . . . while George was waiting for Joseph . . . before The Shepherd went by . . . I was exalted then. You lifted me up to the very top of my bent. Shall I ever recapture that, Esau? Or are you doomed to have a dud for a wife?"

"My darling girl," I breathed, "what do you expect? Think of the punishment which you have taken since then. You wouldn't be human if you could stand up and shout. We're out of the wood, you and I. But we have been through—tribulation of a very exceptional kind, and though I am now more thankful than I thought a man could be—well, I'm not singing any pæans . . . I only want to sit quiet—with my eyes on your face."

She gave her short nod.

"I expect you're right. Never mind. Tell me more about Jonathan Mansel. I'd heard of him—we all had. More than one crash was said to be due to him. But no one could ever prove it. He moved too quietly, and he covered his tracks too well."

"That's why we're leaving this evening. That's why he isn't here now."

"What is he doing?" said Katharine.

"He's gone to Paris," I said, "to change his Rolls. Both cars are privately garaged—at different places, of course. When he picks us up this evening, he will be able to prove that the car which he is using, which will be shipped at Havre, has not been out of Paris for over a month."

"The presumption being, of course, that neither has he?"

"A very strong presumption. D'you know that he's actually taken the trouble to go up to Paris *to use it* twice a week?"

Katharine nodded approvingly.

"I don't wonder he gets there," she said. "But it's just as well for the public he isn't a crook."

... ...

That night I stood with her on the deck of the ship and watched the lights of France sink into the sea; and we both remembered another summer evening, when we had strolled on the deck of another ship—and I had kissed her fingers and they had closed upon mine.

"Don't ever leave me, Esau."

My heart leaped up.

"Never, my darling. I'll never leave you again."

"I hope—I'll never have to leave you . . . I don't know whether the jewels will do the trick: the police don't like doing deals with people like me. But I have grown selfish, Esau. I'm ready to ruin your life, to save my own."

I put my arm about her and held her against my heart.

"Always be selfish," I said. "It's all I ask."

"'Greater love hath no man than this.'"

"My silly Kate! Would it matter to you if *I*'d sailed too close to the wind?"

"Very much—for your sake."

"But not for your own," said I.

She shook her head.

"All the same, it isn't fair. I have no right to allow you to make an honest woman of me. But I can't help that. I can't do without you, my darling. I know that now. And I'd rather let you down than let you go."

I set my cheek against hers, and we stood in a bitter-sweet silence, until the last light had gone out.

At length—

"It was nice of him," she said slowly, "to—to think of me . . . at the last. I'm glad—to have that to remember. . . ."

"He said he hoped we'd be happy."

"If he said it, he meant it. He had many faults, but he always meant what he said."

... ...

We reached White Ladies the next morning at nine o'clock—an immemorial manor, sunk in the heart of the forest which William the Conqueror made. Its charm was strong and gentle—and ministered to the mind. Gray, carved stone and winking lattices, time-honoured lawns and timber older than they, topiary work and flags and a park of blowing meadows, where cows were cropping the shadows of English oaks—

'the same yesterday, to-day and for ever,' as George most truly said.

Mansel's sister was there, to bring us into the house—the simplest, most natural beauty I ever saw. She and Katharine fell for each other at once, and George and I were her slaves from that time on. At least, we should have been : but she would not have that : and, though she was our hostess, she managed to make us forget that within the hour.

Indeed, I shall always remember the blessed halcyon calm of the next ten days. We made no effort, for none was asked of us : no visitors came to the house—or if, in fact, they came, they were not received. Once or twice we drove out—the first time, to purchase some clothes : but for the most part we stayed in the beautiful grounds, absorbing their ancient peace and breathing deep the odour of sanctuary.

Though I think these things saved Katharine from breaking down, she did not make the progress I longed to see. Her flesh recovered. She ate and slept as she should, and the colour came back to her cheeks. But her spirit was burning low and the light in her eyes was dim.

George tried to comfort me.

"Give her time," he said quietly. "Formosa will come again."

As usual, he drove the nail. The girl who sat upon the terrace and seemed so glad of us all could never have bluffed the Customs, to smuggle a bottle of scent.

And then the eleventh day came. . . .

Twice Mansel had been away for twenty-four hours :

but he had not said where he was going or what he was going to do. In view of what he had said, I had but little doubt that he was putting pressure on Scotland Yard: and there it seems I was right, for on the eleventh morning, he put a registered letter into my hand.

VERY SECRET.

Commissioner's Office,
New Scotland Yard.

My dear Jonah,

My opposite number in Paris agrees with me, and the dossier in question has been accordingly indorsed. So far as the past is concerned, Formosa has nothing to fear.

The underwriters are quite bewildered: it means the return to them of thousands of pounds. Indeed, the whole thing has caused an immense sensation, and once again I congratulate you with all my heart.

You mentioned more than once that you were not alone in the matter. If you see fit so to do, pray tell your subordinates that the services which they helped you to render are quite inestimable. The monster was mythical: to end such a being's existence was heroes' work.

Yours ever,
James.

I looked up to meet Mansel's eyes.

"That all right?" he said, smiling.

I moistened my lips.

"A new heaven and a new earth," I said, "are

always acceptable. It was a good day for us when George and I got stuck with a drunken Marseillais who talked to himself."

"I think it's equally clear that it was a good day for him."

I sighed.

"May I show it to her?"

"Do," said Mansel. "And tell a brave lady this—that she has herself to thank for what that document says."

Katharine was in the stables, talking with Mansel's sister, whose name was Jill, and watching six spaniel puppies staggering round the loose-box which was their nursery.

She read the letter through, without turning a hair.

"Our first wedding-present," she said. "And I never thought I'd get one from Scotland Yard."

When I gave her Mansel's message, she shook her head.

"I can't allow that," she said. "I have to thank three people: but I'm not one. Will you take me to Brooch after lunch? Jill says there's a hairdresser there."

"Of course I will, my darling."

"I don't have to have my hair waved, so I shan't be long. And I'd love to think you were looking for me to come out."

That was a sweet thing to say; but I was so much disappointed that I could hardly smile. I had hoped so very hard that the letter from Scotland Yard would kindle the light in her eyes.

I returned to the library—but not by the way I had gone. And I heard what Mansel was saying, before he knew I was there.

"I have an uneasy feeling that she ought to have had a break-down. Our one idea was to save her from such a thing. But that was thwarting Nature. She needed some violent reaction to sweep and garnish her soul."

I did not hear George's answer. The backs of the two were towards me: and neither knows to this day why, when we sat down to luncheon, I could not eat.

... ...

It was three o'clock when we entered the city of Brooch. Jill and George were with us, for both had odd things to do.

The hairdresser's shop was near the Cathedral close, and there we agreed to gather at half-past four.

I saw my lady settled and went off to see the Cathedral, before I did anything else. Though Jill and George would have had me, I made some idle excuse, because, to tell the truth, I was anxious to be alone.

If a man would meditate, I know no better place than a great cathedral church: and I fear I did not consider the many peculiar glories for which the shrine is famed. Pacing the endless nave, I strove to remember the mercies which I had so lately received; but the grave words Mansel had spoken obsessed my mind.

I had little doubt he was right.

We had suppressed the explosion which ought to have taken place—driven back into her system the humours it should have discharged. And now it would never discharge them. The poison she should have thrown off, was being absorbed.

Katharine would always be Katharine—nothing could alter that. But her wonderful drive was gone. She leaned on me, when she should have stood by my side. And her lips were never parted. The glorious, eager look was out of her beautiful face.

For nearly an hour I wrestled with what I knew was the truth : and then I left the Cathedral and made my way back to the streets.

I had plenty of time to spare, for Katharine had made it clear that to cut and to wash her hair would take an hour and a half ; so when I had purchased the two or three things I required, I wandered about the city, observing its fine memorials of olden days.

It must have been a quarter-past four and I was turning my steps towards the row in which the hairdresser's stood, when I saw Katharine coming towards me on the opposite side of the way.

I could not cross over at once, for, because it was market-day, a flock of sheep had just begun to go by : so I stood upon the edge of the pavement, ready and waiting to catch my lady's eye.

I supposed she was looking for me and wondered how she had divined the way I had gone, and I thought how fine she was looking, although the frock she was wearing was one of Jill's. And then, as she came abreast, I saw the look on her face. . . .

The width of the street was between us—some sixteen feet : had I called her, she must have heard me : but

I was so taken aback that I could not find my voice, for, as I live, her delicate chin was up, her eager lips were parted, and the light I had longed to see was back in her eyes.

She looked a little puzzled, but almost debonair, and a rogue of a smile was hanging about her mouth : she seemed so glad to be living, so pleased with all she saw, and when a sheep mounted the pavement, to nose her bag, she laughed and stroked its head and spoke it kindly, before it trotted away.

Her lovely head was bare, and the sun was making the most of her glorious curls : this, with her striking beauty of figure and face, made her conspicuous : but it was her vitality—that indefinable flame which had seemed to be almost quenched, that made her stand out of that simple thoroughfare, as the jewel stood out of the dunghill in Aesop's tale. And if it is thought that I imagined these things, because I loved her so much, I can only say that others were staring upon her and that as the drover went by, he took off his hat.

And then she looked round and saw me, about to cross. . . .

But a glance was all that I got, and she went on her way down the street, with her chin in the air.

... ...

At first I was too much dumbfounded to make any move, and I watched her retreating figure, as a man in a dream. Then I started off in pursuit—and, thanks to my dazed condition, was very nearly knocked down by an oncoming 'bus.

This *contretemps* delayed me, and by the time I had gained the opposite side of the street, she had almost come to a crossing some forty yards off. But if the flurry delayed me, it shook my wits into place, and I saw that I must be careful if I was to come at the truth without doing some harm.

By the grace of God, my sweet was herself again. What magic had wrought this marvel, I could not conceive : but the shining fact remained that Katharine was well. What was equally clear was that Katharine was playing a part.

She must have encountered someone who knew Formosa by sight and she was about the business of throwing him off her trail. If she had waited for me or had gone to the close, she would have been traced to White Ladies before the sun had gone down : but by avoiding us all, she hoped to be able to shake the enemy off. He could, of course, do her no harm—her past was dead. But Mansel and George and I had lately done rough justice, and she had no intention of leading him up to our lair.

The pavement was fairly full, so I had little chance of deciding which of the several pedestrians was following her ; but I saw no harm in reducing the distance between us, and as I set out to do this, the traffic played into my hands.

Just as she came to the crossing, a policeman on point duty beckoned a waiting line on, and Katharine was checked on the kerb, until it had passed. By the time she was free to proceed, I was only four paces away: and I had come to the kerb before she was halfway across.

And then, to my great surprise, I saw her speak to the policeman. . . .

I could not hear what she said, but I heard his reply.

" The General Post Office, madam ? " He lifted an arm. " That red-brick building down there, that stands by itself."

I saw her smile and thank him and go on her way: and I crossed over the street, six paces behind.

Now when she came to the Post Office, I saw her survey its façade: then she did not make for its door, but stepped instead to a window in which there were notices pasted, for people to read.

She stood there, scanning these papers, finger to lip, as though she were looking for something which she had hoped would be there; whilst I passed slowly behind her, revising my late conclusion and wondering what on earth she wished me to do.

This was not the way to give a pursuer the slip. The window was too high up to reflect any passers-by, and since the building stood back, she was out of the stream of pedestrains and so conspicuous. If I could see these things, Formosa could see them, too. And so it was clear to me that the action which she was taking was due to some other cause.

To give myself an excuse for standing still, I took out a cigarette and felt for a match: and when I glanced over my shoulder, I saw that she had turned round and was standing with her back to the window, with her eyebrows raised and the rogue of a smile on her lips.

I think it was the smile that made me determined to act. Danger—finesse be damned. There was Katharine standing, and there was I, her fiancé, six paces away. The thing was ridiculous. We were in Brooch—not Rouen. And The Shepherd was dead.

I threw down my cigarette and stepped to her side.

"Kate," I said, "what is it? What's on the mat?"

The smile went out of her face, and she looked me full in the eyes.

"Did I hear you call me Kate?"

I could hardly believe my ears.

"Why not?" said I, wide-eyed. "You've never objected before."

"I'm not sure that I object now. It's quite a good name. But it looks as though you knew me—and knew me well."

I put a hand to my head.

"My darling," said I, "what on earth are you getting at?"

"Steady," she said. "Let's take one step at a time. Is it a fact that you know me?"

"Don't be silly. You know I know you," I said.

Katharine regarded me straightly.

Then—

"In fact, I don't," she said. "But you look very honest and so I'll take your word for it. If it's true, I've fallen soft. But you'll have to go easy with me. I've lost my memory."

... ...

To this day I cannot remember crossing the street. I rather think she guided me over. But I know that we were across and were walking the way we had come.

"D'you mean to say," I said, "you don't know who I am?"

"I don't know who *I* am," said Katharine. "I've no idea. I've looked in my bag, but there's only a flap-jack there. And I don't know where I am. It seemed so silly to ask—I thought people'd think I was mad—so I asked where the Post Office was. I thought, perhaps, the name would be posted there."

"This place is called Brooch."

"Brooch. Well, that's in Hampshire. And who are you?"

At the second attempt—

"Well, you used to call me Esau," I said.

"Esau?" she said "*Esau?*"—and tried not to laugh.

"Damn it," I said, "it's your fault. You gave me the blasted name."

She laughed at that, till the tears came into her eyes.

"Well, I'll take it away," she said. "It doesn't suit you at all. Have you any other—pet names?"

"Some people call me 'Thunder.' In fact, I'm Jeremy Solon of Savile Row."

"Thunder's better," she said. "And now who am I?"

I shot a glance about me.

I was not dreaming. We were in Bear Lane, Brooch. People were passing by us, and cars and bicycles were crowding the narrow street. And a clock said 'Half-past four '—which meant that Jill and George were in the Cathedral close.

"You're Miss Katharine Scrope," said I. "Your home is in France, at a village called Cardinal. I've stayed there with you—it's a very beautiful place. But just now we are both at White Ladies, a manor-house in the Forest, not very far from here."

I saw her weighing my words.

Then—

"Where are you taking me now?"

"To join the others," I said. "When I left you to have your hair done——"

"You seem," said Katharine, "to know me extremely well."

I swallowed before replying.

"If you ask the others," I said, "they'll tell you how that is."

"Tell me yourself."

I looked up to meet her eyes.

"Well," I said somehow, "of course it's all off now. But, as a matter of fact, you and I were engaged."

I heard her catch her breath.

Then she laid a hand on my sleeve.

"I seem to have . . . torn things up. But please don't take it to heart. I can't say anything yet. It wouldn't be fair to you, and it wouldn't be fair to me. But if, my dear, I fell for you in the past, if you'll give me a little time, perhaps I shall do it again."

CHAPTER XV

OF the four who drove back to White Ladies that afternoon, by far the most level-headed was Katharine Scrope: and when I brought her to Mansel, at work in pipe and shirt-sleeves, siting a bathing-pool, she asked him to let her help, and the three of us worked together for half an hour.

Such self-possession went far to reduce embarrassment: but, what was more, it showed us that we need have no fear of telling her the whole of the truth.

When all is said and done, it is, as they say, a tall order, to tell a dependent young lady of high degree that for three years past she has been a well-known crook: but Katharine's smiling composure and sure address encouraged the utmost frankness where she was concerned.

That night, with the others for audience, I told my lady the story which I have set down in this book, while Carson patrolled the terrace, in case of eavesdroppers. I told her her own story, as she had told it to me. And I suppressed nothing at all, from beginning to end. For the second time that day she took and read through the letter which Mansel had had that morning from Scotland Yard, and all the time I was speaking she never took her eyes from my face.

At last I made an end.

"To my mind, this loss of memory is the perfectly natural result of all you have undergone. Your father's death knocked you out—I can vouch for that. On the top of that came your abduction and your imprisonment. We could not understand why you did not break down. And I was terribly worried, for though you seemed so fit, at heart you weren't the Katharine that I had known. But now you are yourself. And I hope to God you won't fret just because you can't remember a lot of unpleasant things; for we are so very happy to see the light back in your eyes."

There was a little silence.

Then—

"It's clear," said Katharine, "I've much to be thankful for—a very, very great deal." She looked from her host to her hostess. "For one thing only, it's very handsome of you to let me inside your house."

"Oh, Katharine, how can you?" cried Jill. She caught my lady's hand and held it in both of hers. "You see, we know you, although you don't know us. And anyone's only to know you, to know that it wasn't your fault. Besides, you did try to get out: and I don't believe I'd have tried, with my father like that."

With a manifest effort, Katharine controlled her voice.

"Don't be too good to me, or I shall burst into tears." She lifted her eyes to mine. "What a mercy you saw me, Thunder, this afternoon. But for that, God knows where I should be now. And think of the ghastly publicity, when I was found. Photographs of

Formosa all over the yellow press. The very last thing we wanted." She closed her eyes. "Instead, I'm here, safe and sound, with nothing to worry about—except how to try and thank you for all you've done."

"Would you like to repay me?" said Mansel.

"How can I ever do that?"

"Ask me to Cardinal—one day. I've a weakness for fairy castles, hung in the woods."

Katharine turned to Jill.

"Will you come with him?" she said.

"Of course."

"Good. We'll explore it together. Or else perhaps George and Thunder will show us round." She rose to her feet. "And now I must go to bed."

I opened the door for her and Jill to go out: but she stopped when she came to me and looked me full in the eyes.

"Good night, Thunder, and thank you so very much."

I managed to smile.

"Sleep well, my lady."

She put out her hand for mine.

"I'm sorry," she said. "Give me time. But please don't think you're not free. However I come to feel, I couldn't bear you to think that you had to stick to an offer which I have forgotten was made."

... ...

The days that followed were the strangest I ever have known.

I had made up my mind to withdraw, but Katharine herself had begged me not to do that.

" I count upon you," she said. " You know far more about me than anyone else : and unless it upsets you to be with me——"

" Good God, no," said I. " But I—think it's so awkward for you."

" I'll tell you when I find it—awkward."

" Promise ? " said I.

" I promise."

And there the matter was left. But though I was thrilled to see her not only herself, but utterly free from care, there were times when I felt I should have to throw in my hand.

The contrast between what had been and what was now was not so much sharp as savage—a hundred times a day, it plucked and tore at my heart : we had loved one another so deeply . . . but now—she had been taken, and I was left.

She did her very best to temper the wind : no one could have been sweeter or more understanding than she : but half a loaf seems meagre when you have been accustomed to have the whole of a cake.

And then, after dinner one evening, when we were walking on the terrace, under the stars, she slid her arm through mine and spoke very low.

" I'm going to Cardinal, Thunder. I want to see it so much. Besides, from what you say, there are things to be done there which only I can do. George has written to Conrad, saying I'm safe and sound, but that, as a result of what happened, my memory's not too good.

He said he thought it was better to put it that way. Well, that's all right, of course, so far as it goes. But I feel that I must have someone to, so to speak, induct me, when I arrive. I don't even know where my room is. I don't know Conrad from Joseph—I don't know anything."

"George and I will go with you. I'm getting another car, and if you would like it, my lady, I'll drive you both down. But what about Jill and her brother?"

"They can't come till October: but I can't wait till then. Besides, I can't play hostess, when I've never seen the place."

"All right," said I. "The car will be ready on Friday. When would you like to go?"

"On Friday evening. But I want George to go by train."

I raised my eyebrows.

"All right. But why d'you want that?"

"I want to have a day there with you, before he comes. The whole of one day. He can come by the Paris train: you told me that gets into Cruise about nine at night."

"That's right," said I. "That's how he came down before. If we stay a night at Nevers——"

"Did we stay at Nevers last time?"

"No," I said, "we didn't. We didn't stay anywhere."

"Oh. Well, never mind. But I'd like to get in in good time."

"If we stay the night at Nevers, we ought to be there for lunch."

"Oh, that's no good," said Katharine. "I want the whole of one day. I want to be there for breakfast. Why—why shouldn't we drive through the night, and get in at seven o'clock?"

I laughed.

"As we did before? On a Sunday morning, too. When all the . . . ."

And there I stood still in my tracks.

"Was it Sunday?" I heard her say.

I turned and looked at her.

"You know it was Sunday," I said. Her clear, gray eyes met mine. "You know it was Sunday: and—I'm not going to do as you ask."

She turned and set her hands on my shoulders.

"I beg you to do it, Thunder."

I shook my head.

"For my sake, Thunder. Wouldn't you like me to get my memory back?"

"No," I said. "I wouldn't. And I hope you never do."

"That's a strange thing for you to say."

"I suppose it is. But it's true. You see, I have come to believe that your loss of memory actually mended your heart. I believe that your heart had been broken by what you went through: and I don't think it could have been mended as long as you could remember those terrible days. And so I believe that your loss is really the biggest gain that anyone ever had. Nature's made you a present, my lady. D'you think I'm going to help you to try and throw it back in her face?"

Her hands slipped away from my shoulders.

"Perhaps you're right," she said quietly. "Shall we go in?"

With an aching heart, I followed her into the house.

... ...

And so new arrangements were made.

George left for Cardinal on Friday: that meant he would get there on Sunday: and we were to travel by road, stay one night on the way, and get there on Monday night.

Thus George would have twenty-four hours in which to advise the servants what to expect and to see that all was in order for Katharine's homecoming; whilst if she and I went quietly, by the way which I meant to take, the last twenty miles of our journey would have to be covered after the dusk had come in.

I did not think—and Mansel agreed with me—that Cardinal by itself would bring her memory back: but the repetition of history, the revival of atmosphere, the reconstruction of big moments in the very surroundings in which they had really occurred—such things to our mind were dangerous. I use the word advisedly. Oblivion had done what only oblivion could do: and we had all come to believe that it would be a major disaster, so far as she was concerned, if Katharine recovered the memory which she had lost.

And there I will leave the matter, except for this—that George Laking and Jonathan Mansel supported me during those days, as if I had been some king and they my gentlemen. In deed as in word, the two of them showed me an unobtrusive kindness not often met with in an indifferent world.

I needed fellow-feeling.

With their help, I had freed my darling from the power of the dog—only to find that she was no longer my darling, but a beautiful, fancy-free stranger to whom I meant no more than did either of them. The ties which had bound us were cancelled, as though they had never been. The thousand precious moments which had conspired together to bring forth love were blotted out. Our meeting, our flight, our searchings of heart upon the ramparts, the heights we had touched in the bracken, the tender hour we had passed by her bedroom fire—all these and their lovely burdens had been expunged from her mind. But not from mine—and there was the bitter rub.

... ...

Katharine looked up from the map.

"I make it," she said, "two hundred and twenty miles."

"Thereabouts," said I, and set a match to my pipe.

It was Monday afternoon, and we had just finished our lunch by the side of the way. In fact, we were sitting in a meadow, beneath the grateful shade of a whispering lime; and the car was ten paces away, on the opposite side of a hedge.

It was immensely hot, and Katharine was dressed exactly as when I had seen her first, in a shirt and well-cut slacks, with a gay, green handkerchief over her chestnut curls. (It was very strange to me to see how she had thrown back and, going to London with Jill, had chosen the very apparel which she had favoured before.) And now she was sitting sideways and was propping herself with one arm, with the map spread out before her and an eager look in her face.

"You're taking no risks, are you? I mean to say, we've come miles out of our way."

I shrugged my shoulders.

"Last time," said I, "I had someone to tell me the way to go."

"Be honest," said Katharine. "You mean to get in after dark."

"You're too—perspicacious," said I.

She put her chin in the air.

"I don't think you're very kind. I wanted to see it so much—from the gap in the trees."

"We'll walk up there to-morrow."

"I wanted to see it to-day."

"I know," I said. "I'm sorry."

Katharine glanced at her wrist.

"It's only half-past two. If you like to drive all out, you can do it yet."

"Please don't press me, my lady. I'd—rather not."

Katharine was up on her feet.

"I make a point of this, Thunder. I've counted on this for days. I especially wish to see my home this evening, before the daylight has gone. If you like to do it, you can. If you don't want to do it, you won't. But if you deny me this pleasure . . ."

"Go on," I said quietly. "What then?"

"I shall know where I stand."

There was a pregnant silence.

Till now we had done so well: and I had almost fancied that there was more in her kindness than pity alone. But this was no fancy, but fact. And if I refused to give way . . .

I had never thought she would take my precaution so ill. Since that night on the terrace, she had never referred to the question which she had put, which I had answered so plainly—for better or worse: and I had believed that the matter was at an end. But now she had raised it again, in a different guise. A very awkward guise. 'I have gone a long way to meet you: I ask you to come a very short way to meet me.'

I knew her eyes were upon me, striving to read my thoughts: but I stared straight before me, striving to weigh things up.

The risk itself was as slight as the stakes were high. If I liked to put down my foot, we could be at the gap before dusk. And then she would have the great pleasure of viewing her lovely castle, as castles should be viewed—*as she had let me view it*, before we drove down to the valley and up to the gates. And the time of day would be different. . . . The risk was slight. And the stakes were so very high.

For one terrible moment, Temptation had me by the arm. . . . And then I knew that in this I could take *no* risk. Katharine must think and Katharine must do as she pleased. But I could not put in peril the light which the grace of God had brought back to her eyes.

"I'm sorry, Kate," I said quietly. "But I think it's better that we should get in after dark."

She gave her short nod and sat down.

"In that case we needn't hurry," was all she said.

In fact we got in much later than I had meant, for we picked up a puncture just after night had come down; and since, like a fool, I was travelling without a torch, there was nothing to do but change the wheel in the dark. The car being new to me, the tools were unfamiliar, and the spare-wheel was fastened to the boot in a way I had never seen: and though Katharine supported me bravely by striking match after match and burning her blessed fingers in her efforts to make them last, nearly an hour had gone by before the change had been made.

Indeed, it was getting on for eleven o'clock, when we slipped by the famous cross roads and into the hanging forest keeping the Cardinal road.

"Nearly there, now," I said.

"I'm glad of that."

I slid down the hill on which the Mercédes was burned, severed the sleeping meadows and slowed for the gray, old bridge. Then I lifted the car through the village and up the road of approach.

As the head-lights showed us the gateway, I sounded the horn. Then I drove slowly through it and into the little courtyard.

Joseph was by my side, before we had stopped.

"Well, Joseph," I said. "Here we are."

The poor fellow spoke through his tears, but I could not understand what he said.

I turned to Katharine.

"Will you translate for me, please?"

"He says that they never doubted. That he and Conrad knew that you'd save me and bring me back."

Joseph opened her door and she left the car.

As I did the same—

"Damn it," I said, "where's George?"—and sounded the horn again.

Katharine was speaking to Joseph.

As I came up to her side—

"George isn't here," she said. "He got a wire about three and left as soon as he could. For Paris, of course. Joseph was to make his excuses and say that he hoped to be back before very long."

There was a dreadful silence.

Then—

"*Monsieur* Laking was desolate, *Monsieur*," said Joseph, anxiously.

"Desolate be damned," said I. "Get *Madame's* stuff out of the car."

As he flew to the boot, I heard Katharine catch her breath.

"But you're not going, Thunder? You can't leave me here alone."

"Why not? There's no danger now."

"I know. But you were to——"

"Look here," said I. "We both of us know what happened this afternoon. D'you want to twist my tail, until it comes off in your hand?"

She bit her lip.

"I didn't mean to hurt you," she said. "But I beg,

as a personal favour, that you will have something to eat—before you go."

I hesitated.

Then—

"All right," I said. "I'll have a wash, if I may, after changing that wheel. And if Joseph's got any dinner, I'll share it with you."

... ...

The champagne was good and cold and lifted me up: but we did not talk much through a dinner which Joseph served very well.

At length—

"Conrad," I said. "I forgot. Will you ask him how Conrad is?"

"Conrad's all right. I've seen him. He sent his respects to you."

I felt ashamed. I had forgotten Conrad. But she, who could not forget, had made her butler's acquaintance before she sat down to meat.

And she had found time to change—into one of the frocks that I knew: a dark-blue linen dress with little patch-pockets of white.

"I'm sorry," I said. "I ought to have thought of Conrad."

"You've had a good deal to think of," was all she said.

No doubt by George's orders, her place had so been laid that she sat in her father's seat and was facing the opposite way to that she had faced before. And I sat upon her right hand, while Joseph stood back in the shadows behind her chair.

As he offered a pile of raspberries—

"Serve coffee on the terrace, Joseph," said Katharine.

"Very good, *Madame*."

But when we left the table and Joseph opened the door, she did not know where to turn, and I had to give her directions and tell her the way to go.

"To your left, and up that first flight: then to your right, and under the baby arch."

So we came to the little terrace I knew so well, with the oriel hanging above it and the beautiful staircase-turrets on either side.

She stepped to the balustrade, and I did the same.

A crescent moon was lighting the truly exquisite picture the landscape made, and a peace that was not of this world was enfolding village and meadows and the breathless cliffs of foliage rising beyond. Except for the lisp of water, there was no sound at all, and the fragrant air was as still as that of a crypt.

I watched her survey perfection with parted lips.

"Good enough?" I said quietly.

"'Behold, the half was not told me,'" was all she said.

I do not know how long we stood there, but when at last she turned, the coffee and brandy were there, and Joseph was gone.

As we took our seats—

"Does Joseph know," she said, "that he's leaving with you?"

At first I could only stare.

Then—

" What ever d'you mean ? " said I.

" I understand he's your servant."

" Don't be absurd," said I. " Of course he's not going with me. He's taking Conrad's place."

" If I can't have the master," she said, " I don't want the man."

There was a little silence.

Then—

" I don't need him," I said, " and you do. Do me the favour to keep him, at least until George comes back."

" Aren't you coming back ? "

I shook my head.

" Not—not even to get your luggage ? "

" No," said I. " Joseph can pack my things and can send them on."

" Where to ? "

" I don't know at the moment. Carcassonne, perhaps. But I'll send him a line."

" You're going on with your tour ? "

" Why not ? " said I. " I don't have to be at the office until the end of next month."

" Was that why you got a new car ? "

" No," I said, " it wasn't. But what does that matter now ? "

She made no answer to that : and after a moment or two I held my wrist to a candle to see the hour.

Half-past twelve.

" Good God," said I. " I'd no idea of the time." I

drank my brandy down and got to my feet. "You must get to bed, my lady. I'll see myself off."

"Don't go for five minutes," she said. "I've something to say."

Whilst I was hesitating, she left her chair and stepped to the balustrade; and when I came slowly after, she turned about.

"This afternoon," she said, "I did an unpardonable thing. I've no excuse at all, except that I am a girl. And where their hearts are concerned, girls have a weakness for doing unpardonable things.

"A week ago to-day, a man in love with me rejected an excellent chance of my falling in love with him, in case the process suggested should do me harm. Well, that sort of love's worth having. One woman in fifty thousand is loved like that. And I was like a dog with two tails, although, because I'm a woman, I tried to cover it up. And then, this afternoon, out of pure caprice, I determined to put my man to an even more savage test. I chucked—not chance, but certainty into the scale. More. I loaded the dice against him, and dared him to throw.

"Well, we know what he did. He won. And if it's any consolation to you, I never felt so mean in my life. I had no pleasure in my triumph. I felt as though I had beaten a faithful dog.

"And that's all I've got to say—except that, if you will take me, I'll do my level best to make you a model wife."

I put my hands behind me.

"Thank you very much," I said quietly. "I don't

suppose I'll ever be done such an honour again. But I can't accept it, Kate: and I'll tell you why. You see, you love me, my darling—but I am in love with you. You're moved by my devotion: you're carried away by my—unselfishness. Well, that's very nice: but it's not what I want of you. *I'd sooner have one of your gloves* . . . because it would smell of your perfume . . . because it had touched your wrist. . . . And that's the difference between us. And that is why I'm going to leave you to-night."

She had been looking down, while I said my piece; but now she looked suddenly up—with a look I had never seen in her beautiful face.

"I'm short of a glove," she said shyly. "But here's a—a scrap of paper. You may care to see what it says."

Not knowing what to think, I took the folded slip and walked across to the table on which the candles stood.

The thing was a telegram—the telegram which George had received that day.

Laking c/o Scrope Cardinal

Please leave before we arrive stop think what you like of me but I want him all to myself

Katharine

I looked up to see her watching me, finger to lip.

"Oh, Kate," I faltered. "My darling . . . my darling girl."

And then she was in my arms, and her lips were on mine. . . .

"My silly Thunder," she breathed, and took my face in her hands. "I've been waiting for more than a week for you to do that."

"How could I, sweetheart? I had to wait upon you."

"And how could I make the running? You were well into the straight, when I ran out and had to go back to the start."

I strained her against my heart.

"Tell me," I said. "How soon did you—catch me up?"

"D'you want the truth?" said Katharine, and held back her head.

"Of course."

"When the sheep were passing between us . . . in Bear Lane, Brooch."

And that is the end of a tale which, to tell the truth, I have written to please my wife: "for you," she said, "can remember the biggest days of our lives: but I cannot: and so I must have a record of all that took place. And when I say 'all,' I mean it. I want the rough stuff, of course. But I trust you, my darling, to put in the twiddly bits."

And since I can deny her nothing, I have done as she asked.

THE END